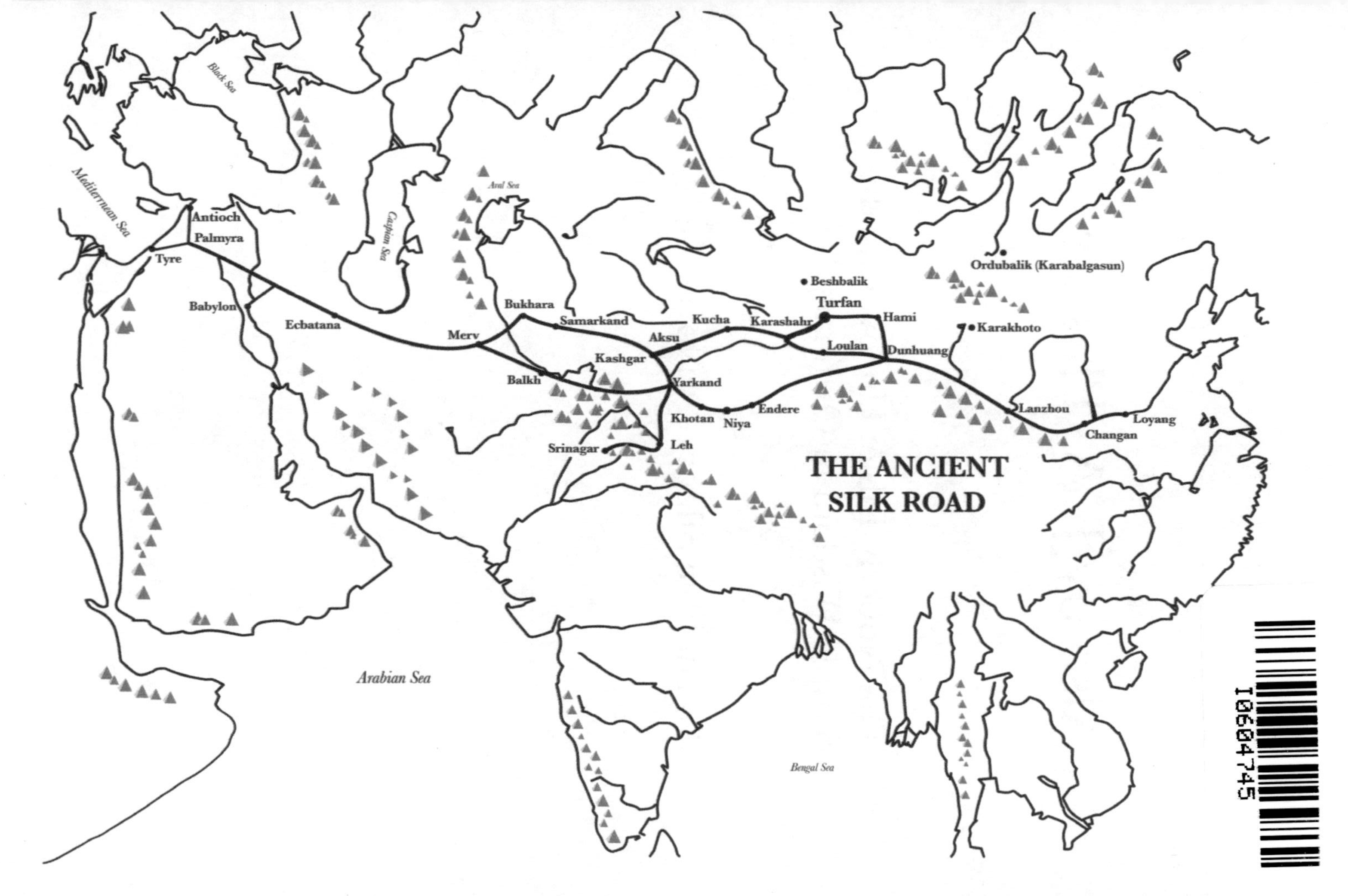

THE ANCIENT SILK ROAD
Antioch
Palmyra
Tyre
Babylon
Ecbatana
Merv
Bukhara
Samarkand
Balkh
Kashgar
Aksu
Kucha
Karashahr
Yarkand
Khotan
Niya
Loulan
Dunhuang
Turfan
Hami
Beshbalik
Karakhoto
Ordubalik (Karabalgasun)
Endere
Lanzhou
Changan
Loyang
Srinagar
Leh
Mediterranean Sea
Black Sea
Caspian Sea
Aral Sea
Arabian Sea
Bengal Sea
I0604745

Also by J. A. Plosker

The Nobody Bible: Uncovering the
Simple Wisdom in Ordinary Life

An Audible Silence (A Novel)

Tea in Turfan

a novel

J. A. Plosker

nobody
press

Published by Nobody Press, LLC
Contact us at: info@nobodypress.com
To find out more about this book, visit: www.nobodypress.com.

Print ISBN: 978-0-9987283-6-0

*For those brave enough to explore, and bold enough to
embrace the wide world of ideas*

Chapter One

Philip nodded, and his henchmen pushed the women aside before dragging the men away. Another group heaved three crosses over and dropped long metal stakes and mallets beside them.

"I have to say, John, I find this irony simply beautiful." Philip tapped the spikes with the tip of his foot, showing little regard for their piercing points. "I showed you such hospitality back home and now you have done the same. You've given me your friends, your mission, and the satisfaction of furthering Meletius's noble work. I don't know how I can ever repay you. We will put Sol in a grave tonight and I'll see that Bo lives to tell of your fate far and wide…though his words may not make sense, since he will soon be missing his tongue."

John looked up from the ground where blood spilled in a raging river from his lip. In the distance, a cloud of dust and torches silently broke the horizon behind the assembled mob. He did not know if it portended trouble or salvation, but as it neared, he knew he needed to stall for time to save his friends.

"You can repay me by doing your best, Philip," John said.

"Stop!" Philip raised his hand to his henchmen. They ceased dragging the men to their crosses, and let them drop in heaps at their feet. "I want to hear what this pathetic excuse for a Christian has to say."

John gathered himself and tried to focus.

"I said, do your best, Philip. Any man willing to go this far for a cause must truly be dedicated. It is an honor to be in your presence."

"Are you mocking me?" Philip made to kick John in the face, but John put up his arms in supplication against the blow.

"No! No, Philip. I realize now that you are a man who is passionate about Christ and his work. You are my opposite. You are right. I was trying to befriend people on the road instead of converting them. I let myself get lost in relationships and not in my mission. I owe the Church more than making friends."

"Oh, so you see that now, do you?" Philip spat.

"I…I do." John winced at the pain in his sides, but knew he had to maintain his strength.

"Why should I believe you? Why should I think you are not just saying this to save your own life?"

"Forgive me, Philip. I forgot my place in the Lord's kingdom."

Chapter Two

One year earlier

Painful sores accompanied John of Antioch since he'd left home months before. They were his kin. His closest friends. Constant companions as real and engaging as any human company, although human company would be a joy.

The road to Antioch from Jerusalem was long and lonely, and he had been traveling for what seemed an eternity. Believers were plentiful in places of comfort, but on the long stretches in between larger cities, friends in Christ were scarce, even after Constantine's decree. The roads were safer now, with angry mobs somewhat quelled by zealous emperors and loyal local authorities. John at once resented the criminals and their wicked ways, yet lamented their relative disappearance. They were always a fertile source of conversion, as well as an opportunity to practice patience. Alas, the paths were now quite pleasant to travel.

This last trip to Jerusalem gained many souls, but not as many as he had hoped. It was always a puzzle for John: How could people hear such beautiful truth yet not want to follow it?

John rested his weariness on an obliging rock and took in the splendor of the valley stretching its arms wide before him. He twirled the wooden cross around his neck, twisting the wheel of grace. Around and around it spun, sure and solid in his hand. It was well worn, bearing the sins of many in its shallow depths. The simple symbol carved from bright wood contained the shadowy confessions of those who never dreamed of whispering their secrets to themselves, let alone to a stranger with a strange belief. But John was talented. When he talked of spirit and the world to come, people in the here and now listened. And repented. His vision became their own. When he drew a crowd, scarcely a breath was drawn, as his words were the very wings of the Holy Spirit.

In the arid breeze, short, brown curls bounced gently against an olive complexion. Wide brown eyes that could penetrate the heart of darkness sat fixed and sure under long lashes catching traces of dust. This face had seen hardly thirty years, but it bore the telltale signs of late nights with holy books, and a man searching for ancient truth by fading candlelight. John held features more prominent than his contemporaries, and abilities more polished, yet, unlike many of his friends, he had shunned a life in politics. His was a world now forged moment to moment in the crucibles fashioned in Christ, his mind growing sharp on the ever-spinning whetstone of man's search for the eternal.

He dropped the cross to his chest, freeing him to cradle fatigued feet. They knew the road, and they knew the tender massage of his hand. The red, burning ulcers cast his mind adrift to the story of the leper in the Book of Mark.

"Christ, if you heal these sores, I will not speak of it in any town. I assure you." A childlike laugh escaped his lips as he savored the image of keeping the Lord's confidence.

He cast a silent prayer to the heavens that he might find the strength to continue. The sun was low to his weary eyes. He needed a bed for the night.

He prayed aloud. "Dearest Father and Son in heaven, please guide me to shelter friendly to Your holy names." John regarded the sun now dipping in earnest. "Or any shelter friendly to my name."

He dropped his feet, gently settling them upon solid ground. They could barely support his thin frame as it rose to its full height. He surveyed the valley with renewed urgency. Brown huts aglow from fires within interspersed with green fields that burst forth from the desert like gems in earthen gravel.

John was a silent dove descending into the small village. The humility of these dwellings was comfortable and familiar, and his heart leapt with joy to again be in the company of men who knew land and simplicity. At one home, he found what he so desired – a cross, painted on a lintel. Taking this as a hopeful sign, he knocked without abandon. A barefoot young woman with eyes deep and familiar opened the door. Dark, curly hair hung down over her dirty tunic. John was struck by her look of youthful innocence as she clung to the door as if to her life in this lonely country.

"Yes?" Her voice was almost silent, almost unexpected.

"My name is John, and I have traveled many miles from Jerusalem on my way to Antioch. I wonder if you might have shelter available for the night."

She surveyed him from his windblown hair to his bloodied feet. John, ever mindful of his imposition and keenly aware of his disturbing appearance, submitted to inspection without protest. She met his inquisitive gaze before opening the creaky, wooden door to admit him. Inside, the warmth of the one-room hut enveloped him – an embrace at last from so far away. It was a home that knew the simplicity of the world, but to him it was a palace of possibility. There was a fire in here, and to John, that was a small fortune in a life of poverty.

"I am Philip." A tall man with sandy blonde hair thrust a strong, eager hand forward. "This is my wife, Rachel."

John took Philip's hand before bowing slightly to Rachel. A half-smile flitted across her down-turned mouth, but it soon disappeared into the shadows.

"I am John, and I appreciate your hospitality. When I saw the cross on your door, I hoped I had found friends in Christ."

"Indeed, you have. And you are most welcome here, Brother

John." Philip pulled a sturdy wooden chair close to the fire and, with a humble gesture fit for royalty, motioned for John to sit. The flames renewed him, encouraging life into his beleaguered body. John felt as if he had been summoned to the right hand of the Lord. "So, Brother, what brings you out this way?" Philip sat next to him, plainly thirsting for news from beyond his town's borders.

"I'm traveling," John began. His attention was carried to the sound of Rachel placing a plate of fresh bread and olive oil and a glass of blood-red wine on the small table next to him. The drink was as warm as the room and brought a smile to his gratified lips. It fell into him like a smooth elixir, and John followed its pleasant burn down his throat, igniting him as flint into flame. He found an eager tongue and ready voice in the wake of the rich shower.

"I'm following in the way of our elders. I have spent the last few months traveling the route of Paul the Apostle, spreading the word of our Lord. And now, I make for my home in Antioch once more."

John took another drink from the shimmering well, feeling a blessed lightness as the liquid nestled in. His unwillingness to relinquish it was short-lived once the smell of bread reached his nose. He dove into the round, steaming loaf with a satisfying crack. It was hard on the outside and soft within, like a reluctant yet ready convert. He drew a tender piece in smooth form through the oil, then brought it home in a sensation of spices long forgotten and so near to memory. The food was nourishing to his body and soul, and John said a hundred silent prayers of gratitude.

"Your search for converts and the fight for our Lord's victory is a wonderful endeavor, Brother John." Philip took John's glass, still half full, and filled it to the brim, pulling John back from the brink of flour-and-oil ecstasy.

"Thank you, Brother," John said. "I would walk to the ends of the known world and further beyond for the One whom I love, though I admit to wondering where I will find the strength to continue. My feet..." John extended a hand down his leg and rubbed his ankles, emitting an unintended sigh. After so many years, the action had become no casual act, but a habit of which he was hardly aware. Rachel, whose presence had passed almost unnoticed, rose from a chair in the corner and hurried to the washbasin, taking up a pitcher of water and a cotton cloth. She knelt beside John, taking his bloody feet in her hands. John pulled away.

"Sister Rachel, there is no need for that," he said.

"John!" Philip raised his hand, staying John's protest. "You are doing the work of the Lord. This is a noble mission. No small action can further it enough. Shelter, food, and clean comfort are the least we might do for you. Please, Brother. May it be done."

John relented and guided his foot into Rachel's waiting hands. She gently cleansed his sores, much improving before his very eyes under her caring and deliberate attention. At her soft touch, he noticed her hands had seen hard labor. Her palms were rough, and her nails worn to the quick, but John thought she had the caress of an angel as she wrapped his feet in pure, white cloth.

"Thank you." John smiled in gratitude, but Rachel did not meet his eye. She simply dipped her head in acknowledgement until her curls brushed the floor, gathered up her supplies, rose to a hunch, and bustled into the corner to busy herself once again.

"It is our pleasure and our duty to help you, Brother John," Philip continued. "Our community must stand together, though separated by many miles. If we can ease your journey, so be it."

John and Philip talked late into the evening, sharing news from far and wide. John discovered this house was no random stop, but a destination for many of the faithful in the region. Philip told John that he had once been a local missionary and had met Rachel, then a young Jewish girl, at a small church gathering. Smitten with the word of Christ, she converted to the Way under his tutelage, and they had been married two years.

"Do you miss serving the Lord?" John asked.

"I can think of no greater pursuit. Nothing worthier of love.

However, I gave up preaching and missionary ambitions for the married life." Philip cast a wry smile at Rachel. He stared in silence as his expression melted away into nothing. John waited, fidgeting in the long silence. "Want to raise a family," Philip resumed, bringing some unnamed dream back to the moment. "That is a great pursuit too, is it not?" Philip's voice was louder than John expected. Rachel did not turn from her work, engrossed with her tasks in the small kitchen. "Still, I'd like to take up the crucifix again and return to the road. The truth is out there for the taking, and I'd like to take it forth for the glory of Father and Son."

"I understand your urge to return to the Lord's work," John said. "It is truly glorious to serve Him."

"It is, indeed, Brother." Philip softened. "It is, indeed."

That night, John lay in a soft bed in the quiet house, listening to the wind whistle over the thatched roof. The sounds of the night were few and far between, the world long since asleep. He silently cursed his throbbing feet, but the curses turned to feelings of guilt.

"These feathers beneath my head feel like thorns," he whispered. "The Lord had such physical suffering, and here I lay, complaining over bruised feet. How did poisonous expectations of easy comfort so quietly replace a clean life of discipline?"

He berated himself until finally, sleep overcame him. In his dreams, John was greeted by a transparent figure, tall and imposing, the height of three men. Though its form was surreal, the presence and emotion it evoked were real enough. John made to kneel, but the being stayed him with a hand. The mysterious figure bent low and touched John's wounded feet.

"Thank you for taking on my burden, Brother John." The voice was calm, yet forceful. "Now, take your wounds and your words to the East and share in the fullness of the kingdom."

"But Father," John protested, "there is much to do here in the Empire!"

"You will find, my son, that the essential extends beyond the empires of man. Go forth strong. A fire will ignite in the fires of the desert. A tall flame will light atop the mountains. The world of man is one in truth. There is a great wisdom in your hands, and you will come to know this."

"I will do as you say, Lord, but how will I—?"

"Penetrate the world of appearances, and you will find the center of the world."

The figure touched John's forehead with its right hand, setting his vision alight. John was overcome with intense emotion. He saw a large mountain rising tall in the desert. He was in the company of foreign men, their faces aglow.

He awoke with a start, his breath heavy and deep. Sweat trickled down his face and his heart pounded as a thousand drums urging him onward to action. He took a moment to re-discover the quiet and the tranquil. He peered into the far corner of the room where Philip and Rachel lay. In the dim glow of the remaining embers, he could see her, raised up, looking at him. As their gazes met, she turned her head to the floor and again lay down beside her husband. Had she seen the presence or heard the voice, he wondered?

John could not rest the remainder of the night, his mind adrift in confusion and excitement. For a moment, he forgot about the sores on his feet. Right now, he could run to Antioch.

Chapter Three

A h, Brother John. Sit."

Meletius of Antioch waved a casual hand to a chair in front of his desk, keeping his attention fixed on the contents in front of him. It seemed to John a rehearsed motion, necessary for great leaders sworn to uphold both God's duty and the duties of earthly matters at the same time. The great Bishop was poring over documents, mumbling incomprehensible frustrations into thin air.

John knew Meletius, through rumor, to be a man of outstanding character and moral fiber, and the unceremonious welcome did not offend. Furthermore, John was aware that Meletius was currently at odds with the young Emperor Valens, the Arian, and did not at all blame him for being distracted. Meletius's recent exile, and the looming threat of another, appeared to have extracted a small yet significant toll on this great man.

While John waited for Meletius to finish, he glanced around the room. For years, John imagined how this chamber might look, and he was unsure what to think now that the moment had arrived. Bare stone walls set off a sudden chill, yet dusty books and ancient, ornate pictures engendered a warm, somewhat musty, quality. The history was palpable, as was the grave weight of generations of great men struggling to uphold the Lord's kingdom while so much of petty politics weighed it down.

Meletius finally raised his eyes to John. Sunken into worn cheeks, they pierced through him. His visage carried convictions battle tested in the militias of the mind. Meletius garnered great respect from supporters and opponents alike.

"Brother, do you know why I have asked you here?" The lightness of the question rattled John, who steadied himself.

"No, your Holiness, though I am honored by the invitation." John's voice quavered, but he felt sure he would be forgiven his nerves in this most holy place.

Meletius stood, his wooden chair scraping across the stone floor. John, tall in his own right, felt he was gazing up to the heights of the tallest hill just to see the Bishop's face. John took in this imposing presence – earned more from years of learning and legend than actual living. Meletius drifted to the far end of the cavernous office and gazed into the courtyard, his back to John.

"Brother John, we are in a time of turmoil. Did you know?"

John held his tongue. He had learned through his many years of preaching and conversion the advantages and grave dangers of hasty conversation – how people are so quick to ask and slow to listen. He took advantage of the Bishop's back and contorted his face, straining for a response that would neither betray ignorance, nor offend.

"Sir, I don't quite understand—"

"Turmoil, Brother!" Meletius turned on the spot, transforming John's gaze to a blank stare. Meletius glided back to the desk and reached for the back of his chair, his bony appendages tapping mindlessly against the hard wood. "A time of dissent," he added, looking into the air, as if addressing the dust particles in a beam of light through the window.

"Forgive me for asking your Holiness, but does this have to do with Emperor Valens?"

Meletius rolled his head slowly toward John as an owl in the night, one eyebrow raised as though he himself had been the subject of the question. "Among other things." He slid back into his seat. The end of the sentence trailed ominously, sending a pang of uncertainty slithering through John.

"Heretical doctrines abound and there is unrest, John. Unrest similar in scale to the times of Julian, but different in scope."

"I have heard." John's tone carried a new confidence. He took advantage of this opportunity to show solidarity. "Emperor Valens is at odds with your doctrines, is he not?"

"Indeed, Brother. It grieves me to say that the ghosts of Nicaea do not sleep soundly in these days." Meletius gazed over John's head, his face clear of emotion. "I consider this most unfortunate."

"Forgive me, but how does this concern me, your Holiness?"

Meletius leaned forward, resting his elbows on the desk. His right index finger and thumb supported his long head, softening his gaze into a grandfatherly aura.

"Brother, I have heard of your missionary journeys throughout the Empire, following the paths first blazed by Paul. Your record of conversion of souls for the Lord is legendary, as is your rhetoric. I have heard your words rival those of Gregory of Nazianzus."

"I am honored." John bowed his head under the weight of commendation. He resisted the urge to let a smile break over his face. "I had no idea such praise had reached these halls or your esteemed ears. I am humbled."

Meletius drew a deep breath. John waited patiently.

"Brother John, as you may know, Valens adopts the Arian fallacy that God and the Son are not coequal in substance. He believes that Christ was brought into existence by God."

"I am aware of this, your Holiness. He holds that our Father is eternal, but that there was a time when Christ did not exist and was created by the Father."

"Indeed, Brother. This heresy is as dangerous today as it was at Nicaea. The salvation of man depends on the idea that Christ and the Father are one in their essence. Christ is no creation. We must harness friends East and West to restore our strength in the truth that Christ is one in equal substance with the Father and that both are eternal." John thought he detected a glimmer in Meletius's eyes − a light shimmering in God's aspirations for mankind. "Much is at stake. Our claim is not academic, but lies at the very heart of the fate of the souls of men. It is the very heart of faith!"

"I agree, your Holiness. Long has this battle raged. Too long."

Meletius furrowed his brow. A faint, guttural groan escaped his throat before continuing.

"Furthermore, and equally as troubling, John, are the stirrings of paganism. Strong voices urge the pagan gods back into our midst. These are none but the scorched remnants of Julian and a deceased Roman history best left in the grave. Yet its hand reaches out to us from the dead." Meletius narrowed his eyes to slits. "We must not allow the faithful to grab ahold of it. We must not let this cold, lifeless appendage strangle the spirit from all we hold so dear."

"This is troubling, your Holiness. Julian's tolerance of pagan cults was terrifying. These embers continue to burn, though they provide no lasting warmth."

"We have worked too hard and too long to support our faith in Christ to see the old ways return, Brother John."

John knew how much Meletius had invested in the Church. Years of exile, infighting, and study showed in his face – each wrinkle another setback, another battle, another treatise. John looked upon him with both awe and pity.

"How may I best be of service, your Holiness?"

Meletius looked him straight in the eye, exuding a piercing resolve. John felt sure Meletius could ask anything of him in this moment, short of murder, and he would accept.

"Brother, I called you here to send you on a mission of great importance."

John allowed himself the joy of elated thought. He was overwhelmed with the realization that his whole life had led to this moment.

"You want to send me to the West? It would be an honor to again gain support for—"

"No. I will send you to the East."

John's mind froze still before the gap. A chill radiated from his heart, shearing through his limbs. Rooted to the spot, his vision in Philip and Rachel's hut was here resurrected in vivid detail. The very arms of the Father embraced him tightly now, and he could not say if he longed for closeness or escape.

John made to share the dream from that little hut so many months ago, but thought better of it. He had not dared to speak of that most precious of visions to a living soul. It was his fiery golden coin, polished and clean. Its brand upon his memory, still hot and simmering, was the only trace of that night. The dream had portended an eastward journey, but for some reason, something deep inside him still resisted the reality. Even now, in the face of its truth…its clarity….

"Why to the East?" John forced a casual, inquisitive tone.

"Brother, I believe these pagan stirrings, and the accompanying unrest, are fueled in part by religions on the roads that come to our empire from the East. The spirits of China and Persia exert too much influence here, and I am afraid that those such as Julian were, shall we say, aroused by these seductive, yet false, ideas. I want you to travel as far as Samarkand and spread the word of Christ. I want you to spread the word of Christ's co-existence with God the Father to the heathens of the East, and reinforce it amongst the faithful."

A wave of confusion and fear swept through John's mind. He knew of these distant gods and the powerful grip they held over foreigners hostile to the Church. However, as reluctant as he was to admit it – even to himself – he was not always comfortable debating those from outside the Empire. Nevertheless, in this moment, he was determined to keep his words even, so as not to give Meletius a reason to change his rather positive opinion of him.

"There is much work in the Empire, Holiness. Do you not want me to speak against the Arian cause closer to home?"

"Yes and no, Brother. Your work will accomplish many important goals. It will spread the truth ordained by the Father in Nicaea, and it will stem the tide of dangerous ideas from the East. I feel you are just the man to take over this duty."

John found an inner resolve in the wake of Meletius's confidence. "I will go where I am sent in service of the Lord, your Holiness."

"I expected you would. Long have I prayed on this, Brother John. I know for a certainty that you can embrace this task and find success. You will join others who already preach in the loneliest of places. But always remember, you will not be alone. You will not be forsaken."

Meletius removed several scrolls of parchment from a shelf. He returned and unrolled them ceremoniously in front of John.

"Brother, I want you to look closely at this map. It illustrates the route I would like you to follow."

"I would be honored."

John joined the Bishop on the other side of the desk, taking great care not to step on Meletius's long, ornate robe with his own dirty sandals. John stood to just above his shoulders, yet he felt dwarfed in his presence. Meletius produced an engraved wooden utensil with a silver finger on the end and used it to trace a path on the map. John had seen similar instruments used in Jewish synagogues when followers read from the sacred Torah scrolls.

"I have decided you should follow routes that will ensure regular contact with traders and armed men from our own empire. The forays of our emperors against the Sassanid Zoroastrian Shapur will no doubt have left scars, but rest assured, our religious presence is still felt in many cities along the way. We have churches and guards all along the route, owing to hasty truces and local bribes. You do not travel as a soldier, so you should be able to travel in peace. We still have magistrates established in large cities to which our countrymen can appeal."

"Yes, Holiness." Meletius's reassurances did little to quell John's uneasiness. Roman and Sassanid soldiers had been clashing for years, battling for territory and control of trading routes. It was even said that Emperor Julian himself had been killed at Sassanid hands. John was unsure how hospitable the climate would be for Christians, as Shapur was a champion for Zoroastrianism. This would certainly not be like preaching in Jerusalem.

"You will start here, in Antioch." Meletius pointed to an area near the Mediterranean. "Then, you will proceed to Tyre where you will hire a caravan. From there, you will go to Palmyra, then head east to Ecbatana, near the Caspian. From that point, you will go to Merv and Bukhara, before reaching your final destination in Samarkand."

"Yes, Holiness." John winced inwardly as his thoughts drifted to his legs, and the sores he had experienced on his travels from Jerusalem. This was a tremendous distance, and he was quite concerned about how his feet would fare. Nevertheless, he kept such reservations to himself. He knew he must find the strength.

"Brother, these lands are populated by Jewish merchants, as well as followers of Zoroaster and Mani, the Buddha, and the pagan gods of the Hindu near the Arabian Sea. Conversion will not be easy, but the work of our Lord seldom is. As I mentioned, there will be others out in the wilderness with you, whom I have sent, and am sending, from this city. You will all be in a foreign and hostile empire, but you will have each other. I want you to take comfort in their counsel and their companionship. Remember, we are all brothers in Christ. Can you perform this task?"

"I can, your Holiness. And I will."

A full smile finally broke across Meletius's face. "Excellent. I want you to take these with you." The Bishop handed him the map and the other scrolls of parchment. "These are scriptures containing the truth and light of the Lord, as well as the Psalms of the Old Testament. They will be your constant companions. Read them before you leave, and let them guide your way."

Chapter Four

John bid the last of his guests farewell, waving as parent to beloved children as they dispersed into the night of Antioch. Though there were grander gatherings in town, his humble prayer meetings were always well attended, his mastery over scripture and history respected far and wide. Followers often praised the thrilling winds of faith that blew through them at evening's close. His home was more a community church than living quarters. He had given permission for the locals to assemble here in his absence, and they assured him they would pray for his swift and safe return.

John sat by the light of the dying embers in silent prayer, the powerful quiet of the room taking him completely. After concluding his devotions, he moved the chairs back in place against the four walls with great care and precision and cleaned up the immaculate spaces around his meager possessions. He stoked the fire until the flames danced high, once again settling himself in front of the hearth.

Basking in the warmth, he let his mind drift to his meeting with Meletius. For many hours, he had tried to resist its intrusion into his thoughts, but now he could no longer avoid pondering this new direction in his life. Endless questions swirled within him. Could it really be? Was he really receiving such an important charge from none other than the Bishop of Antioch? Had he really seen a prophetic vision of the Father that had come true? Would Christ's fire really ignite through him in the fires of the desert? Would he be protected as an unwelcome guest in another empire?

He felt an ever-familiar pang of uncertainty. The guests at the evening meeting supported his new quest and displayed confidence in his abilities, but John was plagued by doubt. Am I really ready to take on Zoroaster, he thought?

He stood tall and stretched to the heavens. Rubbing his temples with deliberate intention, he tried in vain to banish foreign gods and prophets from his mind. Yet, as he unrolled the parchment map for the tenth time and traced his route to Samarkand with a trembling hand, they came alive in vivid detail as he silently mouthed the name of each city, struggling to speak them plain.

"How am I to preach where I cannot pronounce?" he muttered.

John knew the names were only a secondary concern at this point. He was aware that believers in Christ met in these cities despite persecution and intolerance. Before he left the Bishop's study, Meletius reminded him of standing church meetings all along the route. This provided some comfort, as did the bag of gold Meletius provided for the trip. He glanced at the purse, then back at the map, wondering if it would be enough money to cover such a wide distance. He was looking at a journey of many months.

"Christ," he whispered, trying to exile his insecurities, "if you could feed thousands with a paltry amount of bread and fish, I can certainly manage the miles with this gold. It will be enough, and I am thankful."

An uneasy feeling persisted, born of a shadow of doubt that often accompanies the bravado of professions of faith. He quelled it with the knowledge that he would be doing God's work. The far reaches of the East were creeping closer every day, and what was once mystery was now fertile ground for conversion, even if he could end up buried beneath it. He was not the first missionary to be sent to Samarkand, and he would not be the last. He once again ushered in friendlier thoughts of communities in Christ along the road, already coveting their company.

He unrolled a second parchment and read the familiar scriptures. Meletius had given him a list of stories and teaching points from the

Gospels to help prepare sermons and answer questions. John was already well versed in all the arguments from his dealings around the Empire. He had debated the Gnostics and Arians, and despite his pronounced misgivings, held his own against the followers of Mani and Zoroaster. He had deftly navigated the gauntlets of the godless that attempted to sway him with pagan ideas. John was not Meletius, but he knew his way around a conversation and a conversion. He had no reason to believe this would change on the road to Samarkand, though he knew the stakes would be higher as he would soon be the foreigner.

Sleep came in fits and starts. In the deep night, he gave up his pursuit of dreams and revived the fire. He warmed the house before going to a corner of the room to retrieve his familiar cloth sacks. Slowly, and with his mind filled with visions of unknown lands, he packed light and tight for the journey ahead.

Chapter Five

Tyre bustled. Jostling. Moving. Animals, people, and carts. Everything. Everywhere.

John had been here briefly in his travels but had never spent a prolonged period of time in the seaport. He was aware, however, of Christ's ministries in this city, including his healing of the demon-possessed. His passion for the Lord was not just for word, but also for deed.

"Perhaps Jesus stood in this very spot," he said to himself, as he traced his sandal in a cross through the dirt. At that moment, a scraggly Molossian appeared at his foot, sniffing the ground. John bent low. "Hello, yellow dog."

As he scratched the dog's ears and then worked the grime between his fingers, he realized the coat underneath was probably white, but living in the streets had given the dog a dirty, yellow color. He felt pity for the creature as he wiped his hands on his clothes to remove the filth that clung to them.

"I see you are not the color of your noble, darker fellows," he said, as the dog nuzzled his palm. "That will be my fate in a few days' time. Are you hungry?" John pulled some dried meat from his pack and gave it to the dog, which wolfed down the offering. He stroked the beast's smooth coat and admired its large, muscular build. "What's a hunter and protector doing all alone in this place? Shouldn't you be guarding your master's possessions in the dead of night? But perhaps your bright coloring has seen you more fit for the streets."

John looked around for a sign of an owner, but none appeared – a full sea of empty faces with no use for an uncommon guardian. The dog nudged John's hand, licking him.

"Yes, yes," John said, reaching for more meat. "Why don't you come with me? We can hunt for converts together! Perhaps you can protect me from Shapur himself." John continued on toward the stables near the port. The dog circled him, jumping up on his tunic and leaving muddy prints on his white robe. John looked down at him and frowned. "Don't get too excited, dog. I see in you the same zeal I felt inside when I thought my journey would take me westward. But we're not heading west to the safety of sea." John knelt down to face his new friend. "We're going into the East. Into the unknown. We'll flow against the grain like the mighty Nile, following a river of exotic items and beliefs in reverse to find their mythical source. We will explore the roads from China paved with silk and spices, convert the sons of Shapur, and greet the subjects of Samudragupta and followers of Mani, with their heathen wares on display." An icy tingle of nerves caressed his spine. This one-way conversation made the trip more solid. Tangible. He was not yet ready to acknowledge that his dream would soon be reality. "We must keep our minds on Christ, Molossian." John stood, hands on hips, taking a serious tone with his new companion. "His feet blazed the true paths into the unknown, my friend."

John removed a wax-sealed note and two gold coins from his sack. He walked into the stable to which Meletius had directed him, taking care to avoid stepping in the fresh piles of camel dung that lay on the ground. The dog sniffed at them gleefully and ran around visiting the stalls to harass the animals therein – showing the strength and purpose of his breed. John walked up to a man working on a camel's foot. A small bald spot at the top of his head shimmied as he vigorously worked a pumice file across the camel's nails.

"Are you James?" John asked, swatting away flies.

"I am." The man did not look up from the camel's legs.

"I'm John. Bishop Meletius has a message for you."

James's hands instantly stopped their work. An indignant camel took advantage of the pause and flicked its half-sanded foot, setting it back on the ground. James made no effort to reclaim it. Instead, James stood to face him – a short man rising only chest high to John. His skin was very dark, but John assumed this had more to do with his time in the sun than his heritage. He had a gruff demeanor, and his dark eyes squinted as he sized up John, who handed the parchment to James. He slit the wax seal with a stubby, blistered hand. The dog returned to John's side and sat in expectation, as if he had handed the letter to James himself. He licked his chops in some abstract anticipation.

"This your dog?" James asked.

"Um…" The dog looked up at John, panting. "I suppose."

"What's his name?"

John took in the dog's yellow color and said the first thing that came to his mind. "Flavus."

"Two gold coins for my fee, Brother John. We leave for Palmyra at dawn. You ride. Flavus walks."

Chapter Six

John entered the stables just before sunrise. A dim fire barely lit the central walkway. Flavus, still half asleep, lazily sniffed garbage piles for scraps. The inn where they spent the night had been most inhospitable, reluctantly allowing Flavus inside. This morning, John was more than happy to be in the company of camels. And James. Although for now, the building appeared quite deserted.

"Hello?" John's voice disappeared into the shadows. "James?"

A grunt echoed through the stables. James appeared out of the darkness working leather straps between his pudgy fingers. He passed John without a word and began working with three two-humped Bactrian camels in a nearby stall. Hands that had no business with such skill were amazingly adept at readying the animals.

In minutes, two were prepared for riding. Atop the third, James placed sacks of food and canteens. Even though he knew camels could hold hundreds of pounds, John still watched in disbelief as the size of the load grew. He surveyed the bags of flour and the water supply, as well as assorted dried items. It seemed enough food for a year. James swiftly mounted his ride, then waited expectantly for John to do the same.

"On." James motioned for John to mount his own camel.

"Me?"

"No other man will embark on this journey, Brother, and I doubt very much if Flavus can jump with such skill."

"James, I'm sorry. I don't know how to get on. I'm rather used to walking." John's attempt at levity to dispel the awkwardness fell flat. James was obviously a man of little patience.

James sighed with unveiled frustration and dismounted. "It's really very simple."

James came to the front of John's camel and grabbed a leather strap. He emitted a clicking sound from somewhere in his throat and the camel stooped to the ground, tucking its long legs underneath. James motioned with his hand for John to mount.

John moved to the side of the camel, unsure what to do next. Flavus looked on with interest, cocking his head at the strange scene. James seemed to enjoy the confusion, as he offered no help. John tried to jump and swing one of his legs over the saddle, which was deep in the middle and high in the front and back. He fell backwards to the other side, narrowly missing a pile of dung. James snickered. Flavus barked with glee, sniffing at John's head. Even though John knew James was laughing at him, it was the first sign of warmth James had shown, and his own folly was a small price to pay for the sound of mirth.

"Brother, look." James showed John a metal loop hanging from the side of the saddle. "Put your foot in this loop, hold this strap near the side of the head, and lift yourself in. Watch me again."

John looked on as James mounted. John turned to his own camel. After a brush with the awkward and foolish, he began jumping up and down to find a mounting rhythm. Soon, he was high in the saddle. A moment ago, he did not think the space between the humps would accommodate even him, but he soon realized that two riders could fit comfortably. He held on to a metal loop in front of the first hump to steady his frame. His stomach turned as the camel stood and lurched forward. John now envied Flavus with his four paws on the ground.

James flipped a gold coin to a stable master who had just arrived, and in moments, they were on their way.

Chapter Seven

"Are we in Samarkand yet?"

James was apparently not amused with John's second attempt at humor of the morning. He grunted and kept his eyes focused on the horizon as if that were his only job in this lifetime.

"I'm sorry, Flavus." John looked down at his friend, bounding along the rough terrain. "You followed so willingly. Yet, when I invited you, I did not think about the sand and the long distances. When we reach an oasis, perhaps you can stay there, and I will pick you up someday."

Flavus showed no interest in John's awkward apology. He seemed completely oblivious to the gravel underfoot. John was astonished by the dog's unusual hardiness.

John wanted to ride up next to James and ask him questions about the terrain and the journey ahead. He wanted to know about the legendary rolling dunes and rock formations. He wanted to know when the flatter lands would give way to the mountains near Ecbatana. He wanted to know so much. However, the camels were tied in a line with straps, so John was left to ponder his own thoughts in this barren and sparse landscape.

The subtle comfort of dawn's glow gave way to a determined red sun. The chill in the night air would soon be erased and John did not know whether to welcome or dread it. He knew he was beginning his travels at a time of year when the heat would not be so oppressive, but he felt that cold and hot were relative states in this landscape. He feared the heat would not be the worst of his concerns. According to stories from other missionaries, there were worries far worse than sun in the wilderness. Tales of sandstorms, raiders, scorpions, and other horrors of the desert had reached his unfortunate ears, engendering in him a permanent paranoia. He struggled mightily to put these images out of his mind and let his thoughts drift to preaching the familiar word of God.

As the path stretched on, John found himself mesmerized by miles and miles of rocky sand. Scrubby bushes scattered here and there reminded him of gravestones marking this deathly landscape. He wondered how many travelers had perished under them, seeking shade, but finding a darker end. As John's mind was concocting a strange fantasy of death in the desert, James let out a shrill whistle. The camels stopped, stooped, and the men climbed down from their mounts. Flavus, seemingly unaffected by the journey, ran up to John and licked his hand.

"Where are we?" John asked, stumbling around on the uneven ground trying to find his balance. He felt as though he was still bobbing up and down on his camel.

"Nowhere," James grunted.

"James, I—"

"Brother, we are at a stop. If I told you where exactly we are, would it make a difference? Would you suddenly be oriented?" James's face flushed a deep red beyond the effects of the sun.

"I'm sorry," John replied. "This is all new and rather strange to me. I'm a bit disoriented." John took an uneasy step and almost fell on his face. "As you can see."

James took in a big breath and let it out in a long push through clenched teeth. "We're at a resting point. It's the mid-part of our day." The men looked around. John could feel the silence pounding in his ears. "Show me your map, Brother." James's tone softened into an implied apology.

John took out a parchment, unrolled it under the midday sun, and handed it to James. "Thank you, James. I appreciate it."

"We started here. Tyre." James placed a stubby index finger on the map. "We're heading here." He traced a line to Palmyra. "That will be a minor stop for us on the way to here." James traced the way to Samarkand. "Along the way, we need to stay watered, fed, and safe." He rolled the parchment up and handed it back to John. "I've been leading caravans on this route for almost a quarter of a century, since I was a boy. I'm famous for it now, even in the mighty halls of Meletius. I know where to stay and when to stay away. I know where to drink and where the water is poison. I know who might kill you and who definitely will. I've found some places. I've met some people. I know some things. I've performed this long journey many times." James looked directly into John's eyes. "And I will do my best to keep you alive as Meletius has ordered."

"I appreciate that, Brother James." John dipped his head slightly.

"We have many days ahead." James's voice was grave. "This is only our first resting point, 15 miles outside of Tyre. You see that place over there?" James, who was tying the camels to an obliging bush, distractedly pointed into the distance.

John squinted his eyes in the bright sun. "Yes, I see it. The trees, right?"

"Come with me." James took a bronze canteen from the pack camel and handed it to John. "It is time to drink."

John took a long swig, then put some water in his hand for Flavus before handing the canteen to James. He tilted the water to his mouth for only the briefest moment and for the smallest drop before capping it off. John figured James's body had adapted to the heat and that he, like his camels, could go a long way on little water. When they finally reached the trees, James pointed to the ground.

"Look down, John."

"Shade!" John rushed with childlike excitement to sit under the tree, where Flavus was quick to lay beside him. It was only slightly cooler in the thin lines of darkened sand, but John was grateful for any relief from the punishing sun.

Suddenly, one date, then another, hit him on the head. John looked up. To his great surprise, the squat James had shimmied up the tree and was now tossing down sweet fruit. "Flavus!" John snapped at the dog, busily gobbling up the dates James was tossing at John's head. "Flavus, don't eat them all!" John managed to grab a handful and bit into heaven itself. "Thank you, James. I needed this."

James and John sat in the narrow shade of the palms and ate their fill in relative silence. Finally, as the sun started to dip past midday, James helped John back onto his camel.

"Fifteen more miles to go today, Brother John. We must be with others by nightfall, or we will have a dangerous night."

"Others?" John asked, a tinge of insecurity in his voice.

"We aren't the only souls on this great road, Brother…no matter how desolate she appears."

Chapter Eight

In the lingering daylight, John stretched his saddle-weary back. He smiled, watching Flavus scamper up the side of a tall dune, appearing less affected than he by the thirty-mile trek.

John was going to question James about stopping for the day when James exclaimed, "Down there!" John looked below and saw fires blazing in the night. Rising up to greet them was the sound of laughter and the smell of mutton. A swath of blackness against the landscape separated rings of men and camels.

James anticipated John's question. "Two directions, two sides, John. This camp is split into caravans heading east, and those heading west. Makes trading easier."

"How so?" John asked, taking in the scene.

"Well, those coming from the Far East are loaded down with exotic food and spices. Those beginning their journey eastward can cross the middle path and find supplies. Ingenious, isn't it?"

John was only half listening. As they descended into the camp, his mind was distracted by the artistry of the moment, captivated by the sights and sounds – all the legends, all the stories, now coming alive. He saw scraggly men eating gruel from common pots, and princes dining like kings on purple carpets. There were litters and camels, servants and slaves, men and women bound, and men and women free. There were figures in veils, figures in masks, and turbans piled high. Languages melded together like the stews boiling in the pots. The constant sound of laughter tied it all together like a silken bow. It was a landscape of paradise and evil, all in one place.

"Brother!" James's voice startled John out of his trance. "Dismount!" John did not even realize his camel had stopped. If not tethered to James, he may well have lumbered all the way to Samarkand on this night. "John, this is our site."

John looked around his temporary home. James had picked an isolated spot on the periphery of the eastbound side. Their closest neighbors were roughly 20 feet away. He saw their dark faces glowing in the firelight, and could hear whispers in a strange tongue. Are they talking about us, he thought? Are they hatching a plot or telling jokes?

James, oblivious to foreign conversations, unpacked one of three calfskin tents. "Got this from a friend in the army. Years ago. I cut pieces of an eight-man tent and had three smaller tents fashioned from the materials. They pack easily and only take a few minutes to set up. We'll blend right in with the Roman garrisons out here. At least the ones that are left." James slapped the tent hide. "They don't smell too great, but they are nice and waterproof. I should know. Tested them all the hard way." James handled the tent expertly, pounding small, U-shaped iron stakes into the ground with a mallet. John thought the noise was enough to wake the dead, but those around them paid no mind, too engrossed in their own talk; too taken with their own tales of the road behind, and ahead.

"Thank the Lord for these stakes, Brother John. Don't want to blow away in the night. I'm afraid our weight is useless against the winds in the wilds."

His words had an ominous undertone. It wasn't blowing away to great distances that worried John. It was sandstorms that were known to bury men alive in their very tracks that were the bigger concern.

James had altered the tents to suit life on the road. One improvement was the need for only one or two wooden poles that could be erected inside to create a low, sloping roof. He wasn't housing eight men, so the modification worked well. After the tent was up, John watched James take stacks of woolen mats off the camels and place them inside.

"It gets that cold out here?" John's voice held a tinge of nerves on a mild evening that suddenly felt troublingly cool.

"Well," James looked up at the sky, hands on his hips, "maybe not *here* exactly. But it can be cold where we're going. There are high mountains and long winters to the east. Might as well get our bodies used to the habit of sleeping under them. Besides, their weight and cover will keep out…unwanted creatures." He shot a look at the dog. "And I don't mean Flavus."

James fastened the front flaps of the tent together and double-checked his work on the structure. Next, he headed over to tighten the camels' leads on three additional U-shaped stakes he had driven deep into the earth. John was amazed at the fastidious care with which James carried out camp duty. It was a side he did not expect to see. He was clearly in his element as he prepared the site and the camels.

"Is that enough to hold them?" John asked, imagining the blisters he would have if they had to walk back to Tyre. "I'm not like Flavus, here. My feet can't take this terrain."

"No, it's not." James replied with a grin. "But don't worry yourself over it. I haven't lost one yet."

"Terrific."

"Family loyalties, John. Their grandfather and father were loyal to me, and they are, too. Anyway, I had better see to a fire. Our neighbor's light was enough to set up camp, but we will need our own flames for our other business. Stay here, Brother."

James wandered away into the night, leaving John and Flavus quite alone in the darkness by their tent. John was unsure what he could do to help, and he certainly did not want to make a mess of James's progress so far. He simply waited patiently, forcing conversation with Flavus to maintain the illusion of company.

"Your stamina is strange and inspiring, Flavus." John stroked Flavus's belly as it rose and fell in his sleep. "I'm not sure how you're keeping up. Promise me you'll tell me if you cannot continue, and I will give you to a trader heading west." John looked up at the sky, the stars shimmering overhead. "I wonder if this camp looks like a small constellation to the eyes of our Father in heaven, Flavus. What do you think? Do the twinkling fires around us hold only individual stories, or do they merge into a grander narrative? What is our part in the tale, boy?"

Flavus opened a groggy eye and peered briefly at John before returning to sleep again. Moments later, James appeared with a bundle of wood and tinder. He dug into the ground and cleared out remnants of a small fire ring left by some other group and piled wood in the small pit, adding tinder around the base. He produced a flint, striking it true until sparks rained forth, setting a fire before them.

John looked on lazily. He considered asking James where he got the wood bundle, but thought better of it. He had a strange feeling about James – never sure if his warmth was genuine or forced. John thought about their first meeting the previous day and James's gruff demeanor. He dismissed any notion that he himself had brought about this standoffish affect in James, and decided that long days in the lonely desert would eventually reveal true personalities…whether or not he wanted them to.

Chapter Nine

S it," James commanded. He brought a cotton blanket from the tent and laid it out by the fire. John took a seat as instructed and waited as James laid out a picnic by the firelight. The cotton did not protect his buttocks, now raw from his first long day on the camel. Nonetheless, he knew the cotton fabric was better for sitting in the sand, since they could shake the dirt off easily, then quickly wash and dry it. The wool would need to stay clean and dry for sleeping.

"Eat, Brother," James directed with a casual flip of his hand. "It was a long day, and you will need long strength. I cannot impress this enough upon you."

"What are we having?" John surveyed the buffet before him, trying to appear happy and hungry. The heat of the day had exhausted his body and appetite, but he attempted light conversation and made an earnest effort to summon his hunger. Flavus, smelling food, roused his tired bulk and lumbered lazily over to the fire, taking his place next to John and licking his chops.

"Dried fish, wine…and placenta."

"Placenta?" John's mouth watered, yet the sticky sweet, honey and cheese bread made his conscience wince. "Brother James, I hardly think pagan recipes offered to dead Roman gods such as Jupiter are appropriate for our mission." John fed Flavus a piece of fish, trying to avoid James's eye, which he knew would be full of ire.

"*Our* mission? Brother John, you are here to convert souls. I'm along for the ride. To set up hides." He gestured with his head toward the tent. "And to watch yours."

"James, I don't see how any of that—"

"There is a woman in Tyre who bakes Cato's ancient placenta recipe to perfection, and I always celebrate first day's end on the road with this treat. Consider it my reward for starting another long journey away from home and in strange company. We will likely not see this delicacy again once we cross the Roman frontier, so come. Let us eat sweetly off Meletius's gold before it must be spent on foreign delights."

John was indignant. He hardly thought a pagan temple offering befitted the start of a journey such as this.
"But James—"

"We have many days ahead!" James cut the protest short. "There is more in this desert than sand and rock, and more in this sky than sun and brilliant blue. Though the love of Christ may hold sway in our motherland, a nod to an ancient king of gods cannot hurt our journey in other places."

John looked him in the eye. "If you, Julian, and Valens had your way—"

"What are you implying, Brother?" James shot him an angry look that nearly toppled John backwards.

"Nothing."

"If I were you, John, I would wash your remaining words down with wine, and—" James caught himself and took in a deep breath. He let it out slowly, pushing the air from his lungs deep into the fire. His face melted into calm. "John, please. Honor my tradition on this night."

He handed John a piece of the flaky bread and John ate obediently. He had to admit the sensation of bread, cheese, and honey was incredibly satisfying, and it brought a smile to his face. He chewed slowly and smiled at James, who forced an uneasy grin – a silent truce forged in the sight of Flavus, who licked John's hands and face clean.

That night, lying in the tent under a pile of woolen blankets, John replayed the events of the day. It was an easy task, as it had pretty much consisted of sandy, rocky hills and blazing sun. John thought of home, and James, and how quickly one's bed and company could change.

Only a few days ago I was in Antioch with kin in Christ and word received, he thought, and today I am in such strange lands with the oddest of company. He regarded James sleeping on his left, and Flavus to his right. He uttered a prayer to Christ that his journey would prove safe and fruitful, then added another that the wool blankets would do their job, before drifting off to sleep.

Chapter Ten

John awoke to odd sounds – groaning, clanking, voices. All mixed and none pure.

He looked to either side and saw that he was alone in the tent, flaps open to the camp. He pulled on his robes and stepped outside. James was nowhere to be seen. Flavus was curled up on the cotton blanket beside the smoldering fire. Dawn broke into a cloudless sky.

He turned to look at the entire expanse of the main camp, now illuminated in sunlight. What was striking in yesterday's night was now indescribable in the wake of the new day. The sleeping ghosts of the Colosseum were now awakened, their storied sparks re-struck. The colors. The carnival. There were men and women moving. Everywhere. Much like the previous evening, daytime did not decree equality. His eyes were drawn to the people – some riding, some walking, some bound, some with heads covered – slaves, sinners, princes, and thieves. All here. All at once. Legend and caravan met at this crossroads where traders passed his gaze in all directions.

"What do you think, Flavus?" Flavus perked up at his name. He plodded over and stood at John's side, his frame rooted to the spot – an animal-like mirror image of his new master.

Flavus wagged his tail and barked at the passing camels while John's gaze settled upon a lone rider. Like Moses clearing a route across the sea, the man and his creature opened a path through the expanse of bodies. John shifted his weight as the camel came closer and closer, until it was within six feet.

The camel's master clicked his tongue, and the camel stopped and bent low. The rider, dark-skinned and dressed in a thin white robe, dismounted with great precision and care. He set his sandaled feet on the rocky ground and John noticed that he wiggled his toes and tapped them, as if setting anchors in the sand. The stranger drifted toward John, an apparition of Aryan lore — an ancient spirit from a distant land — seeking company in lonely places.

"Greetings," the camel master said. His eyes pieced into John's, creating a connection. After the formal address, he bowed slightly, hands clasped as if in prayer. He had a gangly appearance, standing to John's height. Various bones and joints were visible under a thin skin, mimicking the look of the poles holding up John's tent. A short beard matched the salt-and-pepper hair on his head in both length and color. A red dot graced the space between his eyebrows. To John, he was a character from a long-forgotten lesson in myth, come to life before him.

"Hello." John nodded slightly. He looked around uncomfortably for a sign of James. What if this camel master asks me for directions, he thought? John felt a faint anxiety rush to his stomach.

"My name is Sri. I wonder if you could assist me."

"I am John. How can I be of service?" Oh, no! I only know the road to Tyre, he thought.

"I am traveling eastward, many days from here. I have lost my party to tragedy and am now traveling alone. I wonder if you might allow me to join you."

"Um, Sri, I…" John stammered, taken aback. He recognized Sri to be of Indian descent and was not sure he wanted to travel with a devotee of foreign gods.

Sri seemed to sense John's discomfort, as he gave a look that was as soft as a man could conjure.

"I assure you I mean you and your party no harm. I have lost my possessions and have been slightly injured." Sri lifted his leg to show John a small puncture wound, crusted with blood. "I have naught but my camel here. I have none to ask for aid, but I saw you and your friend ride in last night from the west. You are a small party, and you seem to be traveling light." Sri nodded at John's small campsite. "I will make an assumption your business on the road here is not the regular course of business, and I would be glad to be free of the shackles of the crowd at this point."

John's heart felt for Sri, but his mind still resisted the idea of taking on another traveler. He wanted to ask Sri the details of what misfortune had overtaken him, but thought better of it. Somehow, not knowing made it easier to face the long journey ahead. After fighting with his conscience and a childish notion of foreign threats, his sense of Christian hospitality got the better of him.

"I suppose we have room for one more."

"Thank you, John." Sri bowed low. "Your help is most appreciated." Sri got to his knees and extended his hand to Flavus, who approached him with excitement and profound interest. "Hello, Sir. I have never seen a large dog who could roam free on this road." Sri wore a youthful smile. "And what might your name be?"

"That's Flavus." Sri and John were startled by the voice of James who blew into camp like an icy wind. "And you are?" James made no attempt to mask the suspicion and irritation in his voice. John noted that the presence of this stranger cast James back into his old demeanor.

"I am Sri." He stood to face James and accorded him the same bow John received minutes earlier.

"I'm James. Why have you come to our camp?"

Sri's friendly gesture and tone passed through James's consciousness unimpeded, as his words held their cold edge. Sri was unfazed by his new acquaintance's brusque manner.

"You are certain, James, that I came to your camp? Perhaps I was brought here." John and James looked at each other, puzzled by the remark. "I approached your friend to ask for your assistance. I lost my party and my meager goods to raiders. And, I have suffered an injury."

"Raiders are a risk of the road and a constant threat to commercial caravans," James said flatly. "Surely, you knew that when you set out. So, what do you want from us? Food? Water?" James addressed these questions to Sri with his back, as he was busy packing up the tents and supplies. "I hope it's not money, because you would be wiser to—"

"I would like to travel with you." Sri's voice was quiet, his tone matter of fact. Still, his request cut through James's tirade like a knife. James froze still in the face of this statement, as welcome to him as a camel with a broken foot. John held his breath. James turned slowly and glowered at Sri.

"Travel with us?" he spat. "I do not think so, Sri. We have miles to go." James resumed packing the camels, as if he had stamped out the fiery request like a dull ember.

"I too have a long distance to travel." Sri remained unperturbed, amicably pursuing his quarry. "I have therefore been brought to the right company."

John looked at James's back and said, "James, why not? No one should travel alone on this road." John was surprised to hear his own voice defending Sri.

"As you can see from my stature," Sri added, "I do not eat nearly my weight in food, and I can provide conversation along the way."

John smiled to himself and thought it would be nice to have Sri along if only for the amusement of watching another person attempt to sustain civilized conversation with James. James stood with his hands on his hips. John was coming to appreciate this stance and thought that it somehow made the already shorter James look less imposing.

"Fine," James grumbled. "I assume you are heading to your homeland on the subcontinent. In that case, we'll be rid of you by Merv, where you can take the southern route to Srinagar."

"Thank you for your graceful assent," Sri said. "But actually, I am heading east of Bukhara and Samarkand."

"For the love of Christ," James mumbled. John took devilish

delight in watching James's face drop and turn a beet red, as he realized their destinations were similar.

"Indeed," Sri whispered.

"Come with me." John approached his new acquaintance. "I will clean your leg and wrap it with cotton."

"Thank you, but that will not be necessary. My leg will be how it is, until it is otherwise. At that time, it will again be how it is to be."

"Are you sure? I too have had problems walking around and am no stranger to crimson sores on my lower limbs. I know a thing or two about leg injuries. I can help you to heal that wound."

Sri's stare penetrated deep into John. "You already have…Brother John."

Chapter Eleven

The sun dipped behind them.

The party had not made a sound since their last stop hours before for a light meal and water. Only the slow, methodical clop and occasional huffing of the four camels could be heard. There was a breeze that John longed to feel when it came. When it departed, he felt a tinge of loss.

Flavus continued to trot beside John's camel, never showing any sign of fatigue, even as the terrain became increasingly difficult. His companionship was as constant and unwavering as the sun to the desert sand. John gave up wondering how Flavus could possibly endure walking in these conditions, and had abandoned his attempts to lift him into the saddle to ride. He kept him well fed and watered, simply marveling at the dog's determined strength.

John looked back at Sri, whose eyes were closed. He once again beheld a face that wore a constant smile and look of calm. Every once in a while, a guttural hum was audible, but John assumed it was Sri's stomach growling.

James's piercing whistle brought the camels to a stop. The men dismounted at an oasis where other groups had gathered for rest and relaxation.

"Are we stopped for the day?" John asked, relieved to finally climb from his camel. His legs and buttocks were growing increasingly more painful, even though James insisted that the discomfort would eventually pass as the days wore on, the body growing accustomed to the awkward postures and relentless jerking and bouncing.

"Yes, Brother," James said. "Fill the canteens, while I make camp."

"Come along, Flavus!" John slapped his leg and Flavus came running. "Sri?"

"Of course I will join you. Where you lead, others may follow."

The trio walked to the bank of the spring and John dipped his canteen, drinking long and deep. The water was sweet, but he had to spit out flecks of dust and dirt.

"John, like this…" Sri took the end of his own garment and dipped it in. The hem bowed under the weight of the clear water. He held a canteen under the trickle as it filtered through the cloth, pure and clean.

"Now why didn't I think of that?" John asked, shaking his head with a smile.

"You would have, John, but you have only been out here a few days."

Sri drank his fill on the sandy bank. John sat next to him, Flavus's head in his lap.

"How long have you been out here?" John asked. Sri did not answer right away. He turned his head to the setting sun and uttered a phrase. "Sri?"

"How long?" Sri's voice had a sing-song tone as he repeated John's question. "How long? How long am I on the road?" Sri pointed to a stand of date palms. "As many dates as are on those trees, it seems."

"Sri, that's silly. There must be thousands of dates there."

"Do not assume, Brother, that I have only been on this road once." Sri looked at John and raised his eyebrows. "I ripen as they ripen."

"Sri, I'm not up for riddles. I'm tired."

"This trip has been about two years. But this is only one excursion, which is part of a bigger journey."

"What are you doing out here?"

"The same things you are, I think."

"Sri, how could you know why I'm out here? We have not discussed that.”

“My eyes see more than sand. I see you do not have foreign cargo. You only have goods from home and gold to buy water and shelter, and to trade for necessities. And I have seen you with the scrolls of your holy book. You are out here to celebrate.”

“Celebrate? What am I celebrating?”

“What you should always celebrate, Brother. Your connection.”

“My connection to what? James? Flavus? Those are really my only connections right now.”

“No. I mean your connection to your Christ.”

“Oh…right,” John stammered. “I do have a strong connection with Him.”

Sri dipped his hand into the clear, cool water. He held his hand high, and watched the droplets bounce and bubble back to their home.

“You are out here to share that connection with others, John. I can tell you live your life in that celebration. Your lack of comforts indicates you did not have much to bring in the first place. There are many on this road that carry their wealth with them – material wealth that can be lost to hostile tribes. It makes them the men they are, and binds them to the world. If the raiders strike and steal, it is as if they steal away the very heart of the prince. But you and I have left much of the world behind to seek other treasures. We are not so different from each other. We do not bear fruit in material ground. We seek only to grow the ever-present soul.”

Sri produced a cotton cloth from a small sack and dipped it in the water. He gently washed his leg, while mouthing an incantation. John was amazed that the wound appeared to be healing so quickly after seeing it so fresh.

“How do you know of Jesus, Sri?”

Sri continued to tend to himself. “You are not the first of the West to travel to the East. You are not the only Roman heading into the hostile empires. I know of your books. I have read some of them.”

"You *read* them? How?" John knew the holy word had traveled along the road, but it was shocking to meet a Hindu who actually acknowledged reading the parchments.

"In addition to my native tongue I have learned not only to speak, but to read, yours, and those of your ancestors. Although, there are Christians in my land who have translated the texts for our benefit."

"I'm sorry, Sri. I forget there is another world out here."

"Same world. Different view. I come from a vibrant place. A place of wealth, riches, and knowledge. The borders of my lands have allowed amazing advancements to slip through. You already know through the wars of history that we have our own kingdoms toward the rising sun. But it is often custom that does not enter easily into the histories or cultural consciousness of men."

"Have you considered Christ as a savior?" John's mind began to make chatter about receiving a convert. What better prize than a learned Hindu soul?

"I beg your pardon?"

"Christ, Sri. You mentioned you are familiar with some of the texts. Surely, you have read of Jesus's deeds."

"I have." Sri looked up from his leg, now drying in the evening air. "He was a man of great wonder. He knew how to celebrate."

"But what about his other side?"

"What other side, John?"

"His divine side. He was the Son of God, as you know. The only begotten, ever in existence. As such, he is God and man. He died for our sins and our salvation. Life everlasting, Sri." John relished this opportunity to start a debate with a learned man of foreign descent. It would be good practice, he thought, for debates to come.

"Ah, you refer to your creed."

"That's right. The creed from Nicaea."

"I have heard of this creed – one Father, one Son, one incarnation, and one salvation. It states your beliefs so succinctly, ensuring less talking and more celebrating."

"I suppose you could look at it that way," John laughed.

"John, I would like you to say a word for me. A Sanskrit word. Will you, please?"

"Of course. What is it?"

Sri closed his eyes and took in a slow breath. He let it out in a gentle tone. "*Om*..." He held the silence at the end.

"How does that word go again, Sri?"

"Oh...mmm..." Sri contorted his face to emphasize the shape and sound of each syllable.

"Oh...muh..." John tried. Flavus, on hearing the strange sound, looked up and cocked his head sideways.

"Try again, Brother. Leave out the 'uh' sound at the end. It is Om as in home."

"Oh...mmm..."

"Good, John!"

"What is that? What did I just say?"

"You might think of that as my creed, John. It is at once the shape of things, like Flavus, or that date tree; it is also shapeless things, such as the air we take in, or the water we just drank; finally, it is that of no form, but in existence – the concealed places of the universe to which we are bound. Then, of course, the silence at the end has something profound to say to us. We have to take into account the whole—"

"Wait, Sri." John's face flushed. "You're telling me I just said the creed of another religion?"

"In a manner of speaking."

"I should not have done that." John stood up, visibly agitated. Flavus also jumped to his feet, fully alert. "I cannot profess faith in another like that. Come, Flavus!"

Flavus and John stormed off, leaving Sri alone by the edge of the water in the encroaching darkness.

Chapter Twelve

So, John's a Hindu, is he?" James's unceremonious welcome greeted Sri as he wandered back to the campsite where two tents stood. James and John were sharing one tent, and James had set up a second for Sri. Sri placed himself with a smooth, deliberate motion onto the cotton cloth and took in the firelight. "I'll tell you, it was worth bringing you along just to see the look on John's face when he told me what you did! A few more nights like this, and I swear, Sri, I'm hiring you permanently. John's a Hindu now. Terrific!"

The stinging remarks aroused a fiery glare from John, who consoled himself with leftover placenta.

"Perhaps you are as well, James," Sri said.

James sputtered a few drops of water, sparking a fleeting smile from John's lips.

"What does that mean?" James asked.

"What do you believe in, James?" Sri tossed the question quiet, yet true, casting a tense net about the group.

John, in a gesture of peace and veiled appreciation for James's sudden irritation, handed Sri a piece of placenta. Sri tossed a portion of it to Flavus.

"I believe in myself," James said. "I believe in the stars. I believe in the power of hard work and a good map. I believe a man is only as good as he stands before you. And I believe a full stomach is the key to an early start."

"That's good, James." Sri sat back and looked at the moon

dangling over the desert. "All those items you mentioned have an origin, I trust?"

"Sure they do," James replied.

"Is it God, James?" Sri directed his relaxed eyes from the moon to James.

"God? I don't know. But it all has to come from somewhere, I suppose. Could be God. Could be gods. Could be anything."

"Hinduism would tell you the same thing," Sri said. "The infinite, creative source of being, Brahman, has willed creation, and the gods watch over the things of this world. There is birth, preservation, and destruction." Sri picked up a clay cup. "It is like this vessel, Master James. It was a lump of clay, inert and void of function, though not void of potential. Then, it was molded through a master's hands into something useful. Fired in flame, it hardened and was prepared for a journey in the world. And here it is now, unique, receptive, and ready to serve. When its lifecycle is complete, it will break into pieces that scatter to dust, and once again become part of the earth. Maybe someday, the remnants will find their way into the hands of another potter. Am I so different? Is my body so different? Is my life force so different? I am a Hindu, yes, but all possibility is one in me."

"Interesting," James said, as he grabbed the vessel and took a drink of the water inside.

"So there you have it, John," James laughed. "We're all Hindu. James the pagan. I wonder what Meletius would say right now."

"Wait, Sri." John could no longer hold his silence. "Are you certain we are all Hindu? Maybe the truth is you are a Christian and don't know it."

"Interesting." Sri looked thoughtful.

"It could be so, Sri," John continued. "The creative force of your Hindu culture could be the Holy Father wrapped in Hindu clothing. The will of your creator might be the very same will that begot Christ."

"This could be," Sri nodded. "This could be the case, of course."

"Sounds like you're both saying the same thing," James interjected.

Sri and John looked over at him, surprised at his philosophical contribution. "Well," James continued, "listen to yourselves. Does it really make a difference what the hell you call it? A cup is a cup." James put it down on the blanket. "Mold it, make it, use it. Then, send it home to dust. If you can do it, why worry about how it's done?"

"You make a good point." Sri took the cup back and twirled it in the firelight. "I don't know who made this cup, John, but it holds water. In the end, does it matter who made it, so long as its purpose is served?"

John stared into the fire. He did not like the feeling that James and Sri were teaming up against him. He struggled with the idea that origins did not matter, but did not want to say it out loud. A shadow of fear crept into his mind that if he conceded this point, he would enrage God.

"I don't know, Sri," John shook his head. "I don't know."

"Sit here you two," Sri said. "I am going to get something." Sri went to his small satchel and rooted around. He came back to the fire moments later with a little book – little, but thick. He opened it and turned the pages, a look of amusement on his face as he worked his way to the middle section. "May I?"

John nodded.

"I don't have time for bedtime stories," James said in a huff on his way to bed. "We have an early day tomorrow."

Sri and John watched him disappear into the tent, and Sri began to read.

"As the sun rises in the west, I am filled with confusion. As the sun sets in the east, I am perplexed. As the twinkle of stars begins my day, I am amazed. As the light of the moon shines at noon more brilliantly than any fire on earth, I am puzzled to my core. Yet, I am not afraid. I do not fear the new, for I know that it is but a dream, and that 'new' is merely a way of seeing – of perceiving, just as I know the flow of my past is a dream. Morning's eastern suns of old were only an expectation. My evenings gazing west at the setting fire dipping into the horizon were only habit of the self. The stars at night always had a brilliance, but not to my sleeping eyes. And the moon…oh, how the moon had so much to share, yet, I was convinced darkness held more sway. So now, as Brahma creator desires to create a new dream, decreed from his very lips, who am I to fear his pleasure? Who is Sri to summon the usual in the face of the unique? Indeed, who is Sri? Sri is only that which the Lord Himself has preferred in this moment, and in the next moment could cast to the changing winds of fate."

For a moment, neither spoke. Even the wind was silent as it considered the prose.

"That was beautiful, Sri." John smiled in the firelight. "Thank you."

"It was my pleasure."

"Sri, I know what you said before…by the water…I know you didn't mean offense."

"I am glad you know that." Sri clasped his hands together in front of his chest and dipped his head.

"I guess my discomfort is me fighting with…the changing winds, as you would say."

"Take comfort, John. Take comfort in change and uncertainty. If you believe you live life by a divine decree, do not question even the smallest changes in fate and fortune. In that way, you save yourself for good works and save yourself from a troubled mind."

Chapter Thirteen

How can this be happening? I want answers!" Meletius sat in his study, head in his hands, screaming down at the table. His advisors looked at one another with blank stares and blank minds, clearly sharing a palpable discomfort between them. Their silence over the last few minutes was a sure sign they could not suggest how a group of men in a room could possibly stem the tides of conflict, but no one wanted to admit this to Meletius.

In the pause, an anonymous throat cleared. A single nose sniffed. Someone's weight shifted.

"How in the name of the fires of hell can Valens advocate for the Arian cause?" Meletius asked no one in particular. "And how can paganism still be gaining so much support? Isn't Julian in the grave?" The Bishop looked up and into the faces of his supporters, fully taking in their blank stares. His voice took on a tone of supplication. "Is our work for naught? Do we act in vain? Is our constant struggle against the Arians a futile exercise? We put our necks under the axe every day for this cause. Does that not count for something?" Meletius caught his breath and calmed himself. "I feel trapped in a narrow room, evil closing in from all sides. Did not the Father shine His face upon us in Nicaea? Why have men turned their own faces from His will?"

"If I may, your Holiness…" Basil, a short, rotund man and one of Meletius's closest advisors, raised his hand with a ginger hesitation. Because of his longstanding association with Meletius before and after the Bishop's recent exile, the other advisors acknowledged Basil as one who could speak freely. Meletius gave him a weak nod of recognition. "Your Holiness, Valens has persecuted the pagans, but he has never tried to suppress their ways completely. Placation of certain factions is politically expedient in difficult times. His Catholic persecutions have not seen similarity among paganism. This creaky, wooden Arian doorway has remained ajar for years."

"I am aware of that, Basil. I stand in its shadow every day awaiting my punishment to walk through. Thank you for your striking carpentry metaphor. I shall ride to the Sassanid frontier and share it with our fledgling Emperor."

"Your Holiness, I know all has not been easy lately. I know there is constant talk of exile and war. What would you have us do?"

Basil's lament was reflected in the expressions of all present. It was clear Meletius was troubled, but no one was sure how to act. They were accustomed to Meletius's strong anchor, but now they were all adrift.

"I would have you support the cause of Christ, men." Meletius was quiet yet convincing. "His true cause. I would have you put your vows into practice for the sake of the Lord, damning fear of reprisal."

"In what form, your Holiness?" Basil asked.

"We must cast heresy from before our sight in the name of the Lord. Factions loyal to our cause must root out heresy where possible." Meletius's rage was slowly escalating to vengeance.

"Your Holiness, how do you propose we do this?" Basil cast a quizzical expression. He looked to the others for help, but no one would dare to meet his eyes.

Meletius stood purposefully from his chair and paced like a lion behind the men seated at the table before him. His long, lean body moved in determined stride, straight and stiff as a compass point true and unyielding.

"It has come to my attention that various missionaries sent out over the years have been doing the opposite of that to which I entrusted them. Even those I believed I could trust beyond a shadow of a doubt.

They have been sitting in sympathy with pagans and heretics while out of my sight."

"Your Holiness?"

"Reverse conversion, Brother Basil!" Meletius slammed his fist into the table between two advisors, sending them aside in shock. He strode to his desk and gathered letters into his hand. He went back to the table and cast them unceremoniously into the assembly. "Have you not noticed that half our missionaries do not return? Why do you suppose that is? Surely, it is not for a love of sand and heat. Surely, they are not taking up arms against Shapur on the frontiers. Surely, they are not carried to heaven in storms of dust."

"Agreed, your Holiness, but what is your plan?" Basil asked.

"For the last few years, I have identified emissaries loyal to our cause, separate from the official missionaries I have sent onto the road. Many are bound to the Church through debt, or oath stronger than preference, or desire to practice rhetoric." Meletius bent down so that his head was level with the others. His voice was almost a whisper. "Some of them just have a strong desire to be away from Antioch…for various reasons." Basil and the others exchanged uneasy glances. "They have, these past months, been moving through the eastern routes, mixing in with my more…academic missionaries who were meant to spread the highest word." Meletius's tone took on a conspiratorial air. "They have been attending missionary meetings, ascertaining the truth, or lack thereof, emanating from the mouths of the supposed faithful."

"Spies, your Holiness?" Basil looked at Meletius with some surprise. "You have sent spies into the East?"

"Do not think of them as spies, Basil. Think of them as…interested congregants and supporters. Objective critics for the eager audience in this room."

"How will they report back, your Holiness?"

"They already have reported back, through these letters in front of you. Through traders and guards, through loyal church leaders, and through our networks in other empires. We have outposts and garrisons all through that part of the world, men, and not every soldier is a friend to Julian or the Arians. News has already reached me. It takes a long time, but at least we know that someone is looking out for the interests of the Church. We should not feel so…helpless. I cannot assure you our friendly voices are not also tainted, but at least we have hope."

"And what do we do now, Holiness?" Basil asked.

"Now? *Now?*" Meletius sat back down in his seat, picked up a bundle of letters, and waved it around while looking each man squarely in the face. "I assure you, when enough evidence reaches my ears, I will take the only action I can."

Chapter Fourteen

T he good Lord has brought us another day!" John emerged from the tent and greeted Flavus, Sri, and James already up and by the fire.

"Good morning, Brother John," Sri said. "You are certainly in a light mood. I dare say you are the very sun rising to greet the day!"

"Wonderful," James said. "Two happy Hindus. I can see we're in for a simply magical morning. Next, you'll tell me Flavus has converted, and then I'll really be in trouble."

John's mood remained unmoved against the hard wind of James's sarcasm. "Not even your spears can pierce me this morning, James. I can't wait to set about God's work today!" John took in a mighty breath before sitting down next to Sri and helping himself to some bread.

"Setting about God's work?" Sri looked at John with a raised eyebrow. "My dear Brother, more ages have passed on this earth without the feet of men, than those under his sandal. What makes you think God needs us to do his labors? Are we central to a plan?"

John felt his stomach drop. He had hoped for a new start today.

"Sri, please. Does not your walking mind ever escape your stalking thoughts? It's so early. I just awoke. Can I not have a few minutes before we start the philosophical debate?"

"I am sorry, John," Sri said, bowing his head. "I will try to have more respect for your morning hours."

James looked across the gap of silence toward John, a malicious gleam in his eye. He knew there was a glimmer of hope that the conversation would end here, but he simply could not resist an opportunity to goad his poor companion.

"Answer the man, John," James smirked.

"What?" John was visibly agitated.

"Why do you think you are central to the divine plan?" James asked. "You are the great John of Antioch, broker and barterer in the bazaar of words and salvation. If you really stand by your words, no hour is too early to defend yourself or the noble work you so dearly love to perform. What if the heathens up ahead want to argue before daybreak? Will you tell them simply to come back with their questions at noon?" James let out a quiet cackle and returned focus to his breakfast.

John let out a deep sigh and threw his crusts to Flavus. "It's not that I think we are a necessary part of a plan, Sri, but surely the Lord created us for a reason. Why put man on earth if not for His glory? If not to attend to His doings?"

"Perhaps," Sri said.

"Perhaps?" John smiled. "For what other purpose is man?"

Sri picked up a handful of sand and let it filter lightly through his fingers. "This sand, Master John, serves a purpose." Sri swept his hand across the eastern horizon. "The sun also serves a purpose. If God brought all this about, then surely sun and sand also live for His glory. Surely, they serve Him. Surely, they sing His praise in the simple performance of their assigned duties. Do you not remember Psalm 148? Sun, moon, and stars all praise God."

"I am aware of that passage, Sri, but they don't praise Him like a man will," John protested. "They do not sing of His glory. Is not a person greater in that respect? Surely, that is the gift of man – to sing the praises of God. The Psalms are clear on this, Sri. Man is to praise God with trumpet sounding and with tambourine dancing. Without man, instruments could not praise the Lord. They would simply be a collection of cold and lifeless hides and bells. Our life is a performance for the greatest director…the greatest orchestrator. We are the very instruments of praise. Our voice is the first and greatest tool for worship. It is our birthright. Our gift received, and gift to give."

"Ah, Master John, Psalm 150 begs everything with breath to praise the Lord. Is not Master Flavus included? And what about your prophet Isaiah? Did he not suggest that mountains, hills, and greenery come to life for the righteous? If all things sing praise or can praise, maybe the message is that it is all one thing praising itself. Why would the voice of all voices need to hear ours for its satisfaction? Furthermore, why would the eye of all eyes need to see our prostrations and performances? Perhaps the one who praises, and the one who hears it, are the same."

"That is bordering on blasphemy, Sri."

Sri turned to meet John's eyes. He found in them the very trace of indignation he expected. He put his hand on John's shoulder. "Master John, we are the voice. We are the eye. We just cannot hear or see this truth. We are too busy speaking and searching. Too busy performing."

John pushed away Sri's hand and returned to his tent. Flavus stood and lumbered in after him. Sri looked over at James who shrugged his shoulders, a smirk of resignation crossing his lips. Sri excused himself and wandered into the desert.

＊ ＊ ＊ ＊ ＊

John sat, thinking. Fuming.

"I knew that conversation last night wasn't the end of it," he said to Flavus. "Who is Sri to tell me the business of the Lord? I know the Scriptures, but surely the sun does not praise God through emission of warmth the same way man praises through word and deed. It is simply the sun's duty to be warm."

After he calmed down, John emerged, Flavus at his heels, to continue the discussion – which by this time, had become an argument in his mind.

"Back for more?" James muttered.

"Where is Sri?" John asked, in no mood for sarcasm.

"Over there." James tipped his head to the east unceremoniously, opting not to instigate John any further.

John squinted into the distance. He watched Sri, standing tall on a distant dune, back erect, hands clasped above his head. Sri separated his hands and arched his back until his hands almost touched the ground behind him. After a pause, he bent forward to touch his feet before extending his hands back to the sky. Sri held the pose until John thought sure the very dune would shift beneath him. He repeated this action three more times before returning to a resting position.

"Flavus, come!" John and Flavus walked to Sri.

As John approached, Sri changed postures. He was now standing with his spine perfectly erect, arms extended in a diamond overhead, legs bowed in a diamond underneath. Sri's body was firm and stable. Unmovable. His eyes were closed, and he had a peaceful grin on his face. His body was as still as the sand. John thought the postures and movements looked uncomfortable, but he was impressed with Sri's flexibility and capacity to withstand what seemed a tremendous amount of discomfort.

"Good morning again, Brother John." Sri opened his eyes, but kept his gaze fixed in the distance.

"Good morning again, Sri. What are you doing?"

"Greeting the morning with discipline and balance…in abbreviated fashion, of course, as we have miles to go soon, but a greeting, nonetheless. How can a man say he is devoted to his creator when he does not make the simplest of efforts to acknowledge creation's first act of the day?" John was silent. "Pray with me now, John." Sri released himself from his pose with a deep exhale and took John's hand. Together, and in joy, they faced the sun. "Master John, will you do the honors?"

John focused on the horizon and mustered a feeling of gratitude for the sun that would warm another day. "Lord, we acknowledge Your glory this day. We ask for Your guidance and protection as we seek to spread Your word. We ask for Your favor today as we carry out Your will. In Jesus's name we pray. Amen."

"Amen."

Chapter Fifteen

After the monotony of desert trekking, with only occasional outposts marking the countless days, the group climbed into the plateaus surrounding Ecbatana.

"There," Sri said, pointing. The settlement lay in the distance, heat vapors disturbing the level horizon into billowing movement, as if the city waved upon a flag.

A large mountain loomed ahead. There were peaks to the southwest and east, and plains directly to the south. After so much desolation, it was almost shocking to see hills and valleys teeming with the promise of life – with the promise of human contact on a scale rarely seen on this lonely road.

Though no one in the small caravan spoke, the excitement was palpable. Endless dusty, rocky trails were the hallmark of the difficult journey. It was hot and unpredictable, and John said a prayer of gratitude for the change of scenery, and for his companions. They had become like family after so much time together. He glanced down at the ever-moving Flavus, who trotted alongside the party with unwavering loyalty.

"Your spirits are always up!" John smiled down at his friend.

The wide paths leading to the large city narrowed toward a gate flanked by two massive stone lions.

"Monuments of the Great Alexander," James said, tipping his head toward them. "Built in memory of his friend, they say. Today, they welcome you to the summer home of the Sassanid rulers. If we stay out of their palaces, we will pass unnoticed."

Their small party merged with other travelers as they neared the city. Hundreds, perhaps thousands, came together at this legendary place. John wondered where all these people had been so long ago and so recently. They appeared like so many mirages, promising and tempting, yet this time, animated and very real. He knew of stories of spirits in the deserts, and imagined they appeared now like traders at the gate. He reached out to touch a passing camel to convince himself that he was not merely a player in a dizzying carnival cast in illusion.

John glanced at an indifferent James, seemingly numb to this sight after so many years. He believed James's familiarity with the nuances of life on the trails had bred in him a patient yet weary countenance concerning matters of the road. His life had been camels, oases, and dust, and John thought there was little he had not seen over so much time.

John, however, was unnerved. After keeping scarce company, it was odd to be among so many in a strange land. He knew missionaries were usually safe on the road, but the city was different. Here, familiar soldiers stood by treaty or tolerance alone. John tried to shake the feeling. After all, he had lived much of his life traveling, teaching, and entering strange city gates. He had just begun the process of counting cities in his head, when Flavus barked at a man in a turban, vending wares. John snapped from his daydream and looked at Sri, who wore a dreamy expression. He was about to share his discomfort with his companion, but thought better of it.

The small band rode in silence. Before they could reach the thriving heart of the city, tantalizing up ahead and just out of reach, James led them toward a side alley on the outskirts of town. John steered his camel, but turned his head up the main route for another look. Colors clashed with the colorless dust and gray constructions. Purples and pinks, greens and blues…truly a city of princes. John longed to know the lands from whence these appeared. What were the stories these people could tell? How different were their traditions from his? The more exposure John had to strange cultures, the more curious he became.

The side path ended at a small gate fronting an encampment of white tents. It was a large plot of land overlooking the city. As they rode up, a tall, thin, well-tanned man stepped into the path, hand raised in an unfriendly gesture. He was dressed in a white robe tied at the waist and worn brown sandals. John felt his stomach sink.

"Stop!" he ordered. "We're full here. Turn back."

John leaned to the side in his saddle to peer behind the man and saw that, although there were some tents set up in the campground, they were interspersed by wide berth, and that there was plenty of room. James clicked his tongue, and his camel bent low. He walked toward the man, and they stood so close, John could barely see a sliver of light between them. John braced himself for a fight.

"James," John said, "maybe we should just—"

"Solomon!" James grabbed the man in a large hug and laughed. John eased into a state of relieved confusion.

"How are you James, you ol' apostate?"

"Fine, Sol, you crazy Jew. Fine. I'm a little thirsty, but fine. I thought the mountains would provide us some relief from the deserts, but alas…" James pointed to the relentless sun overhead.

"I apologize for this heat," Sol said. "The nights will still treat you well. I cannot say the same for the days, however. I must say, I have never experienced such discomfort in these mountains in this season."

"Fine by me," James said. "Maybe it will keep the pagan kings away from their palaces in town."

The men embraced again. It had clearly been a while since these friends had greeted one another. Sol cast a quizzical eye upon the party, then looked back at James.

"What manner of group is this?" he asked. "Isn't this a bit light for you? I hope they're paying you well for a private party. Or, are you retired and now leading Romans to their death under Shapur's blade?"

Sol's affable tone prompted John and Sri to dismount. John called Flavus to his side as James made introductions.

"This is Sri and John. The dog is Flavus. Men, this is Sol."

They shook hands with Sol, who then got down on his knees to greet Flavus. Flavus licked Sol's hand and, in return, Sol scratched the dog's ears. This immediately endeared Sol to John.

"What brings you all to the fair city of Ecbatana?" Sol asked with genuine interest.

"I suppose that's me," John said with a smile.

"John was entrusted to me by Mel," James said. "Official missionary from Antioch."

"Official missionary?" Sol asked James with a tone of sarcastic awe. "You brought a Christian missionary to Shapur's Ecbatana? Brave man. Pray he stays busy in his palace." Sol turned to address John. "There is one church here that sees peace as a favor to Rome, but I don't count on it being there when I get up in the morning. Jews do very well in this empire, but I can't say the same for followers of Christ, even though we are kin."

"You don't need to remind me," John said. "I just hope there is a small Roman garrison here."

"Very small," Sol said. "Just enough to keep an eye on the Roman citizenry doing business here. They are mostly message runners and errand boys for the Sassanid elite. Another reluctant favor from Shapur. Anyway, you're wasting your time with this one." Sol punched James in the stomach. "Unless you are out here to spread the good news too, James?" Sol smirked. "Trying to burn off all that bad karma?"

James eyed an amused Sri. "See, Sri?" he said as he slapped Sol's back. "Even Jews know your work." James cast a wink to John. "I guess that makes for yet another Hindu in our midst! But then again, we're all Hindu, right?"

Sol and James exchanged a few more pleasantries before Sol motioned for the party to follow. Sri and John led their camels behind

James and their new host. Flavus ran alongside, sniffing at various campsites and picking up food scraps from campfires past.

"Is this your place, Sol?" John asked, admiring the plot.

"Sure is. Lots of work, but I have loads of hands. Had it for years. James has been a loyal customer. Like I said, Jews do well in this empire."

"I've stayed at Sol's campground more than any other place on the road," James said with pride. "Like brothers, we are."

"Thank goodness I got the looks and brains," Sol said. "The gut was reserved for you." Sol hit James playfully on the arm and James punched him back. The men play wrestled and laughed. James patted Sol on the shoulder, and John smiled to himself as James showed a sign of true friendship.

They led their camels to a large barn lined with stalls. Sol took the reins of each and led the animals to their accommodations. Flavus ran in and nosed at the ground, as was his custom. He nuzzled each camel before barking and following John. Sol led the group toward two white tents, roped tight to the ground on the edge of the property. There was a small fire pit with a stack of wood at the site. This particular plot was relatively quiet and secluded. John wandered to a rocky path that led away to the city and the valleys beyond. He could see small clouds of dust curling in the distance – a sign of the bustling life in this thriving city. Sri walked up and joined him. John turned and saw James and Sol talking quietly and gesturing toward him.

"What do you suppose they're talking about, Sri?"

"I do not know, but it is comforting to know our guide has friends in strange lands, is it not? Ecbatana is so large. So full of life. So drenched in history. Yet, so isolated. It is far from the centers of Palmyra and Merv. If one does not have a friend here, he may not have one for months. At least there is one recognizable face in this place."

"I suppose. I'm nervous, Sri."

"Why?"

"This place. I know Christians are not favored here, and we already walk with Christ on a narrow blade. These will be my first sermons away from the holy and friendly cities of the West."

"I see. Why should this trouble you?"

"At home, I have different groups. Different people. Friends in Christ. The worst I see are pebbles cast in my direction, not swords."

"Do you speak different words?"

"What?"

"Different words, Brother John. Is your message going to be different here than at home? Does your faith rely on your security?"

"No. Of course not."

"Then, why the fear?"

John looked toward the city. "Sri, will anyone in this place hear?"

Sri turned to his friend. "Let us take a walk."

Chapter Sixteen

After settling into their tents with haste, and receiving some directions and cautions from Sol, John, Sri, and Flavus headed down the path to the city. Sri filled John's ear with stories of his previous forays in Ecbatana. Sri strode toward the city as if taking John on a personal tour of his home. He picked up a fallen branch and used it as a walking stick. John again had the image of Moses, this time leading the Hebrews to the Promised Land. He shared this image with Sri.

"I can tell you, Sri, I feel like I've been wandering in the desert for 40 years. Except this time, it's not my feet that bother me. My back is so sore!" John remembered his days in Antioch, requiring rest upon returning from long walks around the Empire.

"Take my walking stick," Sri insisted.

"Sri, I couldn't. I see those poses you do. You must be sore, too. You keep it."

"Actually, Brother, those poses release pain from my body." Sri tried again to hand the stick to John. "They are meant to be balanced and comfortable, to mirror a state of mind."

John, however, waved off the stick and Sri knew better than to press him. Instead, he wandered off the path to a scrubby tree and broke off a decaying limb. He handed it to John with a smile. John cracked the branch until it was a suitable height, and they continued on.

As they entered the city, sights, sounds, and smells engulfed them. John felt a festive atmosphere, stunned that so much beauty could exist outside his own borders. Up to now, these neighbors to the east had only been the subject of nasty story and terrible imagination. So few Romans, he thought, would be able to grasp so much glory in so strange a place. He regaled Sri with stories of the great games of Rome and legendary tales of heroes and tournaments. John was surprised at the nostalgia in his voice, not realizing he had grown so attached to the Empire and its amazing history.

Sol's directions led them to the Christian meetinghouse. John went inside to make his introduction, Sri and Flavus at his side.

"I am Luke." The community leader extended a firm handshake to both men. He was bald as a weathered stone and John had to stoop to receive his hand and look into a face as sour as a lemon. However, Luke had a confident and friendly air about him that put John at ease. "I would be most honored if you would speak to the community here. We have not had a Meletian missionary of your stature at our small gathering in many months. I suppose that is out of fear more than apathy. Although, I should expect more men desiring martyrdom."

"Is it a big community here?" John asked.

"Big enough," Luke replied. "I should say big enough to stay connected, but not so big that we attract trouble under an uneasy peace. We have brothers and sisters in Christ, and also those foreign to the Word; although, all here in town appear foreign to almsgiving. I must admit to you that we are struggling. Water flows more freely in the deserts than money within these walls. You are most welcome tomorrow evening. Perhaps you can breathe new life into an old and weary congregation struggling under the weight of Zoroaster." Sri and John thanked Luke and departed the humble meetinghouse.

"Do you think I can really make a difference here, Sri?" John asked, as they stood in the dusty street in a wild wind.

"Perhaps. Perhaps not. Come. Let us find shelter." Sri grabbed John's arm and led him to a teashop across the street, Flavus lumbering behind.

They ducked into the shelter of the café where Sri greeted the shop attendant with a gesture John thought displayed a considerable amount of familiarity. Sri handed the man a silver coin after he poured steaming brew into two clay cups. The party retreated to a small table where Flavus lay at John's feet. John tipped his nose to the brew and drew a breath. He was instantly transported – flowers and incense, myth and legend, and all the seasons of the year saturated his senses. For a moment, he was fixed in the timeless, where all memories merge into pleasantry.

"Mmm. What is this, Sri?" His eyes grew wide in wonder. "It's unlike any aroma I have ever encountered."

"This, Master John, is a special place." He waved his hand around the room. "This tea comes from a mysterious blend. The ingredients travel here on a very arduous path from China. No doubt you have had these spices and leaves separately or in other combinations. But they are only combined in this way in one other place."

"Where is the other place?"

"Turfan."

"Amazing!" John emptied half his cup, his face radiant in the tea's lingering spell.

Sri placed a gentle hand over John's cup. "Savor this. Much like our little band, this tea has traveled a long distance to be here. It has seen more of the world than many men, and has an appreciation of culture and an acceptance of change unrivaled in human circles. This tea has touched the hands of planters, harvesters, blenders, and brewers before entering that vessel and your body. This tea has its own very special story to tell, if only we would savor it. Give it the respect it deserves, and it will reveal to you its secrets."

John felt life rushing into his body, filling every available space. He longed to stand ten feet tall to take in more. His back pain was a distant memory, left behind in Antioch. He was a new man in a new land.

"What's in this?" he asked, sipping the cup like a baby.

"Good intentions." Sri raised his cup. "A toast." John raised his cup high as Sri continued. "A toast to you, Brother John, to James…" he raised his arm in the direction of the camp, then looked under the table. "And, to Master Flavus!" Flavus raised an indifferent, weary eye to Sri. "Here's to new adventures!"

"To new adventures!"

They sipped the flavorful brew in blessed unison, eyes closed upon its touch. Under the tea's spell, Sri regarded his friend, taking advantage of the peaceful state between them.

"Tell me, John, now that you have had some time to reflect, how do you feel about tomorrow? Luke seems very pleased to have you here in Ecbatana."

"I'm still nervous, Sri. Strange meetinghouse. Strange land. And that talk of martyrdom? There would be no greater honor, of course, but I do not yet fashion my chest a target for Shapur's hilt. I know this is going to sound ridiculous, but this place is so foreign."

"But it has the same heart, John."

"You are right, but it feels different." John bored a finger into a hole in the wooden table.

"Of course it is different. At home you preached in desert and mountain alike, much like this frontier. Yet, I am sure you could count on one sympathetic soul at each gathering."

"Usually, Sri. Usually. But in this land? There are no decrees of Constantine to protect a man here. And what about the cities further east to Samarkand? Meletius told me there were Christians in congregation all along this route, but what if they have disbanded? What if they are dead, martyred against their will? Still, I think I can make it work. I just don't know."

"Well, take the 'I think' in that sentence as a challenge. Consider your Lord and Savior. Did he preach in the utmost safety and comfort?"

"No. Not always. In fact, He really had no safe havens in His day."

"I want to read you something, John." Sri reached into the small bag strapped to his side and pulled out his tiny diary. "I wrote this when I was facing a challenge of my own." He carefully leafed through some yellowing pages, his eyes nimbly darting from verse to verse until he found his desired destination. "Ah, here we are." He began to read in an earnest, deliberate timbre. "I come to the river to pray. I need courage for life's uncertainty – courage only to be found at the certain waters of heaven. I want to show devotion to the Mother Ganga, that She may bestow upon me blessing. Her very body is the water that once touched the feet of Vishnu, and washed through the blessed hair of Shiva. Here, creation and sustenance meet. As I kneel by the river's edge, She swells without warning, Her breasts pouring forth a deluge of life-giving waters that I feel will now take my own life. I am swept away from all I know, carried by the Mother Goddess to the unknown.

"I wash ashore, awakened, in a place I have not seen in my travels. There the Mother leaves me on the banks. Alive, yet alone and afraid on the shore, I long to return to the places I know. I roam aimlessly amid the buildings and peoples of this strange land, unable to speak to another or recognize even my own reflection, for I am surrounded by such oddity.

"As I cry out to Mother in despair, surrendering control to Her, now beseeching Her for the courage to conquer this new challenge, the very scenery around me changes before my eyes. As I gaze in disbelief, I find I was never away from my village and its comforting, familiar surroundings. Indeed, the Mother waters only washed over me, but carried me nowhere. It was, all along, my own self-doubts – doubts I cast forth from me as a net into the river – that caught only my own expectations. I thought I had no courage to face the fears of my own lands. I was absolutely convinced. Yet Mother Ganga revealed to me nothing less than my very own beliefs. The world became a pure mirror to my own inner convictions, reflecting to me that to which I clung in my core.

"From that time forward never again have I doubted – whether in my own or foreign lands. Never have I pined for circumstances other than they are. Mother's lesson flows in me today as eternal as Her life-giving waters. Mother! Behold! You have answered a prayer that was never uttered. You did not fill me with courage, but have helped me to tap my very own."

John sat in quiet contemplation as Sri tucked his book back into the pouch.

Sri continued. "Brother John, I know your Christ met hostility and had insecurity in his travels. I know He was not always sure about the path laid before Him. He, too, was not honored in every town."

"That's true," John admitted, "but He wasn't totally lost. I think, in the end, He always knew His Holy Father was with Him, even in the darkest hours. And if He forgot, He had disciples that could get Him back on the path, Sri. Friendly faces in the crowd."

"You hear that?" Sri looked down at Flavus. "Your master does not consider us friendly faces."

"Wait. You would come to hear me speak tomorrow?"

"Of course."

"But Sri, you don't follow my tradition."

Sri picked up John's cup for a refill. "Brother John, I follow a more important path. I follow your friendship."

Chapter Seventeen

How did you sleep?"

"Good morning, James," John replied, groggy under the spell of a morning come too soon. "Not well." John stumbled over to the fire and sat down. Flavus was at James's feet.

"Too much tea. You should have come out with Sol and me. Drank the good stuff. Ecbatana has some great beverages, John. They'd knock you right to hell."

John rolled his eyes. "That sounds really nice, but I don't think so."

"Your loss."

"James, it's not the tea for goodness sake. My thoughts are distracted thinking about tonight."

"That's right. Your first official sermon out here!" James pitched bread to John who picked at it sparingly as if pulling lice from a child's hair. "John of the golden tongue, afraid it will turn to lead."

"I don't know if I can do it."

"I know of no alchemy that can save you, Brother, but we came all this way. I'm not turning back now. Meletius would probably have my head. Besides, Flav' needs a rest, right boy?" James scratched Flavus's ears and placed some bread near a water bowl Sol had provided from the stable.

"I'm not leaving. I just need some support, James. I need some encouragement, if that's not asking too much."

"There might be a bottle of encouragement left over from last night that I could spare."

"Forget it. That won't be necessary, thank you."

A wave of pity swept over James. "If it's any consolation, there are probably going to be people there from the Empire. City's too big not to."

"Really?" John felt a glimmer of hope rush through him. "I expected some, but how do you know for sure?"

"Sol. Said he has seen caravans arriving from Antioch, Jerusalem, and other places. Said they have been arriving almost daily. It's the season for it, but not for long. Winter will soon be here. But for now, you may not be the only missionary preaching in town."

"But Meletius sent me." John felt his relief give way to a tinge of jealousy. "Why would others come here now?"

"John, this road is long and the cities are plentiful, but as you know, they are separated by wide berth. Ecbatana is a big place, and it attracts many. Pretty much everyone from the West stops here. And if one is a Christian? Well, he will certainly find his way to the meetinghouse. And that teahouse of yours can't only stay open for you. The days may be unseasonably hot, but tea is still a local favorite, and this place is still crowded."

"I didn't mean it that way."

James stoked the fire as Sri emerged from his tent. He appeared fresh and relaxed as he gave a mighty stretch. John heard cracking noises coming from every corner of Sri's thin and limber body.

"Bad sleep, John?" Sri sat down and helped himself to some bread.

"It's that tea, Sri," James said with a smirk.

"The tea has mild stimulant properties that paradoxically relax the soul, James, but I do not think that is our friend's issue."

James rolled his eyes. "We covered that already." The sarcastic tone returned to James's voice. "Anyway, I'm going to see Sol. We're going to get supplies this morning. I need some things to get us through the next few days until we can stock up for the longer journey. Can I take Flavus, John?"

"Sure. He'll make sure you spend the gold wisely."

"Meletius gave us enough for 10 years. We'll be fine. Anyway, Sol and I are going to be dealing with some interesting characters, and I figure ol' Flav' here will be a good deterrent."

"Deterrent against what?"

"That'll be a secret between Flavus and me. Come on, boy!"

Flavus got to his feet, gobbled up his piece of bread, and followed James down the trail to Sol's, leaving Sri and John by the fire. John stared into the flames. After several minutes, he took out his parchments and teaching points to look them over. They sat quietly for a good hour until John, distracted, broke the silence.

"I had a dream last night, Sri."

"Oh?"

"I've had it before."

"Tell me."

"The details are hazy. It's familiar, but…" John's voice trailed off into the void as he wrestled with the images, clouded in sleepy memory.

"But what?" Sri asked, trying to pull John back from the abyss of the mind.

"Familiar, but strange. I see a figure before me, as tall as three men – as high as a man on a cross. I see a fire in the deserts and mountains, blazing with the strength of a hundred suns, but it is not hot. The ground beneath my feet is cool, and the flames don't consume, but invigorate."

"Can you find a word to describe the dream?"

John thought for a moment. "Truth. It feels like satisfying truth."

"I see. And where do you feel this truth?"

"Where do I feel it?"

"Close your eyes. Think about the dream. Do you feel your heartbeat? Can you feel that energy?"

"Yes."

"Where?"

"In my chest…my heart."

"Spread it out."

"Spread it out? How?"

"Just allow it. Feel the heart energy in all places."

"It's faint. I can just barely perceive it, but...wait...it's in my throat. In my hands."

"Yes. Now, focus it just above of your head."

"It's there. Odd. It feels like it has stopped everywhere else except for that small point up there. It is almost as if my thoughts placed it there."

"That is focus, John. Total focus in the domain of the one creative source. Breathe slowly and feel that. Imagine that sensation is a crown atop your head."

John remained still in the exercise for a few minutes then opened his eyes. He suspected that the feeling of calm he observed in Sri was an outward reflection of Sri's consistent practice of this very meditation.

"I feel relaxed, Sri. Even without the Turfan tea."

"Indeed," Sri said, smiling. "This is a simple meditation exercise you can use to calm mind and body."

"Meditation. I've never done it before in this way. I usually approach scripture like meditation. I read it, consume it, digest it, and feel somehow more relaxed."

"That can work too, as long as it is focused. As long as there is intention behind it."

"I saw you doing some exercises on the dunes that day right after we first met. You told me you were greeting the day. Was it something like this? Why all the twisting and contorting?"

"Yoga."

"Yoga," John repeated.

"It is a series of exercises for mind and body. It is a discipline designed to cultivate inner peace – balance and ease of body leading to balance and ease of mind. You do it, too."

"I do? I can't bend my spine all the way back to make myself into a table, Sri."

Sri laughed. "You don't have to. Your dedication to the living Christ is a form of yogic discipline. It's yoga through devotion and actions in service to your Lord. You have disciplined your mind in devotion. You also practice yoga when you do good deeds for others. Selfless deeds. I imagine you have done this many times in your noble travels."

"Does this mean I'm Hindu again?" John quipped.

"You are what you want to be. Your loving dedication and service is yours to direct where you will. It is your constant and unfailing devotion to your highest ideals that is the hallmark of a strong, personal faith."

"I like that, Sri. Devotion. I always thought of it as prayer. Or as a state of being yoked to the Divine, like our packs are tied to the camels."

"Yes. The words we use are different, but the intention and ends are similar. Whether one talks of sitting beside the Lord or merging with a supreme energy, the goal is to do the disciplined work on the inside so that actions on the outside are pure. With a mere modicum of mental cultivation, one discovers many doors opened wide."

"How do you learn the cultivation?"

"Much of meditation is based on breath and breath control, John."

"Why control it? What is wrong with breathing normally?"

"Nothing. Nothing is wrong with that. But if you are faithful in your practice, you soon find the control becomes normal. When I do these physical disciplines, I concentrate on my breath, and that enhances the exercise. The breath energy I feel radiating throughout my body during physical exertion is a reminder that God dwells within all action, and no matter where I am or what I am doing, I am breathing. In. Out. In. Out. If I stay conscious of that, I know I am just a living, pulsating soul passing through an experience like a ghost."

"A ghost?"

"Yes. A spirit. The breath energy enters my nostrils, full of light and potential…full of penetrating life. It animates the lasting core of me and allows me to appear to do my duty and to pass through the situation."

"Then why be there if you just want to pass through? What's the point?"

"In that way, John, I don't become attached to the situation or its potential outcomes. Let us take your sermon tonight. You have already spoken to the community leader and presented him your credentials. He is expecting you. Now, the only certainty this evening will be that you are present with your truth and that you are breathing. You have no control over Shapur, the crowd, these strange summer temperatures, or a person's reaction."

"But what if they reject me, Sri? I am only aware of one Brother in Christ in this town tonight – the community leader. What if the others don't arrive, or the potential converts reject me?"

"Are they rejecting *you*?"

John mulled over the question for a moment. "Well, if they chase me off, yes. If they put my neck to the sword, yes. If they maintain the Arian fallacy, then yes, they are probably rejecting me."

"John, if you walked into the crowd tonight with a tea cart and people politely refused you, would you take offense?"

"No."

"Why not?"

"It's only tea."

"So, the crowd is not rejecting John of Antioch, tea vendor, but his tea."

"I suppose so. But they would be missing some great tea!"

"It is not your job to convince them of that. They either drink or they don't."

"True."

"Well, how are your sermons any different?"

"Well, they…they're…" John was perplexed. He wanted to argue that his words were more important than tea, as they gave him, and others, a sense of purpose and hope. However, for the first time in his Christian life, he sensed that his ephemeral words, and his lasting identity, might be separate. "Wait, Sri. Are you saying that I speak a truth but that it is not me?"

"Something of that nature. They can be separate, or not."

"Separate or not?"

"If you believe what you speak, then you live it. You are it. In the end, that is all that matters. The living Christ is in you. Through you. In your hands. In your actions. He is essential to your being, and beyond your words, although words certainly convey your meaning. But if those words are rebuffed tonight, it is not a reflection on you. Whether or not others accept your spoken words does little to change your lasting self. Maybe the crowd just does not like the blend."

John stared quietly at Sri. Maybe the truth of Christ to the missionary and the truth of tea to the tea maker are not so different after all, he thought.

"John, if people boo you, it is not you at all. It is a rejection of ideas. Maybe the people simply are not thirsty."

"Well, no one boos the tea man."

"That may be the case," Sri laughed, "but you are not peddling tea. You are peddling a worldview. The rejection feels more visceral, even though rejection is rejection. The burden you carry as a missionary – as a herald of ideas – is that people often mistake a person for his message."

John leaned back and gazed into the clouds. They were rare around here, and these were high and thin – curly wisps of inaccessible moisture keeping distant watch on an arid place upon which they would show no mercy. He tried to imagine Christ Himself looking down at this conversation. John knew in his heart that many considered Jesus equal to His message. Even John believed that. He reflected on the current religious situation in his own empire and all the arguments and bloodshed around the idea of Christ's divinity and personhood. Where was He in all of this? Even if people rejected

Jesus's words of love, why did He not take mercy and rain love down upon mankind? It felt at times as if Christ drifted by like the clouds over Ecbatana – so full of potential, but so hard to reach. These thoughts unnerved him. He felt something shudder in his core, igniting a remote burning sensation deep within. He was at once disturbed and elated.

"That shop owner the other day, Sri."

"What about him?"

"We call him the 'tea man.' We name him his profession. I never saw it before. We made the man his medium. If I did not like the tea, I may have associated him with it, and transferred my discontent to him. How could I do that?"

"John, when you walk into that room tonight, consider that you are a ghost – a spirit passing before a crowd. A spirit with words, yes, but a spirit nonetheless."

"I'll share the tea!"

"You will, Brother. I will drink with you."

Chapter Eighteen

John peered through the curtain. "Many have come, Sri."

"Are you not happy? I am sure the community leader is happy, as is his collection box!"

"Well, yes, but Luke told me it was a small group here in Ecbatana. I wasn't expecting such a large crowd. I guess he was telling the truth. Indeed, they have not had an official missionary here in quite some time."

"Of your stature, Master John."

"Right."

Sri peeked out as John paced nervously. Sri surveyed the diversity before him. There were, to his eyes, followers of all paths in the audience, bearing the trappings of many traditions around the region. Sri suspected many were followers of Zoroaster, Mani, and the Hebrew God. He spied men of darker skin who looked as if they may follow the Hindu path or the ways of the Buddha. Persecutor and persecuted all came together on this night.

"Sit with me, John." Sri tapped the chair across from him.

John reluctantly settled in by his friend. "Now, close your eyes. Where do you feel your truth?"

"All over."

"Where is your breath?"

"In. Out. In. Out."

"What is in it?"

"Light. Each breath in is the incoming light of Christ."

"What emerges from you?"

"Will. The will of the Father."

"John? John!" A voice startled Sri and John from their meditation. The gentle pulsation faded as John shook the shock from his mind, gathering himself to the greeting. "John! It's me, Philip!"

John's mouth dropped. He stood to greet his friend, and they embraced. "Philip? Why…? How…? So many months…such a long time since you hosted me so graciously!" John could only sputter his words through his amazement.

"I told you I wanted to get out here," Philip said with a flourish. "When the calling came from Antioch, I accepted in pure joy."

"Meletius," John whispered.

"Yes. He wanted more emissaries here in the neighboring empire. You are not alone, Brother. You have friends in Christ in these hostile and godless lands."

"Why didn't you come and find me in Antioch?" John asked.

"Indeed, my friend, I left long before you. You were such an inspiration to me, I could not help but take to the road. I wanted to see you but there was no time for delay, even in friendship."

The men embraced again. John turned to Sri. "Sri, this is Philip."

Sri stood and politely nodded his head. Philip's demeanor shifted, grooves forming on his brow. His affect transformed into an implied standoff, unsure what to make of John's present company.

"Sri?" Philip repeated the name disdainfully as he looked him up and down. "Are you a brother in Christ?"

"He's a follower of the Hindu way," John answered with ease.

Philip turned his gaze to John, his warmth completely replaced with an icy contempt that spread about the room like a cold wind that steals the very heat of day.

"John, a word?" Philip turned his back to both men and stormed off.

"Excuse me, Sri." Sri nodded to John as he followed in Philip's hurried steps.

"John, what are you doing?" Philip clenched John's arm in a tight grip.

"What do you mean?"

"You came out here to spread the word of Christ. To win converts in an unfriendly land."

"I am, Philip. I am about to preach in a few minutes. And I've been doing the Lord's work all along the route before arriving here. I've been talking with small groups and teaching at camps—"

"You are here to take up the spiritual sword against the Zoroastrian curse and to stem the tides of paganism washing westward." Philip cut through him like a blade through smoke. "What are you doing with a Hindu?"

"He joined my caravan outside of Tyre. He was in trouble and needed help. Isn't that what we should do? Who are we if not an aid to those in need? A friend to the lonely? Isn't that what sparked our friendship, Philip?"

"You've carried this tumor from Tyre? He needs Christ, John! That's the only help you should give him."

John tugged hard and extracted himself from Philip's grasp, taking a step back. It was as if he were looking into a mirror that shows one's past. He saw venom in Philip's face that made him quite ready to be done with the conversation. .

"Philip, I—"

"John, if Meletius knew. If any of his military loyalists out here knew."

"Knew what?" John stood taller, rising to meet the disguised threat.

"Meletius has sent emissaries like me into the East, along with the steady stream of official missionaries. There have been reports of missionaries joining with pagans and straying from the path." Philip leaned to the side and looked past John to Sri, who busied himself at the curtain. "Some are even rumored to be disappearing into the jungles of the subcontinents."

"What are you talking about?"

"John, I'm not out here by coincidence."

"Wait, you're spying on me?"

"No, I'm not spying," Philip snapped. John found this defensive tone jarring. Philip seemed to catch himself, his demeanor and voice softening to an almost condescending tone. "I'm visiting fledgling churches and prayer groups that suffer under Shapur's persecutions. Just like you, I'm out here to answer questions and check in with our missionaries."

John's eyes narrowed, as if trying to penetrate Philip's soul. "Oh. You're just checking in?"

"Yes. Nothing more."

"Is that why you pulled me from my friend to talk in private? Is that what's going on here? We're just catching up?"

"John, Meletius has made a significant investment in you and his missionary work."

"His work?" John stared at his friend in bewilderment. "I thought we were spreading Christ's message. Actually, I thought we were spreading good deeds and loving truth."

Philip remained unmoved, John's words bouncing off his face like a flat stone flung upon a frozen stream. "I will be in the audience tonight, John. I look forward to your words. Or, should I say, the words of Christ."

Philip turned his back on his friend and marched out from behind the curtain to take his seat. John returned to an empty chair, brooding. Sri sat next to him.

"Are you alright, Brother John?" Sri's voice sent a shockwave through John's agitation, increasing the intensity.

"We're not brothers, Sri!" John snapped. Sri's expression did not change. It remained soft and comforting. "I'm sorry," John said. "I should not have said that." John placed a gentle hand on Sri's shoulder. "I forgot who I was talking to."

"It is quite alright. A more aggressive force has obviously colonized a peaceful empire. No matter. It is just tea, after all."

"Philip was a friend in my travels back home. Now, he is haunting my travels out here."

"How can a ghost haunt a ghost? He has his truth, too."

"You heard all of that?"

"John, your friend did not make much of an effort to keep his voice down. These curtains are cloth, not brick."

"I'm sorry."

"For what? He needs to speak what is true for him. You obviously inspired him, as he rushed out onto this road on the heels of your visit."

"I know. But he hinted that the leader of the Church in Antioch has been sending people out here to keep track of our missions."

"So?"

"So?"

"Will this change your words, John?"

"No."

"Your work?"

"No."

"So?"

"Sri, please. You don't understand. You answer to no one. You're a *successful* ghost, remember?"

"And what is success? I try to do what is best by the gods, John. I try to do what is best by my neighbor. I try to cultivate my body in constant preparation for its journeys through the world. Remember our chat about yoga?"

"Yes."

"Well, yoga is not only a series of exercises. If you recall, we said it was a way of existing in the world. It is exercise, discipline, right living, and the like. I must answer to each limb on the yogic tree. In that way, I answer not to men, but to my integrity. Socially, you are right – that makes me a ghost. When we do not answer to men, they cease to see us."

John considered how Philip's demeanor changed when John

disagreed with him. It was as if Philip was looking right through him, completely unaware that another human was participating in the conversation. As he was about to share this observation, the crowd behind the curtain fell silent, and Sri and John heard Luke giving an introduction.

"John, it's time," Sri said, urging his friend back to the moment.

"I know."

Sri peered out from behind the curtain. "I am going to be in the audience looking for ghosts. Or better yet, spirit. Ah, and I see two spirited souls already. James and Flavus are here!"

"Really?" John's chest swelled with pride in his companions.

"I'm going to join them, Brother. It looks like they are saving me a seat, which appear to be in short supply." John's stomach lurched at this observation. "And you are in luck, as I see no hilts awaiting your chest. Good luck, Brother John."

"Thank you, Brother Sri."

"Where is your breath?"

John closed his eyes and felt his heart beating all around his body, and in his very crown. "In. Out. In. Out."

"Where is your truth?"

"Within."

"So you are never without?"

"Never."

Chapter Nineteen

Friends in Christ, I welcome you." The crowd murmured a warm encouragement as John walked onto the small, wooden stage. He held a parchment in one hand, reserving the other for expressive gesture. Once the dam of anticipation broke, he felt confident, in his element, as he moved about the platform. Though the room and crowd were foreign, he now found his feet treading upon familiar territory.

"I know I am among friends, as I see the smiles on some of your faces. Smiles that say, 'I have found a lasting peace.' I admit, Brothers and Sisters, when I set out for Ecbatana so long ago, I did not know who I would meet. Stories had reached my ears in Antioch – stories of distant lands and strange practices. I wavered, my friends. I wavered in my commitment and assigned task out of fear. Even as Meletius *himself*," John looked over at Philip, who wore a gaze of stone, "guided by *Christ*, charged me with my duties, I wavered. I wavered in self-doubt. Would I know what to say? Would I know what to do?"

There were whispers through the crowd and looks of concern on some faces. John felt a fire blaze within as he spoke his truth. He noticed the few remaining seats filling rapidly, and a host of eager bodies flowing out the back, craning their necks for a glimpse. He knew in these remote areas that religion had become a form of entertainment, and he knew a loud voice echoing in Christ about the empty Sassanid streets would attract attention.

"But then I realized…" John cast a pause among them. A hush of anticipation fell over the crowd as they hung onto the edge of John's precipice. "I did not need to know!" A murmur of confusion rippled through the room. "Why, you ask? Because Christ, in His infinite glory and wisdom, knew. His words would be my words, His deeds, my very own. He has brought me safely into the desert and through her gauntlets of thirst, danger, and unrest. He has brought me safely to you, my friends."

The crowd roared in approval. For John in this moment, Christ's was the only voice on the planet, and he the only mouthpiece. He felt inspired as he continued.

"I know there are some here who are searching, seeking, watching, waiting. You have come out on this night, perhaps to see a show. You have heard of the Christian tongues and are curious to hear them more closely. Perhaps you thought you would witness an execution. Perhaps you thought I would be serving tea." John glanced at Sri, who had a smile on his lips. "Let me assure you, the truth of which I speak can quench your thirst. One has lived who can bring you everlasting satisfaction. I say to you now that He is Christ the Lord!"

The crowd clapped as the rolling of thunder. James looked over at Sri and raised an eyebrow. Neither man had seen this side of John before. They were both impressed with his confidence. It seemed to grow as John spoke into the night.

"Three centuries ago, there was One who stretched His arms wide to gather in all souls. He looked out upon the world, His flock, desiring to embrace them all – to pursue their hearts and spirits. But, He could not." The crowd fell silent, unsure about this apparent lapse. "He could not embrace us, Brothers and Sisters, because His wrists were nailed to wood." The crowd again mumbled a quiet assent. "He could not follow us to preach His truth, as His feet were nailed to this very wood as well." The crowd mumbled louder. "He died on the cross so that we may yet live. But, His spiritual embrace is always around us. His Godly feet always walking with us."

John paused as the crowd united behind his words. He felt the pulse in his heart, above his head, in his throat, as the spirit washed over him. He was the very embodiment of fire, alight to the core.

"Friends! Friends!" John held up a hand in friendly gesture. "I would ask for your silence now." John again looked at Philip who furrowed his brow in annoyed confusion as John called for the excited crowd to settle. "Close your eyes as one, friends, whether believer or not. Do you feel the energy of your heart throughout your body? Do you feel the breath in your lungs? Let it move easily. In…Out…In…Out…"

Philip's eyes were closed along with the rest of the crowd, and he shifted in his chair. He parted his lids a crack to survey the room. Everyone appeared to be completely enraptured, breathing in unison. He allowed his eyes to return to John one more time before closing them again.

"The pulse in you is the very heart of Christ, beating within. Your breath is the very breath of God, filling you with the capacity to speak His praise. Take this moment and meditate on the energy of Christ within you."

Philip this time opened his eyes wide and looked over at Sri, whose eyes were closed. Philip then fixed his gaze firmly upon John, with a look of hostility that could burn the heart of a man.

"Imagine in your very mind Christ Himself on the cross, Brothers and Sisters. Imagine Jesus Himself, arms spread wide. Do not despair at this sight, for His crucifixion ensures always an image of open arms. Ensures always a picture of Christ gazing down at His beloved flock. Ensures always a vision of divinity rooted to the earth, anchoring men's souls in the world to the Holy Spirit that transcends all things.

"Be united spirits now, Brothers and Sisters. You are only a soul bound to Christ. You are only a single energy in meditation. Be one with Christ – in the world, but passing through. As what was truly lasting in Christ was not bound to the cross, so your soul is not bound to the material world. Let your love of the Son and His Father deliver you from the agony of temporary life to the bliss of eternal existence."

John gazed out upon the sea of calm. There was a sense of peace in the air. For a brief moment, his eyes met Philip's intense stare, but he quickly broke the lock, unfazed.

"Brothers and Sisters in Christ, seekers and others among us, I bless you that the truth penetrates your very soul and that you find true liberation. Leave the sins of this world on the cross with Christ, so that your lasting self can be with Him, one for eternity. Amen."

"Amen," the crowd said quietly, and in perfect unison.

For some time, no one moved. John maintained silence, so as not to disturb anything about the moment. He could feel everyone breathing. Meditating.

Chapter Twenty

As eyes slowly opened on their own time and of their own accord, an energetic pulse surged through the crowd. Chairs shifted as all assembled stood to greet one another, bliss upon their faces. John could not tell believer from seeker from non-believer, and had a hunch no one in the audience could either. He had an intuition that no one cared about that just now.

Luke approached John with great enthusiasm and excitement, and stood next to him. A line snaked through the crowd to greet John, who was also charged the task of making community collection. The last two people were a short man of medium build who appeared to be of Chinese descent, and Philip. The Chinese man dropped a silver coin in the box in an unceremonious manner and pulled John's arm, gently. John, however, was distracted as he searched the crowd for his friends.

"Brother John," he said in an excited voice, commanding half of John's attention, "I have never heard a truth of Christ in quite this way. So much passion. So much unity. So much tranquility. Your words remind me of the great Buddhist and Taoist teachings of my homeland. I was transported to her, and away from a scattered, homesick mind. I want to thank you."

"I'm touched, good sir," John said in partial awareness. "Thank you."

"Please. Call me Bo."

"Bo."

The man bowed deeply to John, hands clasped together in front of him. John, in return, fumbled through an imitation of the gesture while holding the collection box and scanning the crowd. Bo smiled up at John then disappeared as a vapor into the night. John found Sri and James lost in conversation in a small group, such that they did not notice the odd exchange. Philip, now flanked by two men John did not recognize, stepped forward, his critical eyes returning to John after watching Bo leave the tent. Philip dropped a large gold coin in the box with a grand gesture, and nodded to Luke.

"Rather a solemn moment at the end, Brother John," Philip said. "Did you cast a pagan spell?"

"No, *Brother*. I simply had the crowd put their attention on their own connection to Christ, and not on me."

"Interesting approach. I can inform Meletius that you have taken his doctrine to new heights, then? Not only are Christ and the Father of one substance; now we are all of one substance with Christ. Or, should I say, Christ's mysterious energy. Interesting."

John's blood ran cold. Philip's words suggested a heretical teaching that, if it reached the wrong ears, could end John's missionary work…or worse.

"Philip, why are you so angry?"

"I'm not angry. Just confused. I hope your association with this Sri character has not changed you."

"Changed me?"

"The texts are clear, John." James picked up John's parchment rolls from a nearby chair and shook them over his head. "At least, the *approved* texts are clear. Have you bothered to read them?"

"Philip, how dare you question—"

"Christ's relationship to the Father and to us should be familiar to you by now," Philip said, brushing John's protest aside, as if a pestering fly. "Others may have their own views, but Meletius, your patron, is clear. You need a bit more clarity, John. Why don't you…*meditate* on it a little while longer. Perhaps that will help."

"I believe I was quite clear." John shook the collection box, now heavy with coins, in Philip's flushed face. He handed the box to the grateful Luke. Philip took in a deep breath, as if to speak again, but simply turned and left the tent, followed by the two men. John exchanged pleasantries with the small, regular meeting group of Ecbatana, who waited patiently until after the formal greeting of visitors. He offered them a blessing and reassurances for their continued existence in the city. They asked him to come and speak at any time and John thanked them warmly. He walked to where Sri and James were still engrossed in animated discussion, Flavus asleep at their feet.

"Good job, John."

"Thanks, James."

"You have some spirit." James smiled.

"Actually, I'm a ghost."

"John, I commend you for your broader vision and powerful energy," Sri said, embracing his friend with a comforting warmth.

"Thank you. That peaceful breathing just seemed natural in there."

"No, Brother. It was natural in there." Sri touched John's chest with his hand.

"Sol is across the street," James said. "Let's join him for some of that tea. Or something stronger?"

John tapped his leg and Flavus hopped to attention, ready to accompany them out of the tent and into the silent night of Ecbatana.

Chapter Twenty-One

I am telling you, John has changed." Philip sat at a café nursing a drink, talking with his two companions. He scraped his cup in jagged circles on the table, betraying a mind that had not seen much rest. His mood vacillated wildly between anger and confusion.

"I thought he sounded devout...I mean, I've never really been...relaxed at the end of a sermon." Mark, Philip's friend, was a stocky little fellow with beet red skin. He wore a wrap on his head and a scarf to cover his face when out in the sun. Philip looked at him in surprise.

"I agree." Philip's second confidante now suffered under Philip's stare of disbelief. Simon had well-defined muscles, but they seemed out of place, attached to his lanky frame like meat hanging on a butcher's hook.

All three men had been assigned the same official duties, and had traveled to Ecbatana together. However, both Mark and Simon acknowledged Philip's place as the de facto leader of their little band – a title he would have assumed anyway.

"Friends, I assure you, I saw him sitting with that Hindu. I am sure the pagan's...beliefs...found their way into that talk last night. And you both best take care. Your words are dangerously close to straying over the line."

"Calm yourself, Philip," Mark said. He shot Simon a look of discomfort, but Simon kept his head down. "We're sorry. So, what are we supposed to do?" Mark's expression was vacant, his mind a blank slate upon which Philip could draw. "Meletius wanted us to watch, listen, and report. He didn't say anything about taking care of problems."

"Well, we have a problem," Philip said, glaring at both men. "And we have to take care of it soon."

Chapter Twenty-Two

Anyone here?" Philip poked around the camp, kicking stones into the fire pit and tracing lines in the dirt with his foot. He tested a pile of wood with his sandal, sending the stack tumbling to the ground. Scowling, he surveyed a scattering of Flavus's chew bones and some assorted trash from one lively night or another. James and Flavus emerged from a tent.

"Can I help you?" James asked.

"I'm Philip." Philip softened his face and strode over to James, hand outstretched. The stranger's confident air immediately irked James as he reluctantly returned Philip's gesture. "The community leader told me about your campsite outside of town, and I thought I'd—"

"I've heard of you," James said, his voice flat. "John's not here. He and a friend went into town. I don't know when they'll be back."

"Could you tell him I stopped by?"

"Sure." James gave Philip his back and set about methodically re-stacking the wood into a neat and tidy pile.

"Thank you. Oh, and can you tell him there's a meeting tonight at the community church? He's invited if he's interested."

"S'pose."

"Well, thank you again. Did not mean to intrude. Sorry about your stack of wood." Philip grinned as he turned back to the rocky path, and headed toward the city.

At dusk, John and Sri returned to the campsite looking jubilant.

They were engaged in lively conversation with much gesturing and excitement. Flavus ran up to greet them, his tail wagging.

Sri got to his knees to accept Flavus's courtesy. "We missed you too, my good friend. But you were better off here where you could rest."

"Where have you two been all day?" James asked. "I have hot water but no beef to boil. I almost sent Flav' out to retrieve you!" James stoked flames in the pit, sending bright orange sparks up into the night.

Sol had joined him in the late afternoon, and he now reclined casually near the fire. He greeted his friends with a smile. John dropped bundles of raw meat and bread near the fire. Flavus sniffed at them then went to lie down, confident his portion would soon come. Sri sat easily and gently took off his sandals.

"Sri showed me a temple!" John was eager to share. "Actually, it was more of a makeshift temple. There was a festival today. Who was it for, Sri?"

"Lord Shiva," Sri said. "Devotees of my tradition have a small gathering in this town as well."

"Shiva," John said. "That's right."

"Your Hindu roots are showing, John." James could not resist hurling the barb as he opened the package of meat. He tossed some lingering fat to Flavus.

"I didn't participate, James." John sat heavily next to Sri and gingerly removed his own sandals. "I just took it all in. You should have seen it. Heard it. What a celebration! What a sight!"

James cast a confused look to Sol. "I'm Jewish, James," Sol smirked. "Don't look at me. I don't know why Shapur lets his guard down with these two."

"Good lord, Sri!" James said with a laugh. "You're converting the greatest Christian orator of our generation!"

"Calm yourself," Sri said quietly. "We are just seeing the world, one beautiful devotion at a time. Besides, it was near the church, so we stopped in to receive a blessing from your Christ, as well."

"Oh, that reminds me, John. Someone stopped by to see you."

"Who? No one knows I'm here. Was it Meletius?"

The group laughed. It rang out clear in the quiet evening.

"Hardly," James said. "Your old friend Philip."

"Philip?" John gasped.

"Yeah. Said there was something going on at the church tonight if you wanted to come by."

"Strange." John looked over at Sri, who shrugged. "Luke didn't mention a meeting when I was there today. I'll go tonight and see what it's about."

"I don't like him, John." James's face had a stern look in the fire's glow. "And not just because of what you told us about him."

"What don't you like?" John asked. "I mean, besides the obvious."

"I don't know. For starters, why the hell was he so interested in where you were staying? Can't he just see you at the church? Can't he just leave messages there with Luke? Also, he has a…way about him."

Sol looked at his friend. "So do you, James, but we still keep your company!" He chucked a pebble at James.

"Trust me, James," John said, "I know what you mean."

"What did you ever see in that man to begin with?" James asked. "Where was friendship possible with such a person?"

"In hospitality," John said quietly. "Simple hospitality. He showed me kindness when my need was great. He gave me shelter when I needed it most. We broke bread and shared news, as only friends do."

"So, what happened?" Sol asked.

"I'm not sure," John replied. "I've been trying to figure that out since our meeting last night. I suppose the business of his life has found him lost. I may not be able to follow him into his darkness."

"Are you sure you want to go to the church tonight to test the waters?" Sri asked.

"I suppose it couldn't hurt to dip my toe in again," John said. "I owe Philip that much for his past kindness."

"We owe men only that which they owe to us," James said.

"And what is that?" Sri asked.

James tossed a sizzling, steaming piece of meat to John. "Freedom from annoyance."

Chapter Twenty-Three

John walked the dark path to town by the light of the heavens. The streets were subdued at this hour, and John forced his attention to the waning crowds as he navigated his way around the strange faces, trying to avoid large piles of camel dung littering the avenue. As he approached an alley a few streets from the meetinghouse, a set of strong arms grabbed him while a pair of hands tied a gag around his mouth. He was dragged, kicking and gurgling, to a nearby building, and pushed inside.

"Sit him there and secure him!" a voice barked from the darkness. John struggled and squinted, but could not see his captors. "Secure him!" the voice yelled again.

Two mysterious figures tied John to a wooden chair with rope, the tight knots sparking a tingle through his fingers. Two candles burned on a table in front of him, but he could not make out any of the three faces. His heart pounded in his chest. A man leaned in close over the table and pulled down the cotton gag, allowing John to speak.

"Philip?"

"John."

"Philip, what, in the name of the Father, are you doing?"

"Saving you, John."

"From what?"

"From yourself."

"Let him go," came a faint voice from the corner.

Philip picked up a candlestick and strode to the far end of the room.

John strained his eyes to see, but only glimpsed a dark shadow. "How dare you question me, woman!" Philip raised the candlestick to a menacing height.

"No!" the voice cried.

John now recognized it. "Rachel? Rachel! Philip, no!" John could only watch in horror as Philip's shadow, imposing in the dim light, brought the candlestick down on Rachel's head. As the candle tumbled from the holder to the floor, extinguished, John could see her in a crumpled heap. "Philip, stop!"

John clenched his fists in rage, feeling the rope cutting into his skin. He welcomed the physical pain, deflecting his mind from the horror he had witnessed. Blood trickled down his fingers. He listened for any trace of her voice, watched for any slight movement, but the corner was deathly silent and horribly still.

"Please excuse the interruption." Philip dragged a chair over to the table and placed it across from John in the glow of the remaining candle. John could barely make out Philip's face – eerily calm, devoid of emotion. His tone, in the aftermath of the assault on his own wife, sent a chill down John's spine. "As I was saying, I'm saving you, *Brother*, from straying from the path."

"You bastard!" John yelled, as he struggled to free himself. Simon and Mark held him in place. "What are you talking about?"

"When I saw you with the pagan the other night, I admit, I was puzzled." Philip casually laid the empty candlestick on the table next to the other, which was still burning bright. John noticed faint streaks of blood and a small dent. He winced in anger. "I saw you with the Hindu at the church and thought how unfortunate it was that you had decided to spend your Christian currency in such a way. But when I saw you today—"

"Saw me where?"

"At the pagan festival, John. You probably didn't recognize me, and that was by design, of course. But I did see you there."

"So?"

Philip stood and walked around the table. The hard, methodical fall of his sandals against the stone floor echoed around the quiet room. He sat on the edge of the table and leaned close. John felt Philip's hot breath against his face. The two sets of hands behind him pushed down on his shoulders, stressing the futility of any struggle; it was as if he was being forced to watch a horrific play he did not want to see. Nevertheless, John stared Philip straight in the eyes, refusing to yield ground to torment.

"So? So, I want you to explain what you were doing there with the Hindu."

John spit in Philip's face. "His name is Sri!"

Philip slapped John across the mouth. He struck so hard John felt the hands on his shoulders loosen their grip for a brief moment. He felt blood oozing from his mouth in a reluctant trickle.

"What were you doing there?" Philip asked, his calm tone intact.

"My business and my company are my own to keep." John was defiant.

Philip swiveled quickly and with a swift, forceful blow, he punched John in the stomach with such strength, it stole the very breath from John's lungs.

"How very wrong you are. Meletius is footing the bill for your little excursion, and I don't feel you are paying him back in a respectful manner. In fact, Brother John, you seem to take great pride in raising your robes high and pissing on the cross."

John struggled to catch his breath, his eyes narrowing to meet Philip's gaze. "I would piss on you if I could. Lay your hands on me, but how dare you lay them on Rachel."

"John, you and I both came out here to do a job." Philip knelt at John's side. He dipped his index finger in the blood from John's wrists and worked it against his thumb. "A job in small repayment for the blood Christ spilt centuries ago." His tone remained conversational. "We are both dedicated men. Of this there can be no doubt. We are different in only one respect. I'm doing my job correctly."

"And what is your job, Philip?"

"To secure the Church. To do what I must to preserve its integrity."

"What in God's holy name do you know about integrity?"

Philip leaned into John's ear and whispered, "I know this much, Brother. If you set another foot in a church on this road, I'll know it. And I'll see you dead."

John studied Philip's face – but for what, he knew not. Philip forced a grin that lit a fire of contempt deep within John's core. Unable to contain himself, John again spat in Philip's face, showering him in blood. The hands upon his shoulders tightened once again as Philip fumbled around in blind rage for the candlestick. Finding it, he gripped it tight and reared back to strike.

At that moment, the door burst in. In the darkness, John recognized the voices of James, Sol, and Sri, but there were also others John did not know. The men grabbed Philip, Simon, and Mark. John heard Sri's voice in his ear.

"Once I untie these ropes, you must flee. Quickly!"

An anonymous body bumped the table and the remaining candle went out. John could hear the angry brawling, as he broke free of his bindings. However, he did not make for the door. Instead, on instinct, he raced to the corner for Rachel. In the darkness he felt for her head, touching the wetness on her hair and face. He prayed to God it was blood from his own hand and not from her.

"Rachel? Rachel!" She was unresponsive as he gently stroked her face.

John picked up the tiny, limp body, cradling her in his arms. His first image of her – an innocent standing in her own doorway so long ago – rushed back to him. Now, he ran for a different door, tripping over bodies strewn across the floor. He could not distinguish friend from foe, but only Rachel mattered, and getting her to safety. As he ran, he felt ablaze, filled with rage, will, and passion, culminating in a sense of purpose.

The herds of people had mercifully dwindled to nothing in the later hours, and John did not stop until he reached the footpath to the campground. He sat down to rest, holding Rachel in his lap, hugging her close. Flavus barked and whined in greeting and licked John's wrists, dangling low under Rachel's weight. The moonlight illuminated her fragile frame. He held her face in his hands and tried for a response.

"Rachel? Rachel!" Nothing.

John looked around like a mouse exposed in the light. He listened and searched the darkness for some sign of either captor or savior.

Three figures approached.

His muscles tightened, his body on alert. He drew Rachel closer as if he could pull her inside of his own body. His heart raced. Panic. Hope. All emotions at once. He shifted her to his left arm and took up a stone with his right hand. He was about to throw it at any unsuspecting head, when he recognized Sol. James and Sri trailed behind. The other men were not in sight, nor did his kidnappers pursue.

"Some night, huh, John?" Sol stepped close and pat John on the shoulder. "Are you alright?"

"Yes, Sol. Thank you." Barely able to speak and flooded with emotion, John surveyed the group in utter relief. "How did you know I was in there?"

"Thank him." James motioned to Sri who stepped forward. "He suspected something was up with Philip and convinced us to follow you. Lucky."

"Lucky, indeed." John wiped caked blood from his mouth and dabbed at the syrupy remnants of a cut. "Thank you, Sri."

"You are most welcome, Brother."

Rachel moaned. The group drew in close to assess her.

"Rachel?" John tapped her face gently. He looked at the other men. "We need to get her to safety. Quickly." James bent down to take Rachel from an exhausted John. John recoiled, tightening his grip on her. "No, James. I will care for her."

"Set her here." James motioned to a cotton blanket.

Sri stoked the fire so the group could survey Rachel's wounds. Sol ran to get water and clean cloth. When he returned, he handed the basin and cloth to John, who sat by the fire and held her spent body close. He wiped her face with the cloth, and dabbed at the gash on her head in exhilarated disbelief that they were reunited, though under such terrible circumstances. Rachel groaned and ever so slightly opened her eyes. She noticed John's hand near her face and suddenly became aware of all the men staring down at her. She let out a blood-curdling scream, struggling in John's arms. He hugged her tightly.

"Shhh…Rachel, you are safe. It's John. It's John from Antioch. Remember? Remember me?" Rachel settled, yet her body shuddered. "Rachel, it's John," he repeated. "I won't hurt you."

Rachel relaxed into his arms, shaking. Her tears flowed freely over cuts and bruises on her face, but John knew she had more scarring than for which this night could account.

He touched his cheek to her forehead as the men stood silently and watched.

Chapter Twenty-Four

S he's sleeping, James." John was adamant. "We can't just go."

"John, we have to." James mirrored his tone. "Thanks to your friend Luke, they know our camp. They know where we are. They could come down the path any minute!"

John was unconvinced. "They wouldn't dare come over here. Not tonight. Besides, I've made some friends here. We'll be fine."

"John, this isn't Antioch for Christ's sake," James roared. "This is Ecbatana, and it's a different justice out here. We will be wanted men in an alien place. There are only the friends who came through the gate with you. You cannot count on being the friend of any man in Ecbatana now."

"Justice?" John hissed. "Wanted men? They got what they deserved. You beat them up pretty badly."

"Maybe too badly," Sol muttered. He looked at James who glanced at Sri. John checked on Rachel, lying peacefully on the cotton mat. He stood to face Sol.

"What do you mean, 'too badly?'" John cast a stormy look into the sea of faces.

"John," James chimed in, "don't you wonder why they haven't followed us?"

John's heart stopped. "Well, I…wait. What? James, what did you do?"

"Well," Sol interjected, "to be honest, we don't really know who did it."

"Who did what?" John's voice grew louder.

"John, none of those men emerged from that house tonight." James looked down at his feet.

"Dead?" John whispered, in a voice now leaden with secrecy. His body crumpled in a heap next to the sleeping Rachel.

Sri knelt down beside him, resting a calm hand on his shoulder. "John, we don't know. All we know is that you and Rachel are safe. Sol's friends did not come back to camp with us. They have fled Ecbatana until the dust in this city settles."

"And so should we," James interjected.

John was motionless for several moments. "James, Philip is Rachel's husband." His eyes looked down to Rachel, a quiet pity in his voice.

No one spoke. The tension was palpable. Only the fire moved.

Rachel stirred to break the silence. "M…must get away." Her words were faint. "M…must leave. Scared."

All eyes fell on John. "Pack. Now."

Chapter Twenty-Five

The camels were not eager to move at this late hour, if at all. They had traveled a long distance to Ecbatana and were clearly intent upon guarding their downtime. Nevertheless, with Flavus's help, the men got them up, packed, and moving. Sol kept watch while Rachel remained on a chair in the stable.

"Sol, do you have a camel to spare?" James asked. "We have no idea what lies ahead, and we may need it."

"I do, James. And I'll be riding on it."

"Sol, no." James walked over to his friend and placed a hand on his arm. "Your campground. Your business…" He knew this camp was Sol's entire life, and it had been such a big part of his very own.

"I know James, but—"

"But what? You'll go on the run and lose all this? It was dark in that room, Sol. They didn't see the faces. They'll suspect the three of us, but not you. You'll be safe here in Ecbatana, but if you join with us? Well, I can't guarantee you will ever see your home again."

"There are no guarantees on this road, James, but I will not argue with you. Time is too precious for fighting." Sol embraced his friend. "Take the camel and leave me here." Sol ran to the end stall and brought a camel to the group. "Take him. Head east toward Merv. There are small settlements along the way where you may find shelter and solitude. No one knows this better than you, I am sure. Bring the camel back my way someday, if you can. If not, God be with you." Sol cast a glance and a nod at Sri. "And may his gods be with you, as well."

"Thank you, Sol," James said. They embraced again.

"Sun is almost up, James," John said. "Hurry!" John bustled around the stable in desperation, urging everyone to make haste. Nerves were on edge in the darkness. "Sri, help me with Rachel. She can ride with me until she regains her strength."

Sri was busily saddling the other camels and packing them with supplies, but he dropped his duties to assist. James and Sol loaded goods onto the new animal to better distribute the weight, before taking over Sri's loading chores. John hoisted himself up on his camel. Rachel was groggy, but lucid enough to climb into the saddle in front of him with Sri's tender guidance. John gripped her tight around the waist and held her close so she would not fall. With the caravan prepared, Sri took his own mount, as did James. Flavus led the way out into the unknown.

"Goodbye, Sol." John waved, and Sol nodded. "Thank you for everything."

"God speed, friends!" Sol stood, hands on his hips, and watched the party recede from view. "May we meet again in better times!"

The caravan made its way to the edge of Ecbatana. They did not have nearly enough supplies, and no plan, except to get as far from the city as possible. Daylight was preparing to break as the group again passed the stone lion sentinels at the gates. The party paid them little tribute as they turned toward Merv.

Chapter Twenty-Six

Day and heat burst upon the group in most unwelcome fashion, stealing away darkness – their one sweet defense on the challenging road. John grew more and more paranoid as the sun rose higher and higher. He was desperate for a sign of safety but knew that was a luxury now well beyond his grasp, even unto the far reaches of the Chinese frontier.

Towering mountains rose into a cloudless sky on either side of the path, and the camels cut through them like knives. The party rode in silence, each man lost down the lonely trails of his own mind. John placed a cotton cloth over Rachel to keep the sun off her bruised body. She sat limp in the saddle, while John kept a hand against her stomach, reassuring himself with each of her slight, yet regular, life-sustaining breaths.

"James!" John, overwhelmed by his own thoughts, was desperate for any word, for any sign of solace or comfort. He wanted answers and he wanted to rest with Rachel. The calm, methodical plodding of his camel was almost too much for his troubled mind to bear. "James, where is the next stop?"

"There are stops all along these mountains," James yelled back. "But I know one where we will be safest. Most people stop six to seven hours outside of Ecbatana, but there is a cave system 10 hours out that will make a good place to camp. Water runs cold from the mountaintops to pools hidden in the foothills. Most travelers rest too early on their first day, and bypass it on their second. Some are just afraid to stop."

John considered questioning this last statement, but was too distracted by Rachel. He had to trust more than his own life now to James's seasoned judgment, and was more than willing to defer to James's many years of experience.

"Fine," John agreed. "I'm forcing water into her, but she looks exhausted."

The group carried on, past the expected oases and encampments. They paid no mind to those already bedding down, as they forged onward. John searched the hills. Replaying the scene from Ecbatana in his mind, he surveyed the mountain passes for signs of life or secret encampments, but saw none. Only soaring birds and deathly silence accompanied them. Nonetheless, he remained resolute in his trust of James and, after the previous night, John knew better than to second-guess his companions.

He reached down for Rachel's hand, dangling from under her soft coverings. He put his wrist next to hers and saw they had similar scars. Rachel moved her head slightly and groaned. John nuzzled her head gently with his through the cloth.

"Christ," he prayed quietly, "deliver her safely."

The sun started its earnest and final westward descent. Ecbatana was now many hours behind and John felt an apprehensive comfort. He looked down at Flavus who had not left his camel's side through the rocky terrain. No sound had passed between the group for some time. The only sign of life, a caravan traveling in the opposite direction, prompted barks from Flavus. Sri had not spoken since the morning, and James did not appear in the mood. Even the camels were quiet and cooperative since Rachel joined.

A light and unexpected breeze carried noises into John's ears – the clanking of a pot, then voices. The sounds drifted across the foothills, reverberating about the desert floor. As the path stretched downhill, John saw a small circle of tents well off the main route. There were sites beyond, snaking along the side of the mountain. John squinted as he searched in the distance. This was a place one would miss, or give little thought, if he was not paying attention on the road, or not specifically seeking it. The group veered off the path to the north toward the distant encampments. John soon realized this was not a formal campground. Small altars dotted trails leading up into the hills. James led the group to a vacant spot against the mountain and dismounted.

"Where are we?" John asked.

"It is a pilgrimage site," Sri said, breaking his hours-long silence. "There are sacred pools in the cave systems. But, as James said, many do not stop here. Some are too busy thinking about early rest or further progress, and others fear the place."

"Great," John said with resignation. "I'm glad we're here then. We need a little more fear in our lives. How do you know about this place, Sri?" John surveyed the tents and altars interspersed against the foothills.

"Many you see are on the road for business," Sri said, "but as I have told you, I travel with a different purpose."

James raised a hand and emitted a shrill whistle, bringing the caravan to an abrupt halt. "I hate to interrupt, but there is almost no sun left, and we have no camp."

"What about Rachel?" John asked, adjusting her in his arms and preparing for dismount. "We need to re-dress her wounds and see if she will take food."

"You're right," James said, "but we know she is alive, breathing, and that you have provided water along the way. Get her into a comfortable position so we can make camp right now. Then, in firelight and comfort, we can properly tend to her and see that she is stable."

"But James—"

"Don't argue with me, John. One thing about the injured on this road – it is good to rush to aid, but not to cure. We must have good warmth, body position, and time to make sure she gets what she needs.

If we are forced to set up in shadow, she will have none of that. Now please, let us get started in what light remains."

"Fine, James. We will do as you say, but if it is alright with you, I will stay with her and do what I can while you and Sri set up camp."

"Fine by me," James said. "Sri and I will make haste." James leapt from his mount and fastened his camels to a nearby bush. He immediately set about fashioning a makeshift fire pit with wood, rocks, and his foot. In a flash, he had a small fire burning to take the chill from the air.

Satisfied that Rachel had a warm place, John now tried to maneuver both himself and Rachel closer to the fire.

"Come over here and help me, Sri."

Sri helped John gently lift Rachel. He took her in his arms. Together, they placed her on a cotton cloth James laid out for her by the fire. She was breathing and peaceful, so Sri yielded her to John's quick care and canteen then devoted himself to his other duties.

"Sri, you never answered my question from before," John said. "How do you know about this place?"

"I am out here on a similar purpose as you, as I told you so many day ago. I was called to the road for spiritual reasons. I, like James, have seen many things. I have made some stops others will not, and I do not often judge before experience, for courage is the soul of change."

James and Sri unloaded the tents. James hammered in posts to better secure the mounts.

"To be honest, Sri, we know so little about you," James said. "You've been with us for so long, yet so much of your life is still a mystery. I have to say, I'm curious to know more, too."

"I will tell you something of my life if you wish," Sri said. "For the sake of Rachel. Maybe a story will make our camp come together in quicker, more pleasant fashion. But these are details that very few men know. Details that are part of another life, and a distant man."

John and James exchanged glances.

"I would like that very much," John said. "Please."

"I first met Gurudev when I was very young," Sri began. He paused, and in the silence, the fire clicked and crackled.

"You met *who*?" James huffed, pounding in a stake.

"Gurudev," Sri repeated. "My holy teacher. But I suppose I must start earlier than that. I was born into a prominent family. Traders on this road and merchants they were – faithful servants of this path for many generations."

"You were caravanners?" James could hardly believe what he was hearing.

"Indeed," Sri said. "My father would say, 'Someday, son, you will inherit my trade and continue my noble tradition.' But I was not interested in money, jewels, and spices. As a young boy, I was at my father's side when he met travelers and traders from various empires. He was ruthless with them, and I did not like to be with him. He demanded swift payment of debts, or he would…" Sri's voice disappeared down the dusty trails of disturbing memory.

James, now bustling about with the tents looked up from his work. Sri stood motionless, staring into the distance.

"Would what, Sri?" James asked.

Sri snapped from his stupor and began unpacking a camel. "He would…well, he was, as I said, ruthless. When I was ten, I saw him beat a man to within an inch of his life over a debt of ten silver pieces. It was at that time I began to stray from him to meet the mendicants, monks, and missionaries, and to hear their tales. They were my people in heart and soul. Their stories were my delight. These were the men who drifted unnoticed among the busy merchants. The men who were often last to exit the ships, yet first to be of service in the ports."

"Wasn't your father angry about that?" James asked. "Didn't he grab you by the collar and drag you back to his business?"

"Indeed. Indeed, he was angry. But I was persistent in my absences. Instead of learning the trade, I learned the stories of these men of mystery. I savored their languages and admired their holy symbols.

Their currency was not the passing fancy of gold and jewel, but word and soul. They traded in the everlasting. After a while, my father's violence was so terrible, I ran off into the forests for good. I lived alone and by my own labors for a long while, making friends with religious devotees of many traditions, studying and meditating upon the holy scriptures.

"At 16, I met Gurudev. I took his holy vows as my own, and I lived with him in his mountain retreat for many years. He imparted to me his wisdom and his commentaries. We would spend time in conversation upon the Upanishads and he would teach me yogic wisdom. Unlike my father, Gurudev led by gentle example and demonstration. One day, in my twentieth year, he called me to his bedside – a simple straw mat covered with dried leaves. He said he was to leave his body in seven days. He told me he had a vision, and I would need to accept it before his departure. I would have to extinguish the flames of desire in my living mind and then I would travel the world. At that time, he declared, an immortal fire would then ignite within my soul in the desert."

"A fire in the desert?" John looked up from Rachel, and stared at Sri, eyes wide.

"Yes," Sri nodded, a hint of nostalgia in his voice. "A great fire that I would tend. I refused to hear this and went about my yoga and devotions in the forest, surrounded by the lush greenery and streams, and animals that had become my companions. I did not want to hear talk of deserts and fire, even internal fires. I already had the flame of my devotions. For what more could I ask? One week later, I came to Gurudev's side. He told me again of his vision and again I was reluctant to accept it. He said, 'You must take what I say into your heart so that I may be free.' I prostrated at his feet and relented, vowing to follow his vision. He left his body that same hour. Before he departed, he touched me between the eyes and uttered, 'Sri.' That has been my name ever since. All names before that time have passed into shadow."

"I've always wanted to be called Pompeius." James slapped the tent hides, stiff and true, and stood back to admire his handiwork. He ran his hands along the smooth, cool shelters. "But I'm not going to find a guru or whatever to change it now. What did you do after the name change?" James asked. "How did you get out here? Sounds like you had it pretty good in your jungle homeland."

"The good life is relative, Master James," Sri said.

"Really?" James laughed. "I don't know about that – a warm night, a cool spring, a cheesy placenta, and adventure upon the next day's ride. I would say that is enough to make any man happy. Wouldn't you agree?"

"I have to admit, Sri," John interjected, "placenta is very tasty. Although, I could do with a little less adventure." John stroked Rachel's face as she slept, and thought he detected a fleeting smile across her lips.

"Indeed, friends. But my life was not so simple then. I meditated on Gurudev's words, and realized, with some pain, that I could no longer hide from my destiny. I left the jungle retreat in the mountains and headed to my father's home."

"You went *back*?" James asked. "To such a terrible person?"

"Yes. Forgiveness dictated that I had no choice." Sri unpacked some clean cotton cloth and brought it, and another canteen, to John, who started to gently clean Rachel's face. Sri then set about stocking the tents with woolen blankets and other supplies. "The home of my youth was in another forest miles away from Gurudev's, and I returned in expectation and regret, my spiritual journey balanced on the edge of a knife. Mother had long since passed, even before my departure years before. Father was now old and weak, and I cared for him for a year, revealing nothing of my life, only serving him in our home."

"You were a good son, Sri," John said.

"Duty is not performed for praise, John. It is performed for duty. I practiced my spiritual disciplines when father slept, and disciplined myself to care for him when he was awake. When he died, his whole estate was left to me, including his caravan. I gave his fortune to the poor and created an ashram from our home, where I led a group of mendicants. I suppose I settled in, but of course, life had other plans for me. One night, Gurudev appeared to me in a dream. He waved his hand before my eyes and revealed to me the great road upon which we now travel. The next day, I mounted a camel at father's stable and rode out into the world. This world."

"And then you ran into us," James laughed. He was now sitting by the fire with Flavus, preparing to cook dinner. "I'm guessing Gurudev didn't see that coming."

"Well, yes," Sri said. "I did meet you. But after many years. Of course, it was all meant to be. All guided by Guruji's sure hands."

"So many travels," John said. "It's a wonder to imagine."

"Indeed. I have spent many years sailing, walking, and riding, visiting with pilgrims from all places and all paths, following the invisible will of Gurudev."

Sri approached the fire where John was now holding Rachel's head in his lap, stroking her hair. Sri closed his eyes and took in several deep breaths before fashioning a pillow out of a long piece of silk that he had received at the Shivaite ceremony in Ecbatana.

"John," he said, "I think we are now in a setting where true healing can begin. Our patience and discipline will see reward. Please lay Rachel's head on this cushion." John obeyed, gingerly laying Rachel down so her head rested on the cloth. "The water please," Sri requested.

John handed his canteen to Sri, who poured some cool water into his palm. He closed his fingers around the liquid and held it above Rachel. He uttered an incantation and moved his hand along the length of her still body. He then brought it back to her head where he dripped droplets down his thumb onto Rachel's wounds. He placed his hand over her face and took in three deep breaths, exhaling with force from his mouth onto her body. Flavus came over to sniff and

John silently moved him away. John and James watched in amazement as Rachel moaned and opened her eyes.

John made to touch her, but Sri stayed his hand. "Wait," he whispered.

Sri stared into her eyes. Rachel's eyelids fluttered in the firelight. Her eyes rolled toward the top of her head. Her breath was irregular and agitated, but slowly calmed down. She blinked, oriented herself, and looked up at John. Her lips, dry and cracked, formed a faint smile, framed by her drooping, matted curls.

"John," she muttered, her voice rough as the mountain, her tone as smooth and glassy as the pools therein. John's heart skipped a beat. Rachel raised a shaking hand and held it out for his. He accepted without hesitation. She gently squeezed his fingers, but only as tight as a child collects a butterfly. "S…" her voice was almost pure air as she struggled to form a word.

"What, Rachel?" John asked, tears forming in his eyes. "What are you saying?"

"Safe."

Chapter Twenty-Seven

The camp now consisted of three tents – one for Sri, John, and Flavus, one for James, and one for Rachel. John awoke the next morning and saw his tent was empty. He emerged to a roaring fire where Sri and James shared a breakfast of bread smeared with camel butter, a treat procured in Ecbatana. Flavus was asleep at Sri's feet.

"Where is Rachel?" An inner panic revealed itself in John's voice.

"Good morning to you, too, John." James said, tossing him a piece of bread slathered in the rich grease.

"Where is she?" John asked again, his tone still urgent.

"She's fine, Brother. Sit." James motioned to a rock beside him. "Rachel is at the baths."

"The baths?"

"I told you," Sri said in a soft voice, "this is a pilgrimage site. Springs run out of these mountains, forming hidden pools in the caves. Rachel joined a group of passing women going to cleanse and pray. Nothing lives in the pools but prayer, Brother. I assure you, she is quite safe."

"Which direction?" John asked. He was clearly not going to rest until his eyes saw Rachel. James, resigned to giving directions, waved his hand west to a path that led into the foothills. John made to go, only delaying long enough to take a drink of water. As he left, James nudged Sri and grinned. Sri shrugged and ate his bread in silence.

John worked his way along the mountainside path until it turned into the hill. He followed the narrow road up to a system of caves, alive with the sound of laughter. He crouched behind an outcropping at the mouth of a cavern, secluded by scrubby bushes, and peered into the pool. There were women of all races bathing and washing clothes in the cold water. Some were holding hands, praying, while others made offerings at an altar near the edge of an inflowing stream.

John's eyes found Rachel among them. She appeared bruised, but fresh. He could hardly believe how well she was healing. She was kneeling in the pool, pouring water from a clay vessel onto her head. As she stood to wring her long, curly black hair, she rose from the water to her full height, arching her back. This simple task unfolded in slow motion before his eyes. She wore a long, flowing white dress that he guessed was a gift from one of her new friends. It clung tightly to her body, grasping her form, as his hands once held her against him on the camel. The water revealed her entire shape in every detail. She opened her eyes as water dripped from her lashes and nose. John felt at this moment he could end his journey and still be saved. Assured that she was safe, he snuck away.

"Did you find her?" James asked with a smile.

"Yes," John said without further revelation. He wanted to keep his vision of her to himself. The moment was the most intimate of his life and he had no desire to share it with anyone.

John took a seat next to Flavus and scratched his ear. Flavus licked John's arm before putting his head back down. John took a piece of buttered bread and sat with it in his hand, unmoving. He preferred to savor his new memory, instead.

Giggling drew the men's attention to a trail outside of camp. Four women walked in conversation, Rachel among them. Her dress was dry, but her hair was damp – her curls silky, shiny, and clean. A woman renewed. She hugged her female companions who veered onto another path, leaving Rachel to enter her site. She sat down by John and immediately took his hand, surprising and delighting. It was soft and cool, owing to the fresh springs.

"You appear revived," Sri said, handing her a piece of bread covered in butter.

"Thanks to all of you!" She smiled and ran her hand along her head. "I still have some bumps and bruises, but at this point, I'm just happy to be alive." Rachel was in good spirits. Her hair now hid the gash on her forehead. She turned to John and looked up at him with clear eyes, as brown as the desert at dusk. John was sure her red lips rivaled rubies from the finest traders. He imagined her long lashes blinking a breeze to cool him. Rachel appeared for a moment as if she would speak again, but instead, she rested her head on his shoulder and looked at the ground.

"Do you remember what happened yesterday?" James asked.

"James!" John's voice was stern. Protective.

"It's alright. He can ask me." Rachel lifted her head, her look soft, yet confident. John's mind was still bent on sheltering her, but he relented and allowed the conversation to progress. "I only remember parts of it. Philip struck me hard, and I blacked out. I don't have many memories after that. I remember some moments being on the camel with John, but not much more." She looked around her. "I'm still not sure how we got here exactly. But I can say, I'm glad to be away from the city."

"We took you out of Ecbatana," John said, "after Sol, Sri, James, and some of their friends followed me to where Philip and his men grabbed me."

"It's a secret meetinghouse." Rachel's voice turned dark. "They use it to talk about their war."

"Their war?" John asked. "What war?"

"Their war against anyone who is not in agreement with their purpose." Rachel took a big bite of bread and licked her lips to take in all of the butter.

"Wait." John sputtered from the canteen he had in his mouth. "Are you telling me they really think they're involved in combat?" John looked at his friends, bewildered, then to Rachel. "Who are they, the Roman Army?"

"Yes," Rachel said, swallowing with a small laugh. "At least that is how they view themselves. A holy army. Luke had already been under suspicion for allowing heretical teachings, and I suppose they were there to look in on him. You coming to preach must have allayed Philip's fears at first, but then when he heard you speak…well, I think it caused quite a stir. I wish I could have seen you. I wish I could have seen Philip's face!"

"It's probably better that you didn't," John said. "Safer."

"Oh, yes. Much safer," she said, gently touching the cut on her forehead."

"I'm still not sure what I did that got them all so angry," John said.

"Philip has been sensitive lately," Rachel said. "He takes his mission very seriously. He measures men now by their adherence to his own views. We've been growing more and more distant as he heads down this spiral. I don't know him anymore. He's like a stranger to me. He kept me in that small house, out of sight. He would go out into the city with Simon and Mark and spy."

"I knew it!" John exclaimed, looking at Sri. "I knew they were spying for Meletius."

Sri tipped his head to John.

"When they were sent out here from Antioch," Rachel continued, "they were charged with maintaining the purity of Church teachings. They were told to collect information." Rachel exchanged a gaze with each man. "But Philip went crazy. He started dealing with matters on his own."

"What matters?" John asked, leaning toward Rachel with earnest curiosity.

"Philip got in the habit of following missionaries and community Christians, and if they said things or did things he felt were out of line with Meletius's teachings, he would have them seized by forces sympathetic to Meletius. Roman soldiers may not have a big presence in Ecbatana, but they are there. Trust me. Many reject the Arian Valens and are loyal to Meletius. When Philip found dissenters in the community, he would have them arrested…or worse."

"Worse?" James raised an eyebrow and looked at Sri and John. "He sounds like Shapur himself."

John noticed a tinge of anxiety cross James's face. John had become accustomed to James's sure-footed navigation of problems on the road. Clearly, Church politics were not an obstacle James had faced before.

"On the outskirts of Ecbatana there is a graveyard." Rachel's voice was now a whisper. Everyone had to lean closer to hear her. "The locals call it 'the Pit.'"

"I've heard of that place," James said. "That's probably where you were headed, John." Sri nodded in agreement.

"Some people deny its dark history and don't believe it is anything more than the final resting place for locals, but they are very wrong," Rachel said, a conspiratorial tone edging its way deeper into the conversation. "It is filled with the corpses of those who have found themselves on the wrong side of various merchants. It's a place people stay away from. No one wants to end up there, and many are superstitious about it. They feel if they don't mention it, they'll be safe. We had only been in Ecbatana a few days when Philip started thinking about using it to bury other kinds of people."

"Like me," John muttered.

"They were sent from Antioch only to gather information," Rachel said. "I swear. It's just…I suppose things get strange out here. We've been out on the road so long that, well, something must have changed in Philip. He was a different man once…he is quite another on this long, lonely road."

"I know you didn't have anything to do with this," John said, reacting to her tone. "You don't have to defend Philip, Meletius, or the Church."

"Defend them?" Rachel was taken aback. "I'm not defending them! I'm simply telling you that Meletius did not authorize Philip to use force of any kind."

"So why would they?" John asked.

"I told you. Something changed. That night when they attacked you, before they left to kidnap you, I heard them talking. They said they were going to put you back on the path or take you to the Pit. Philip knew I had overheard, so he locked me in that secret place to make sure I didn't go to find you."

"Bastard," John muttered. "I admit when I saw Philip again, I wondered about you. But, of course, things went badly, and I didn't have a chance to find out if you were with him or back at home. I'm glad to know you would come find me to warn me. I'm sorry you were locked away, or we would have come for you."

"I don't remember anyone coming in to save us." Rachel looked around at the group.

"It was a few minutes after Philip knocked you out," John said. "With that candlestick. I'm sorry Rachel, there was nothing...I..."

Rachel reached for John's hand. "It's not your fault," she said. "Please don't blame yourself. There was nothing you could have done." John met her gaze and mustered a smile. "Anyway, he got what he deserved, I'm sure." Rachel furrowed her brow and took another bite of bread. The men exchanged uncomfortable glances. Sri cleared his throat, and everyone cast eyes at the ground. "What's wrong?" Rachel searched the group with a quizzical look. "What did I say?"

"Rachel." John could barely mask his quaking voice. "Philip...he...they didn't follow us from that house."

"So what?" She said. "They probably didn't expect that kind of resistance. You probably scared them off."

"I'm not sure scared is the word," Sri added.

"Why? What other word is there?" There was a faint tinge of panic behind Rachel's voice as her eyes darted from man to man – even to Flavus.

Sri approached Rachel and knelt in front of her. He gently touched her trembling hand, mustering his calmest voice. "Rachel," he whispered, "Philip may be dead."

"Dead!" Rachel exclaimed. "Dead? Sri, what are you talking about?"

"We don't know for sure," James said, trying to cut through the awkward exchange. "We freed John, and he grabbed you. Then we all ran. It was dark…"

Rachel sat stone-faced. The men were at a loss for words. Suddenly, she let out what sounded like a giggle stifled under a choking weight. Then she collapsed, eyelids fluttering.

"Rachel? Rachel!" John tapped her face. "Rachel?"

"Dead!" Her eyelids shot open with the word. "Dead?" Enlivened with a sudden animation that coursed through her body, she was laughing and crying at the same time. She rolled over on her stomach.

John gently touched her back as she lay on the blanket, a slight quake radiating just under her skin. "Rachel," he said, "we're not sure…we—"

"Dead?" she wailed. "He's…he's…"

"Rachel, are you alright?" John was unsure what to do. Sri still knelt beside her. James merely shrugged his shoulders, at a loss.

Rachel looked up at John with tears streaming down. "He's been dead to me for years!"

Chapter Twenty-Eight

Should we check on her?" John asked. Rachel fled to the solitude of her tent after hearing the news about Philip, and had not emerged.

"I suppose you can try." Sri tipped his head toward the tent.

"Rachel?" John poked his head inside. "Are you alright? May I come in?" He heard soft sobs and decided the lack of an answer was his invitation. Rachel was sitting with her back to the entrance, her face in her hands. He came up and knelt beside her. "Rachel? Are you ok?"

She turned to look at him, tears pouring down. She grabbed John's arm for support and buried her face deep in his chest. John cupped it in his hands and pulled it away from his robe. He wiped her eyes with his sleeve, gently dabbing at her nose, pink with emotion, and stroked her hair.

"Rachel, talk to me," he said. "What are you feeling?"

"John, do you remember when we saw you back at our home?"

"Yes." Despite his best efforts, his face broke into a smile at the thought of her tending to his wounds. "You showed me such kindness."

"After you left, all Philip could talk about was following in your path. Spreading the word. He was obsessed. We sold everything we owned and left immediately upon your departure. Philip made his services available to Meletius, swearing an oath to protect the Church. We hardly had a chance to stop on the road. He only wanted to get to

Ecbatana. He started talking about having a son and raising him out here. We tried for a few months, but I could not get pregnant. He would call me worthless. He would assault me repeatedly, saying he was determined to get me pregnant. Hitting. Always hitting." Rachel started to cry, and John hugged her close. "Meletius called us 'emissaries' and 'interested congregants,' and he assigned us all to places on the road," she said through her tears. "He told us others had already been sent. Philip drew Ecbatana. Some were sent to Merv, Bukhara…cities all along the route."

"I know," John said. "I am to go to Samarkand. But I was sent as an official missionary."

"That's what Philip wanted. On the way he kept telling people that he was going to be more than 'interested.' He wanted to get involved in deep teaching, public speaking, and rooting out evil at its source. He thought that's what you were doing back home. He looked up to you. It's all he wanted after you left."

"Did you want to do this? Did you want to come out here with Philip?"

"No. I wanted to stay and build the family we longed for. I wanted to try to get pregnant again, at our home, in the safety of our four walls and with the support of our local meeting. Philip didn't want that anymore. He said our little town was too small for his plans. He was obsessed with being out here. He said the reason I couldn't conceive is because I must have been a Jewish whore before he met me, and this was God's punishment. He said, 'I don't want you, but no one else will have you, so I guess you're staying with me.'"

"I'm sorry, Rachel."

"He kept saying he was going to sell me to a caravan or prostitute me. One night at a campsite, I was alone in the tent. Philip was at a prayer gathering. A man stormed into my tent and tried to attack me, but I fought him off, screaming. When Philip came back to the tent, he said he didn't care about the assault and that I was just a prostitute, anyway."

John felt a silent rage sweep over him. His insides screamed in anger. He wanted Philip's face in his hand now, with a rock in the other.

"Rachel, listen to me – I will take care of you, do you understand? I will take care of you from now on."

She put her head on John's chest and cried. This time, he did not stop her.

Chapter Twenty-Nine

That night, everyone relaxed by the campfire. The evening was mercifully cool against the mountains and bellies were full of bread, dried fish, and fresh water from the spring. Rachel had cried herself to sleep earlier in the day, and was now back in the company of the others. She seemed revived, but still withdrawn.

Topics of conversation drifted easily from empires to cooking, as each person consciously tried to maintain a light atmosphere to ward off the unknown. Despite their best attempts, the events surrounding Philip and his men still hung in the air, looming over the camp like a toxic mist. James broke the silent agreement and brought up the inevitable.

"John, where are we going from here?"

"Merv," he said. "It's the only way. For all of the road's terrors, I have to continue my work out here, and Merv is the next major city. If we keep moving, we should be safe." Sri looked at James, uncertain and unconvinced. "What's the matter?" John was taken aback by the sudden lack of unanimity. He was sure everyone wanted to be as far from Ecbatana as possible. "Why is everyone so quiet? Aren't we going to continue east?"

"John, listen to me." James stoked the fire, avoiding John's quizzical gaze. "I think we should go back to Ecbatana."

"What?!" John exclaimed. Rachel gripped John's hand as James continued.

"I've been thinking about what Rachel said to us today. About

Philip and the other men and what they're doing back there. I think they need to be stopped."

"Wait, are my eyes deceived or is this James before me?" John looked at him with an air of complete incredulity. "Is this the same James with whom I left Tyre? You don't care about anything!"

"John, that's not fair," Rachel said sternly.

"He's right." James laughed.

"James, Sri, and I were talking this evening when you went for firewood," Rachel said with an air of genuine calm.

"This is *your* idea?" John was flabbergasted. He could not believe Rachel wanted to go back to danger. Back to Philip. He hoped that the shock in his voice would conceal the jealousy in his mind.

"In part, yes. Philip was my husband. Is my husband. We don't even know if he is alive or dead. All I know is he was doing terrible things to good people, and I think we can do something about it."

John considered this new development and played with the possibilities in his head. Deep inside, he knew Rachel was right. He, too, needed to know about Philip. If he was alive, John wanted to stop him. But he fought this course of action. He didn't want to see Rachel hurt. And, if he was being honest, he was afraid that if Philip was still alive, Rachel, with her sweet nature and sense of loyalty, would return to him. John wrestled with these thoughts as Rachel's eyes pled with him.

"Rachel," John said, "I just found you again. I—"

Rachel placed a finger over John's lips. She knew his mind, but kept her words cryptic. "John, I have experienced torture at that man's hands. Now, he may be torturing others. My soul will not rest until I know the truth of his life or death." She slid her soft finger slowly from his mouth and down his chin. The movement was seductive. And persuasive. "Help me."

"Well, Sri?" John looked to his friend for a balanced counsel. "What do you think? Should we go back to danger?"

"We do not go back to danger, Brother John," Sri said. "We go back to secure the safety of others."

"You know my vote," James said, anticipating John's question. "Ask Flav' what he thinks."

"Flavus?" Rachel called the dog, who lumbered over and put his head on her lap.

"Unanimous," John said. "Now, we need a plan."

Rachel looked at each man. "I think I have one."

Chapter Thirty

John and Sri emerged to the fire and saw only James, quietly stoking the coals. Flavus was at his side, supervising the morning task.

"Good morning, you two," James said. "And John, before you ask…" James put up a hand without looking up from the fire. John froze the words about to leave his mouth. "Rachel went to see her friends. They were heading for early morning devotion."

"Do you think they'll have all the supplies, James?" John asked, sitting down to breakfast.

"We can only hope," James said. "It would be a good start to our plan."

"I can't believe we're doing this," John muttered. "But, I suppose we have no other choice. I just wish there was another way."

"There is always another way," Sri said. "The only question is whether you would risk it."

"Okay, okay," John said, settling into his bread.

The men ate in silence, then tended to the business of the morning to keep their minds active, away from dread. Soon, Rachel appeared with three companions. She had an arm full of dresses and cotton cloth. All four women came into camp, laughing and talking excitedly.

"Friends," Rachel was grinning from ear to ear, "meet Dian, Deborah, and Sejal. Ladies, this is Sri, John, James, and Flavus."

The men stood in greeting and everyone exchanged pleasantries. They invited the women into the circle for refreshment and relaxation. Sejal was drawn immediately to Sri, at whose feet she knelt to touch –

a sign of respect for his age and station in their culture. Sri laid a gentle, steady hand upon Sejal's head and uttered a quiet prayer. She sat next to him, and they began to speak in their native tongue, while Dian took an immediate interest in James. Deborah sat with Flavus and scratched his belly while Rachel took a seat next to John.

"Rachel," John whispered from the corner of his mouth, eyeing the new company, "who are these women? I thought you were only going for prayer and supplies."

"They are pilgrims, of a sort," she whispered back. "They came to the mountain after escaping a trader who was to sell them as prostitutes. They remind me of us. Displaced. They fled here and met a fortune-teller who told them they should settle down in this holy place with the others. They make a living selling dresses. I met them at the pool. Perhaps you saw them the other day when you, shall I say, visited?"

"I…well…" John stammered, and his face flushed.

"John, my eyes were bruised, but I am not blind. Those bushes were not very thick." Rachel gave him a quick kiss on the cheek. John touched the spot gently, as the tingle of her lips lingered. "They are going to help us. I told them about our plight, and they readily agreed to accompany us."

"They're coming with us?" John's whisper was now almost a scream. All conversations ceased and everyone looked at him. He grinned a weak, toothy smile, eyebrows raised. "Sorry."

"We are coming with you, indeed," Sejal said. She was a tall, confident woman, with skin the color of cream with a hint of cocoa, and long black hair in a braid to her waist. John thought she resembled the Hindu goddesses he'd seen painted on silks. "We have been at the mountain for a long time, and we have been waiting for a sign. Our Sister Rachel has found us, and we are meant to help you in Ecbatana. Enough terror is on this road already. We do not want to know there is more, and that we hid in the mountain, doing nothing."

"Perhaps we should go over our plan again," Sri said.

"Excellent idea, Sri." Sejal beamed at the group.

Dian was a very short, thin woman, who stood to James's chest. She had light skin and big eyes, full of endearing joy. She pulled three dresses from a pile, as well as three long scarves and other assorted garments, and handed one to each man.

"These, men, are for you," she said with a smile.

"I can't believe this," James said, rolling his eyes at Sri.

"You'll make a beautiful woman," Dian cooed.

John smiled to himself as he detected a hint of flush rising in James's face.

"We ride for Ecbatana tomorrow," Deborah said. A tall woman with olive complexion and striking features, Deborah's hair was the color of flame. John thought her dark eyes and reserved nature contained a wisdom born from her ancient Hebrew descent. She carried herself as a woman who accepted little trifle and little nonsense. "Each man will shave, don a dress, a scarf…" Deborah's voice was authoritative, stopping inevitable criticism in its tracks. "…and makeup."

"And the women?" John asked.

Rachel stood him up and pulled at the belt around his tunic, so that he stumbled close to her. "We'll be your masters," she said.

John smiled. "Ladies, no disrespect, but this is never going to work."

"I disagree," Sri said. "It is a great plan for getting into and around Ecbatana."

"He's right," James agreed. "This is not exactly how I want to do this either, but unfortunately, so many know our faces. Our names. Bigger cities become smaller outposts when danger is afoot. Even those who would not do us harm cannot be trusted to recognize us and yet keep our presence silent. There is no other way for us to move around."

"Tell me, John, did you look twice at the faces in the crowd in Ecbatana?" Dian asked. "Did you pull down the scarves and lift the dresses?"

"No," he said.

"There you have it!" Rachel said triumphantly, as if this logic was obvious. John's strained expression revealed that he was not so easily convinced. "John, it's the only way we can know the truth," she said, her tone more sympathetic to his hesitation. "That is why we're going back, is it not? To find out the truth?"

"The truth," John muttered. "I thought I had the truth months ago when James and I departed the port city. We went forth from Tyre with nothing but holy parchments, three camels, and Flavus. Now look." John wore a resigned grin as he surveyed his companions. "I don't know what to think anymore."

Sri approached John, putting his hands on his shoulders. "Brother, listen to me," Sri said. "We have been charged with the task – no, the duty – to come to the desert with truth. Now, we can act on the highest principles of that truth. We can ignite a fire of justice to save others from darkness and restore order to a chaotic situation. We owe it to all we hold dear to do this."

"You're right, Sri," John said, looking straight into the depths of his friend's solemnity. "I know you're right."

Chapter Thirty-One

That evening, the women joined the men at camp. They had their own tents and two camels they received as a gift from a wealthy pilgrim to whom they offered a prophecy and blessing of riches that had come to fruition for him. They set up next to the others and sat by the fire. As they talked, each new woman shared something of her past.

"I'm from Jerusalem," Deborah said. "I was taken from my caravan in Merv two years ago."

"Taken?" James asked.

"My husband, a Jewish merchant, sold me into slavery to settle a debt with a particularly ruthless silk broker from China. Dian had a similar fate."

"Indeed," Dian added. "Except my husband was a Christian trader from Tyre. Or, should I say, 'traitor'? He sold me to the same slave driver as Deborah."

"What about you, Sejal?" John asked. "How did you enter their company? Did you have a husband, too?"

"No," Sejal scoffed. "I have never been married. And, knowing what I know from my friends here, I likely will avoid that path. My parents abandoned me to the world when I was eight, and I have been roaming alone ever since. I came to the road following nothing but my instincts. I was kidnapped and forced into Deborah and Dian's slave caravan."

"We all escaped together," Dian said.

"Sejal worked her ropes loose," Deborah interjected. "She was determined to save as many of us as she could before we were prostituted. She wanted to free all the women, but we were all she could save before the trader's assistant awoke and raised the alarm."

"I shudder to think of the fates of those I could not save," Sejal said. Sri reassured her with a gentle touch.

"How did you come to this place?" John asked.

"We fled into the night and eventually joined a friendly monk who left us here," Sejal said.

"And we've never looked back," Dian added. "We were so grateful for our freedom, we turned our lives over to the Divine in this place. That is why Rachel's story touched us, and why we are coming with you. Why we must come."

"There is nothing left for us in this life but service," Deborah said.

Dian pulled a tambourine from a sack and started to tap a light, rhythmic beat. The bells jingled softly through the night, but grew louder and louder until the shaking treble pierced their ears. The women, entranced by the sound, rose like spirits in unison and danced around the fire, to Flavus's barking delight.

"This," Deborah said, her body swaying and floating to the beat, "was how the women of my tribes would dance long ago. We were strong. Free. And now, I spin with my sisters in complete unity. Our bodies now move as one to offer our love to the Divine. We express our love to God through music and dance. It is all we have. It is all we are."

John watched, completely enthralled, as Rachel twirled, light on her feet. Her hair traced perfect circles around her. He was struck by her look of complete ecstasy and liberation. She appeared like a tigress, unleashed into the wild for the first time – exploring the fruits of salvation that come from a truly authentic experience, delivered from the bondage of word, rule, and men.

When the women emerged from the dance, the men cheered – as much for the glow in the aftermath as the devotional performance.

Sri was drawn to his feet, overjoyed at the exuberance. "A blessing on you all who are in this circle," he said. "The Divine is here and is upon us always."

"Always," Sejal said quietly, sitting back at his side.

"Who else wants to share something?" Dian asked.

The men looked at each other.

"You want *us* to share?" John asked. "I'm not sure we can equal that. Besides, I think I left my tambourine in Antioch. Sorry."

Rachel sat beside to him with a smile. "This is not a competition," she said. "Don't you have something you could share? I have seen you writing throughout the days here and have noticed your parchments. Share with us." She pushed John's arm playfully.

"Rachel, it's nothing. They're just notes. Thoughts for my sermons, that's all." John looked at the ground, suddenly bashful.

"Share with us," Dian said. "We are all of one mind, and do not judge. There is no harm in intimacy. Indeed, you will be wearing our clothing soon."

John laughed, happy to finally discover for himself a light moment in the lingering dark circumstance of the coming morning. Realizing he was not going to escape the stage, he went to his tent, retrieved a parchment, and unrolled it by the fire.

"Ooh! Are you going to read to us from your holy Scripture?" Sejal asked excitedly.

"Not exactly," John said. "This is something I wrote in Ecbatana before all of this happened to us. It's nothing, really…just a simple rhyme."

"Please read," Sri prodded gently. "We would like to hear it."

John cleared his throat, and began. "I came to the road to give the truth, not to trade it away. Upon a camel from Tyre I carried it close, too full of fire to stay. I brought it out in places unknown, and showed it the light of the sun. For some it glowed, for some it was dark, but all manner of men are one. I see companions, true by my side, even in difficult travels; those who bear witness to this Antioch man, who stitch him when his life unravels. There was a time when this never could happen, when never such thing could be. But I now know that life, in all of its forms, in the end is only tea. To speak of Christ and all of His deeds, this is the greatest of feats, but to come to the road and live His word among friends, now my life is complete."

There was silence. Dian sniffled and Deborah wiped a tear from her eye. John held the parchment, smiling. He felt calm in the wake of the words, as their truth resonated deep within him – their energy radiating out of him and through the circle before him.

Rachel, squinting in the firelight, looked closer at the page. "John, that last line is not written there."

"I know. This has been bothering me. I was not sure how to end the devotion, but it just came to me in this moment."

"It was beautiful," she said, taking his hand in hers.

"Yes, John," Sri said. "Thank you for sharing that."

The group nodded approval as the fire crackled in the night. Flavus whined in his dreams, as flames flickered. Once again, the mood grew somber as the reality of coming events descended upon them.

Suddenly, but with the tenderness of a loving secret, Sri broke out into a chant. "Lord, I seek Your life. I seek to know You close." Sejal recognized the song and joined him. "Lord, we seek Your life," they chanted in unison. "We seek to know You close. You are the very light of the world, You are flame in the darkest room. Lord, we seek Your life, to know You is knowing the womb."

The chant went on for many minutes and eventually all joined in. They closed their eyes, allowing themselves to be carried away in the melodic spell. No pitch set in stone, no tone required, the repetitive droning of the words took on the melancholy of the group, and became a prayer for their safety and well-being as they prepared to embark on the difficult task ahead. As the song ended, the voices merged with quiet.

It was all to bed, and uneasy sleep.

Chapter Thirty-Two

It was an early start. The ride west would be slow, as there were now more camels and more in the party. The men submitted to the women for a shave, and put on their dresses. The women also applied makeup to them.

"James, dear," Dian said, "you are going to need a big scarf." James laughed, making the task between them easier.

The men relinquished their clothing to the women, who emerged from their tents with their hair tucked tightly into turbans. Everyone wrapped scarves around their faces.

"This is ironic," John said, smoothing his dress. "I came out here to preach in public, and now I have to hope the public does not notice me."

"This is only so we can move about more easily, John," James said. "I know."

The men packed the camels, and the team moved out.

Chapter Thirty-Three

I knew I'd have to head west again someday, but I didn't think it would be this soon," John whispered in Rachel's ear. "I would have at least liked to have seen my destination in Samarkand before riding back through Ecbatana."

Rachel leaned her head against John, speaking softly in his ear. "Honestly, I didn't think I'd ever leave there."

John was only half listening. He heard her words clearly enough, but was more intent on breathing them in. He closed his eyes and was transported to good memories, some of which came from experiences he'd never had. He felt cool nights and soft breezes. He tasted fresh dates on warm sand. He drank his fill from an oasis. There were warm bodies on—

"Woof!"

John was startled from his daydream.

"What is it, Flavus?" James asked.

The party looked up to see a vulture soaring overhead, searching for some dead prey, still and lifeless. John prayed it was not an ill omen.

"Flavus, it's just a…Flavus!" John exclaimed. "Everyone, stop!"

"What's the matter, John?" James yelled from the lead.

"It's Flavus."

"So?"

"So, he's the only dog we know that travels along this road. None other has his strength. Everyone will recognize him."

A silent and sickly knowledge spread through the group. Ecbatana was big, but not that big. It would be a risk taking Flavus back, and everyone knew it. The truth of what was about to happen was a swift punch in their guts.

"We cannot hide him," Sri said to the group, cutting off any plans to include Flavus on the trek. I suppose he has become such a fixture among us, we did not think about that earlier. His constant companionship and loyalty have blinded us. We would no sooner leave him than leave John. But we must."

John clicked his tongue, and his camel bent low. He and Rachel dismounted, and they knelt before Flavus.

"Flavus…" John held out his hand in empty offering. Flavus approached slowly, head down, as if he knew what was coming. John gently stroked Flavus's strong neck, full of soft muscle. "Rachel, what do I do?"

Deborah and Dian dismounted. They approached John, and Deborah touched his shoulder.

"We have not left the mountain yet," Deborah said. "I have an idea. Flavus can stay here with the other women."

Everyone exchanged glances, nodding their heads in assent.

"Good idea," Sejal said from her camel. "The women could use a protector around here. He can run, play in the springs. He will be well cared for. He will be loved as every other denizen of this mountain. His life will be one with the community."

"Sri?" John looked to his friend for advice.

"Brother John, we are going to a dangerous place. It is not just the men anymore. These women about us are strong as stone, yet we cannot put them at more risk than they already are."

"I'm sorry, Flavus." John put his forehead low and Flavus licked him in an implied forgiveness.

"It's alright," Rachel consoled. She kissed John lightly on the cheek. "He'll be alright. His loyal spirit will always be with us." John looked at Rachel, his brow slightly furrowed. "He'll be ok," she repeated, sensing the doubt in his eyes.

Deborah and Dian approached Flavus.

"Flavus." Deborah knelt in front of him. "This place has protected its women for so long. It has given us strength. You will be safe here. You will be a blessing unto the mountain."

Deborah and Dian asked the group to wait while they led Flavus to some distant tents where other women of the village lived. John could see three women emerge from a dwelling. They got on their knees and John watched as Flavus licked them in greeting. Dian pointed to the caravan. With a heavy heart, he offered a solemn prayer that he and his dear friend might reunite someday.

Minutes later, all were again mounted and moving.

Chapter Thirty-Four

The caravan was somber at their first rest, but everyone was alert. It had already been a long day, but so much more lay ahead. They decided to stop where others congregated so that they would not draw attention sitting alone. They needed to hide in the crowds. It was important to stay focused and for each person to remember their role. There was a deep sense that this was not seven individual threads, but one tapestry united in design and purpose. If one end loosened, everyone knew the whole group might unravel.

"Don't lose your senses," James said. "Don't forget yourself. Stay covered from head to toe."

"He is right," Sri said in a grim whisper. "We are going back to the unknown in Ecbatana. That means every stop we make from now on is unknown."

The women, dressed as men, went for water and the men, in women's clothing, stayed behind to keep watch over the crowd. When others approached or passed too closely, they kept their eyes low, mindful of their head and body cover. The women had provided the group with cotton undergarments to cover the feet in case their dresses and robes proved insufficient.

"My makeup is coming off on my scarf," James said. "How do the women wear this?"

"I'm growing nostalgic for my bare feet and waist-covering," Sri laughed.

"Suddenly, I envy Flavus," John said, kicking a stone and looking down disdainfully at his stockings. "At least he can be Flavus." John remembered himself and snapped from his musings to search for the women in the masses. "Can either of you see where they are?"

"Don't worry." James worked to suppress his gruff voice so as not to arouse suspicion. "They are well disguised."

John's mind was not at ease, as he knew that even the best disguise was no match for danger. He felt he would give anything to catch a glimpse of Rachel, safe and sound. He continued to scan the sea of humanity while on the other side of the grounds, the women filled jugs with water.

"These outfits feel so strange," Sejal said. "Everywhere I am, it feels the covering is not."

Dian giggled. "I do have to say, my robe smells like James. I could get used to this."

"I'm done with men," Deborah said, rolling her eyes. "One terrible experience was enough for me. But Rachel..." Rachel averted her eyes, suddenly profoundly interested in the water. "Well?" Deborah asked.

"Exactly," Rachel said. "The well. Keep your eyes on it and keep your voice down."

"Come now, Rachel," Dian prodded. "What is going on with you and John?"

"I'm married, remember?" Rachel snapped.

"To a man who beats you," Sejal said. The women looked at Sejal in surprise, her directness catching them all off guard. "Well? Am I not right? He was terrible to her. We all know what it is like to be treated like animals, Rachel. You do not deserve that. No one does. You are no more married now than Deborah or Dian. Free yourself, Rachel."

"We made a vow to Christ," Rachel said. "I cannot break that."

Sejal knelt next to Rachel. "I do not follow your Christ, but I know of him. It is my understanding that he was a gentle, kind soul."

"He was," Rachel agreed. "He is."

"If I had chosen a path to take a man, I would want to be with your Christ."

"Sejal!" Rachel looked up for the first time in the conversation. "That's blasphemy!"

"I have seen versions of your holy texts and heard stories that refer to Christ with a woman," Sejal said.

"Not any books I know." Rachel's tone cast ice into the sand at their feet.

"What I'm saying is that there is no harm in a good man," Sejal continued. "The true sin is not the breaking of a vow, but living a solitary life of pain while beholden to an oath. Your commitment was to a man who, even if still alive, may no longer exist. I cannot imagine a law in graceful heaven or good earth that could bind in such a way."

Rachel did not respond. Her stomach lurched and tears formed as Sejal's words penetrated her heart. She had entertained this conversation in her mind for many years, but was always too afraid to have it with another. She was about to speak when two men approached. Anxiety seized the women, freezing them silent in their carelessly noisy tracks.

"Excuse me, sirs?" A tall, gangly man addressed them. The women were in a state of near panic. They bent further toward the ground hoping to appear lost in their conjured tasks. Only their eyes were visible, their long hair and their secrets tucked neatly away. "Sirs?" the man repeated.

The women exchanged furtive glances. Each was sure some part of her body showed that would give her away. Eyes darted back and forth, approaching a breaking point. Rachel's heart pounded with he beat of a thousand drums, and she thought surely it would explode. She was ready to strip off her layers of clothing and expose herself. She was ready to meet her fate here at this oasis. She could meet her maker now. She could end all this. She could…

Suddenly, Sejal stood tall. She grumbled a Sanskrit phrase.

"Sirs," the man said, "we are wondering if you have seen three men pass this way. A Hindu and two Romans. We know that description could fit many, but we will make it easy on you. They have a dog traveling in their party. Have you seen them?"

Sejal again harnessed her deepest voice and spoke in Sanskrit. The others kept their faces focused on the ground, praying the strangers would think they were all Hindu.

"Forget it, Simon." Simon's short, beet red companion was clearly losing his patience. "Barbarian mumblers."

Sejal, trying her best to sound confused and annoyed, spoke more Sanskrit phrases as she turned and went back into a crouch at the well. The sky so bright in the light of a plan to seek justice was now overcast, as the women realized this storm was real. Identity had been traded for safety. Lives were at stake. Even if Philip was dead, it was clear his soul guided the living to seek revenge. As the men departed under a rain of curses, the women held their breath, afraid that even the wind from their very lungs could give them away if allowed to escape.

Chapter Thirty-Five

Alone figure sat brooding in the musty, gloomy room near the community church. The cotton coverings over the window slits blew gently in the breeze, occasionally letting in slivers of light that revealed nothing but the brutal reality of an angry man. His wounds, still fresh and stinging, seethed painfully under the bandages about his head. A Chinese maidservant employed by the local church approached to change his dressings and to put salve on his bruises.

"Get away!" he yelled, hitting her on the arm. "Go do something useful for Christ. Crucify yourself!"

The woman, fearful of his vehement tirades, obediently stepped away, lest she be removed in a harsher fashion. Philip, on edge, stood and paced about the room, occasionally stumbling, still dizzy from head trauma. He peeked from behind the curtains in a now-familiar habit of continuous vigilance. He surveyed the streets beyond, watching the people walk by. He considered each one very carefully.

"Where are those bastards?" he muttered. "Where are those accursed souls?"

"Mmph…" A figure struggled in the corner.

Philip spun around and addressed his company. "Have you something to say, Hebrew?" His tone held a thinly veiled disgust. "That's fine. You don't have to say it. I know. I need to be patient. News travels slowly out here. I just like to know what's going on, that's all. I like to know where the enemy is."

Philip pressed his hand against the bandage on his face that covered the empty socket where his eye had been. He winced at the pain under the herbal compress. He cursed John. Sol emitted stifled sounds through the cotton cloth packed in his mouth. Philip's idle wanderings about the room stopped at the door.

"I'd better lock this, my friend," Philip said. "I don't want to make the same mistake this time." He pushed on the small door handle and peered outside to make sure his guards were still posted before shutting and latching it. "They won't get back in here again without me noticing. Next time, I will be ready. However," Philip came over and put his face close to Sol, "to come back to save a godless Jew, a person would have to be crazy." Philip spit in Sol's eye, then stepped back and sat on the table, facing Sol. He took in a scornful breath. "I see the disdain in your eyes," he said. "But I am only doing what anyone would do in my situation. I've been through this before. I've held an equally soulless body in your seat. I can assure you, I am now quite practiced at the art of captivity."

Sol squinted in anger. Muffled mumbles of frustration. Fists clenched.

"I know, Sol. I know. You're right." Philip sauntered over and tapped Sol's knee with his hand. "I am only here in Ecbatana to observe and to make reports for Antioch. You would tell me that Meletius was clear about my role." Philip took in another deep breath and blew it out toward the ceiling as Sol hissed through the rag in his mouth. "But if you had a soul, you would know that the price of saving it sometimes requires us to take…certain actions."

Sol closed his eyes, trying to block Philip from his sight. Philip picked up a parchment from the table and threw it at Sol.

"Meletius seems to think he must take certain actions, too. That scroll is a decree from Antioch. It is a recall of missionaries from this road. These notices are making their way out as far as China. Imagine that. So much effort over the years to reach so many, only to be told we are being called back." Philip shook his head and let out a sinister laugh. "Meletius says he has an accounting of each of us, and that we are to return on pain of excommunication. Any missionary found on this road a year after receipt of this will be shut out from the Kingdom. And why?" Philip's face contorted with rage. "Because of you!"

Philip lifted a wooden chair and hurled it against the wall, smashing it to pieces inches from the maidservant, who let out a cry of terror. Sol flinched.

"Excuse me, Sol." Philip's voice chilled Sol's blood. "That was not directed only at you. You are just part of a much bigger problem. Jew, Hindu, Buddhist, this godless Chinese slave in my house – even my rogue Christian friend, John. All with their own mission out here. So much camel shit piled in the true Christian path…" Philip walked over to Sol, made a fist, and reared back as if he would strike, but stayed his hand. "So much shit and only Philip to clean it up. Meletius may be afraid of reverse conversions, but I assure you, I am not. I know his recall is only temporary – an effort to regroup, retrain, and to clean shit from the Church's stalls. But I assure you I know the truth. I can stay this course, and I will stay in Ecbatana as long as I can before going back."

Sol grunted.

"What? You don't support my decision to stay in Shapur's fair shithole of a city? Well, I can tell you, Sol, I am not going anywhere. Not yet. At least not until I see John hang."

Sol struggled in his bindings and mumbled a string of guttural curses. Philip rushed close to his face, his breath hot and venomous.

"Think what you want of me, pig, but I promise you – Simon and Mark will find John and his pathetic band of traitors. And they *will* pay."

Sol tried to break free, breathing heavily.

"Oh, so you don't want that? I understand. You want to see something more, do you? You think that maybe since you and your damned ancestors put Christ on the cross, *you'd* like to do the honors to John?" Philip grinned a malevolent smile. He relished driving Sol to a breaking point. "Fine. We'll put him on the cross together. You can drive in the spikes!"

Philip laid a hard punch into Sol's stomach. It was so fast Sol did not have time to tense. He slumped forward, his head dangling.

"Bastard!" Philip yelled. "You wouldn't understand anyway. This isn't a Hebrew war. Your time has passed, and your books only lay in the dust under the marching feet of the Christian faithful. And that march? It is the truth going to war to save what's right. It is a fight for Christ."

Philip placed a finger under Sol's chin and casually flipped his loose head upright. The cotton rag in Sol's mouth dripped blood, and his eyes fluttered before coming to. Philip tapped Sol's face to rouse him completely. Philip looked directly into his eyes as he knelt to the growing puddle of blood in Sol's lap. He didn't break the gaze as he stuck his finger in the blood and licked it off.

"This," he said, "is just one small payment of a very large debt." When Sol did not respond with anything more than an angry glare, Philip laughed and made for the door. "Do not tend to him," he yelled to the Chinese maidservant as he walked out of the room into daylight so bright, he winced as it pierced his eye.

Chapter Thirty-Six

How many?" James asked.

"Two," Sejal replied as the women adjusted the men in their clothing. "One called Simon. The other didn't give a name."

"Mark," John said, his tone flat.

"Who are they?" Dian asked.

"Philip's henchmen," Rachel said. "I haven't found the breath to tell you until now. They are loyal to him and to his madness." The women were silent.

"They were there the night we saved Rachel," John said.

"Was there a third in sight?" Sri asked the dreaded question.

"Not that I could see," Sejal said.

John did not know whether to feel fear or relief. He wasn't sure if he wanted Philip alive or dead. There was too much history. Too many emotions. John sought a temporary solace in ignorance. Rachel came over and squeezed his hand, joining their separate fears as one.

"We have to wait," James said solemnly. Everyone looked at James, surprise on their faces. They had already started their preparations to depart. "We wait," he repeated, "and we enter Ecbatana under cover of darkness. That way, we can return to the campground undetected, and set up again at Sol's campsite. We do not know friend from foe now, and we cannot rely on disguise alone. Night will be our safety. Our friend."

"Is that wise?" John asked. "I agree that we should probably wait for nightfall, but once inside Ecbatana, should we stay at Sol's?"

"It's a risk," James said, "but if Philip is alive, he may not suspect that we would return to the same site. If he sent his henchmen out on the road, he obviously thinks we've run. Far. He is betting on Merv. If we do something potentially foolish, we may avoid the fool himself."

"That is right," Sri said. "If Philip is alive, he will want revenge at any cost and his senses will be heightened. We may be better off staying where the terrain is familiar. We know that campground and know how to get in and out in a hurry. We will be vigilant."

The party set up a small camp to eat and wait out the day. They decided the crowds were no longer safe, and rested well away from the main route so as not to be approached again – and to be able to see trouble coming from a distance. All were quiet as they busied themselves around the site. Sejal sensed the anxiety and tapped Sri on the arm. She whispered in their native tongue, imploring him to do or say something to relieve the tension.

"How about a story?" Sri asked.

The group perked up, ready for any distraction.

"Everyone come over here and get comfortable," Sejal said, beckoning them with a parental gesture. She shepherded her friends with reassuring touch into a tight circle, as a goose to her goslings. "But stay aware."

Dian sat down next to James, and Deborah joined her. Sejal remained next to Sri. Rachel and John sat together, holding hands. Everyone clung to the silent threshold before the tale, desperate for the beginning.

"I told the men here that I had a great guru," Sri began. "He was a quiet man, was Gurudev, but he would often tell me tales at his retreat. I try to remember as many as I can, and to keep him alive in the telling. It occurs to me to share this one. Perhaps Gurudev's invisible hand is guiding our journey once again."

Sri closed his eyes and took in a deep breath. A reverent look crossed his face, as if he were in fact facing his beloved teacher once more. The group waited for his calming voice. Everyone tried to relax, but their eyes constantly scanned the horizon.

"A young beggar was journeying through a small village." Sri's voice was just above a hush, requesting their attention, which they gave gratefully. "The beggar was hungry and thirsty, for he had not known food or water for a long time. One day the man was begging and a beautiful woman, bejeweled and covered in priceless silks, walked past, eating a peach. It was ripe and juicy – a brilliant yellow against her hands. The beggar's senses were cast into covetous longing, overcome with desire. This is a woman of means, he thought, and a peach would be such a welcome delicacy in this dry place!

"'Please,' the beggar pleaded in desperation, pulling at the hem of her flowing, flawless robes with his grimy hand. 'Good woman, please, your peach. I have not seen food for days. I will give my life to you, if you but give me your fruit. Please.'

"The woman stood before the beggar and nimbly nibbled the fruit down to the quick, plucking off each golden morsel with utmost care and precision – only enhancing the beggar's voracious appetite. She dropped the pit, dry and hard, into his despondent hands. He beheld the lifeless stone, then looked at the woman with tears that could barely come due to dehydration.

"'Plant that with care in this acreage about you, and you will have your peaches,' she said plainly as she walked away.

"The beggar, hurt and confused, did not know what to do. Out of desperation, he planted the pit in the parched earth. He begged water of the locals and carefully poured it on the dirt, so as not to waste a single drop. He doted upon the seedling, focusing his attention upon it. As its very life became his labor, the people of the town became accustomed to, and amused by, his project. They came from all around to see him tend his small plot and were just as eager as he to see what would emerge. As a token of admiration for his loyal and loving discipline, they brought him grain and water on a regular basis, and eventually he had enough resources to eat regularly and to start a small farm, of which the growing peach tree was the grand centerpiece

– fertile and full of life.

"As the years progressed, the tree grew tall and robust amid his other crops, including grains and beans. The beggar found a wife and had children, and his farm became prosperous. The peach tree bore plentiful fruit, which the man kept for himself. He made pies and candies and greedily stored them for his own enjoyment. The local citizens asked for bushels to help the needy about town, but the man steadfastly refused.

"He grew old. His wife had passed away and his children had families of their own. Laborers, whom the now-wealthy merchant hired, worked the land. One day, he walked to the center of his farm and sat in the shade of the grand tree. He gazed up into its leaves and beheld the fruits bulging under the weight of their plentiful juices, hanging low and seductive. He stood to pluck one to enjoy at his leisure. In the distance, he could see someone open his wooden gate and enter his land. It was a dirty beggar woman.

"'You there!' the man yelled. 'Beggar woman! Away with you! This is my land!'

"The hunched woman approached as he took a bite of the fruit. She held out her hand, famished eyes pleading. 'Please sir,' she said. 'Please may I have that peach? I have not seen food for many days. I will give you my life, if you but give me that one peach.'

"The man nibbled the fruit down to the quick and dropped the pit on the ground, deliberately out of the grasp of her outstretched and trembling fingers. Suddenly, the beggar stood tall and ripped off her dirty rags. Radiant rays shone from the spot and the beggar revealed herself to be the visage of the beautiful woman from so many years before, her silken robe and jewels blinding in the brilliant light emanating from her very form.

"'I am the goddess Annapurna!' she bellowed, shaking the leaves above and the strong roots below.

"The man knelt in front of the goddess of nourishment, averting his eyes in deference to her wonder. 'Holy One, had I known…I'm sorry. You have given me so many blessings! I have reaped your bounty with an eye blind to gratitude.'

"Annapurna was enraged, her voice roaring about the fields. 'Once, you said you would give your life for a peach. And now you see, one pit has given you many. It has provided you livelihood. It has given you your very life.'

"The man did not know what to say. He suddenly felt a pang of regret not only at his treatment of the beggar woman, but how he had kept the fruits to himself through the years. 'How can I repay my debt to you and to your beggar visage, Great One? How can I best atone for my greed in your sight?'

"Annapurna directed the man to look high into the canopy of his giant tree. 'Do you see the hundreds of peaches hanging here?' she asked in a stern voice.

"'Yes,' the man replied, his voice quavering.

"'As many peaches as you see hanging here are as many lives as you must be reborn to this village until you have performed two services in my honor. You must see planted as many pits as are now on this tree, and you must give your future lives in service to those less fortunate.' The great goddess disappeared in a whirlwind, leaving the man alone with his thoughts, and his peaches.

"That day, the man had his servants pick every peach on the tree. Over the next week, they baked them into pies, cured them with curry, and set them out in segments to dry into sweet candies. He baked breads and tarts, and mixed them with vegetables from his plots. He issued an invitation for the town to come to his home for Annapurna puja – a ceremony of honor – so that all, rich and poor alike, might celebrate the goddess.

"The whole town arrived – magistrate, merchants, mendicants – and everyone enjoyed the peaches. After the feast, they all joined together in a great hall on the property. The man walked around to each person, personally handing him a pit from the peaches used to make the fabulous feast.

"'What are these for?' the town leader asked.

"The man told his guests the tale of how he had met a beggar in his grove who was the Goddess Annapurna. He also issued an apology for not being more giving over the years. He ended by imploring the people of the town to plant their pits, and to urge their descendants to give the fruits of the trees freely to all beggars. When he had sealed their word with a solemn vow, the man could hardly contain his joy.

"'In the name of the great Annapurna we will do as you ask,' the magistrate said. 'But tell us. Why are you so happy? You are on the verge of singing and dancing, yet your task seems so momentous — your fate sealed for many thousands of years. So much labor through so many lifetimes.'

"The farmer simply looked at the magistrate and said, 'I am happy, for now I know you all will plant the pits I was to plant. I planted one tree in one lifetime, and it will bear fruit for hundreds more. I am now free to live hundreds of lifetimes without toil in the earth. I have, on this night, satisfied Annapurna's decree of planting. I am now free to give my future lives in simple service to others and enjoy the fruit of your labors.' And with that, he picked up a stick and a small sack of peaches and wandered out in the world to beg once more."

The mood in camp was warm and comfortable as the party pondered the story. For a fleeting, blissful moment, the group seemed lost in the myths of time. Sri uttered a quiet blessing to his guru and to the great Annapurna.

"Thank you, Sri." John smiled at his friend. "That was beautiful. I guess we all need a reminder that we must stay in active service and share what we have with others. We never know who will help us along our path."

"Thank you," everyone said quietly, agreeing with John.

"You are all most welcome," Sri said. "When Gurudev told me this story, it was at a time when I was struggling. I did not know whether to go home to my father's business or keep to my spiritual vows. Paralyzed, I kept my knowledge and my goods to myself, resisting the world. Over time, I realized the right direction was to share my bounty, no matter how small, and to do my best to serve. I followed my intuition and came on to the road as Gurudev prophesied. It has been a good direction for me."

Rachel looked to the western horizon toward Ecbatana. "Are we going in the right direction, Sri?"

The group looked at him hopefully.

"How would you feel if you rode east now, Rachel?" Sri asked. "How would you feel if you left the innocent to a potentially terrible fate?"

She met his gaze and smiled. "All labor and no service – like a woman to be sentenced to many lifetimes of repentance, Brother Sri."

"There is your answer."

Chapter Thirty-Seven

Wᵉ must go." James roused his companions from their fitful sleep.

The group was happy to oblige. No one seemed comfortable with the fact they had to return to Ecbatana, yet sitting idle in wait was even more agonizing. They fixed their clothing and checked each other's appearance. The trail would be relatively safe at night, but they did not want to take any chances. They tightened their belts and turbans, knowing at any minute they may have to be in character. The discomfort of strange clothing was a small price to pay for peace of mind.

"Everyone ready?" John asked.

The group clicked their tongues, setting the camels on alert. The beasts were slow to react, resentful and unsure of packs and travelers in this late hour. They seemed to sense a long night ahead. James helped Dian and Deborah onto their camel. John and Rachel got comfortable, as did Sri and Sejal. The group set off in the growing darkness, and as they took the trail out of the campsite, weary travelers just bedding down cast odd looks from their fire rings. Leaving camp at day's end was highly unusual and could arouse suspicion. The party kept their eyes downward to avoid the stares, occasionally glancing up to see if Simon or Mark may still be lingering. Despite Sejal's assurances that the men would head east on their search, the party was not convinced.

The moon shone overhead, and the stars were bright in a cloudless sky. John took almost as much comfort in these heavenly companions as he did the ones with whom he traveled this night. The mood was quiet as the nighttime hours took hold on the plateau.

"John?" His name rode Rachel's warm breath into his ear. He didn't answer right away in hopes that he would feel his name again. "John, I know we usually cannot wait to dismount, but I wish the distance tonight was infinite." He heard a sniffle, yet did not reply. "I'm scared, John. I'm really scared. Maybe Sri was wrong. Maybe we're going in the wrong direction."

Rachel settled her head against his back, wrapping her arms tight about his waist. He remembered their journey days before, that found him clutching to her very life. Now, it felt as if she was holding fast to his, in blissful repayment.

"I'm scared, too." He squeezed her hand. "But I've been thinking about it…about my journey from Antioch."

"Oh? How so?"

"I came out here wanting to spread the truth, but now, I realize I need to protect it."

"What do you mean?"

"That night in the room, Philip had a look in his eyes. A look of fear. Rage. He was a caged animal, wild and insecure. I wasn't sure at the time what could create animosity to that degree, and that scared me."

"You were sure he was unhappy with you before that moment, though?" Rachel asked.

"Yes. I had words with him at the community church a day earlier and I knew he was angry with the company I was keeping. His disdain for Sri was painfully obvious. He didn't know how new, foreign friendships would affect my work, or how they would affect me. At first, I thought he was genuinely concerned for me as a friend. But he stopped listening to my truth and listened to his own fear."

"What is he afraid of?"

"I know this is going to sound strange, but I think he is afraid of himself."

"I don't know about that, John. I think we're all scared of *him* right now. Surely, he knows that."

"That's not what I mean. It's like Christ. Or, rather, the opposite of Christ. The Lord carried a message of hope and love for all mankind. Not just for a few, but for all. That was over three hundred years ago. Since that time, it has become less about the message and more about the messengers, as Sri would probably say."

"So, what has all this to do with Philip?"

"I think when a man fears losing his power, he turns on people. Even people he once loved."

"Like Philip did with you and me."

"Exactly, Rachel. If you are not for his system, you are against it. If you do not support him in his every endeavor, he grows resentful. He became paranoid, afraid of himself without power. Afraid of losing influence. Maybe he feared I would somehow take it from him. Or, maybe he realized he couldn't control me, my message, or my company, and it was eating him up inside. It's all about power."

"It's not like he had much power to begin with, John. Meletius certainly ranked him below missionaries like yourself."

"Philip may have a lower status in Meletius's eyes, but status is status. And, it is often built on a worldview. One receives recognition because of what one believes, and not because one is simply a human being worthy of recognition like all others. A person comes to depend on a specific point of view for strength, rather than finding the strength to simply hold a point of view. Philip may not have had much power, but he had enough to get him recognition. And when I challenged his worldview and his power, Philip assumed I was challenging his self-worth. I almost pity him."

"You're beginning to sound like Sri, Master John." Rachel squeezed him tighter, pressing her cheek deeper into his back. He smiled to himself. He didn't mind sounding like Sri as long as he got to be John who had Rachel. "Is that really what you think happened to Philip? That he is afraid of losing influence?"

"Maybe."

"But his influence comes from Meletius. His influence only comes from a duty another person gave him."

"True, Rachel. But maybe that is the point. Maybe he is afraid of losing his purpose, no matter where it comes from. I guess if someone gives us direction in a life of aimless searching, we appreciate it so much we stop our own investigations. Philip came out here to do a job, just like the rest of us. But he forgot for whom he did it. Meletius? Christ? It doesn't matter to him. It has simply become about his own power and personal crusade, and not the message of unity and brotherhood. Those messages stand on their own two feet, even if no man supports them."

"I guess we were expendable. We stood in his way."

"Not really, Rachel, but that is what he thinks. That is what is so sad. He could have let me move on. He could have let me speak my truth to the crowds. They would have the power to decide if I am on the path or not. He could have allowed me to peddle my tea in Merv and Samarkand."

"Peddle your tea?" she asked.

John found Rachel's question amusing and endearing.

"Yes. But he couldn't allow it. He thinks I am the enemy. He doesn't remember that we are both brothers in Christ, and that the only thing we are opposed on is the scope of our truth, not its core. I like to think my journey is liberating me and expanding my message. I can run from shore to shore on wide strands now without fear of falling. Or drowning."

"And Philip? Is he on secure footing?"

John thought for a moment, trying to picture Philip chasing him over metaphorical oceans. "I think Philip feels he is walking on a narrow bridge."

Rachel shifted so her chin now rested forward on John's back. She peered up, taking in the stars above.

"The stars are symbols, John. Do you know that?"

"I do. Still, I like that you remind me."

"They are stories that have been recounted over and over, in many empires. They are set in time. Set in space. Open books for us to read night after night. But this…" Rachel fell silent.

"But what?" John turned so that his cheek almost touched hers. "But this story. The one we are characters in now. I don't know how it will end. I don't know what happens. It isn't written anywhere. It's not contained on any parchments. It isn't familiar. All of this talk of fear, anger, violence, truth, uncertainty. Where is it going?"

John turned his head all the way around and looked down at Rachel who at this angle had her chin on his shoulder. Her eyes looked up, her face holding a whimsical expression in the bright moonlight. John bent down. They closed their eyes and kissed. Rachel's lips were tight at first but softened as his hand touched her face. She opened her mouth slightly and John could taste her tears as they streamed down. He felt his body ignite in flames. No words ever spoken from his mouth felt as true as the gentle touch of Rachel's. He reluctantly pulled away from her and put his nose to her forehead.

"No matter what happens in Ecbatana, I will not leave you, Rachel."

Chapter Thirty-Eight

Fire danced high and menacing in the Pit. The Ecbatana graveyard was quiet. Eerily still. Philip and five new confederates nailed together four wooden crosses and dug four deep holes. Each man attended to his work in urgent silence. Philip threw down his shovel and walked over to Sol, whose mouth was still stuffed with rags. Philip knelt beside the crumpled heap – Sol's white clothing now caked in dried blood.

"You see these, Jew?" Philip pointed at the crosses now assembled. "They should look familiar to you. Not too long ago, you put my Lord and Savior on one of them. And now? Well, now, I will repay that favor." Sol shifted on the ground and groaned, as if writhing in the acid from Philip's tongue. "Are you trying to tell me something? Are you trying to tell me what I want to know?" Philip kicked Sol in the side, and he coughed into the gag. "Listen, you dirty pig. All I ask is for a direction. A name. A time. Something. Give me one small clue as to the whereabouts of your friends and maybe I'll show you mercy. Maybe your death will be quicker and more dignified than Christ's. And maybe…" Philip wore a terrible grin, "maybe I will only need three of these crosses."

Philip slipped the cloth from Sol's mouth. Sol coughed the word, "Bastard."

"I'm sorry, Sol. I think I misunderstood you. I'm not fluent in Hebrew. I hope, for your sake, you said 'westward.'"

Sol spat a hard 'b' that splashed red into Philip's face, covering his remaining eye with blood. Philip wiped the spittle away with a steady hand and an icy affect. He stood with purpose and walked over to a cross.

"Men?"

As two of the team continued digging a deep hole, the rest dragged a screaming, gurgling Sol to a cross, forcing him upon it.

"Stop it!" he screamed. "Goddamn it! Stop this!"

"Taking the Lord's name in vain before crucifixion? And just when I thought you couldn't sink below your heritage, Sol."

Philip crammed the rag into Sol's mouth. The men untied his hands and held him down. Philip, with little ceremony, grabbed three razor-sharp metal stakes and a mallet from the ground beside him. As the men held Sol against the wood, Philip drove a spike into Sol's right wrist. Muffled, agonizing screams permeated the hushed graveyard.

"How does that feel? Does that feel like justice?" Philip savagely pounded the stake in as he spoke in rhythm with the mallet, "Dirty...Damn...Sol." The click of metal to metal pierced the night air – each high-pitched ping another reminder of Philip's reverence to his very highest and most precious ideals.

Sol vomited into the rag, gagging and struggling as the surreal shock of a thousand lightning bolts tore through him. Once the first spike was set, Philip coolly hammered Sol's other wrist to the cross. He then stacked Sol's feet, one upon the other, and tied them tight to the structure. When Sol blacked out from pain, succumbing to the horror, Philip poked his side with a hot torch to revive him so he would feel the agony. Sol's side was charred, exposing the scorched tissue underneath.

"One...Two...Three," Philip counted, as the men dragged the cross to a hole. They tied the cross to two camels stationed nearby, whipping their hindquarters to move them. As the animals dragged the cross, the men heaved from the rear until it stood upright. "Whoa, whoa!" Philip stopped the camels as the men held the cross steady. The others rushed over to fill in the gaping abyss. "How fitting that this crucifix and your grave will likely use the same hole." Philip patted the cross with a proud hand. "I may come back tomorrow and bury you myself, dead or alive, just to get your wretched visage out of my sight." Philip smirked as he stomped the disturbed earth with his foot. "Men, get on your knees!" Philip barked. "Close your eyes and let us offer thanks. Lord Jesus and Holy Father, we thank You for Your mercies, and the strength to conquer Thine enemies. Let tonight be only one glorious stop for us along Your holy path. Guide us on our journey to fully rid this road of those who stand against You. In Your names we pray. Amen."

"Amen," the others echoed.

Philip and the men stood back near the fire and looked up at Sol on the cross, admiring their handiwork. His head was slumped forward, and the ground grew red at the base from the steady tapping of dripping blood. Rats scurried about picking at the remnants of flesh and bone. Philip wiped sweat from his brow, streaking blood across his face as he reveled in a job well done.

"Now, Sol," he said, spitting at the base of the cross, "we shall see if loyalty pays off for you…or me."

Chapter Thirty-Nine

Thest gates are not as impressive at night," John said to James as
they rode back into Ecbatana, Rachel asleep at John's back.
"Somehow, these great lions seem even more ferocious without the
light of day to tame them."

"That's true, Brother." James said. "Nor are they too welcome a
sight."

"I agree. When I first saw them days ago, I thought my very soul
would leap from my body and dance with joy. But now, I dread them
as if they are stalking me. What do we do now?"

"I thought we agreed to see Sol again," James said.

"Risky, James. I know that was the plan, but I still say that is not a
good idea. Philip may have spies stationed there waiting for us – other
campers or confederates. Sol would have no way to know."

"We did come back here to see if Philip is alive or dead," James
said. "Maybe that would get us our answer."

"I don't think that is wise," John protested. "We should not risk
safety for knowledge tonight. We cannot risk dying in slumber before
the morning sun. We must change this plan. Please. We need a quiet
place to rest and come up with a strategy. We need to figure out what
we're doing here."

"Alright, alright," James whispered. "Relax. These disguises may
buy us the ability to stay closer to town, if we are careful."

"Do you have other friends here, James? I seem to remember you
and Sol going out a few days ago and meeting with people."

"I'm not sure they are the sort of people we can trust, John."

"We don't have many options. We need to bed these camels and find a camp."

"I'm sorry we can't be of more help," Dian said. "But you all know this place better than we do."

James took a moment to think, his face betraying an inner, fruitless search for ideas. John thought he sensed a flickering of panic from James, which did not settle his own anxiety.

"I may have a solution." Sri's voice startled the men. They had been so lost in their own planning, they did not think to solicit other opinions.

"Let's hear it," John said. "We will entertain all offers."

"John, do you remember our teahouse?" Sri asked.

"Yes."

"Do you remember where I said the tea came from?"

"Turfan."

"I know the trading party that brings ingredients here. They are often in Ecbatana at this time of year on their way back to China. I was to meet up with them and travel to Turfan as part of their group."

"Why didn't you mention them before?" John asked. "We were here longer than a night."

"I was going to stop by and see them soon after our previous arrival, but of course—"

"We got sidetracked," James said.

"Indeed. Their house is on the edge of town, and I did not speak of it before, as I did not think it wise to ride that far into the city upon this arrival. I believed Sol's campsite was the better choice. Now I see we must choose a different option. With James's blessing to travel closer, maybe it would be wise to see if they are in. They have a scholar who travels among them with whom I am friendly. They may be able to hide us, and we can use the teahouse as a lookout."

"Lead the way," James said.

"Agreed," John chimed in.

Sri led the party through the deserted streets, rows of shops and houses passing, closed up tight against the night. With each movement forward, John's awareness heightened. He expected Philip to leap from dark recesses at any moment. Every shadow playing in the street caught his attention…every single one, another menace. On the far edge of town, well off the main route, Sri whistled just loudly enough to stop the camels. The moon shone on a doorpost with a Chinese character painted upon it.

"This is the place," Sri said.

"It looks dark in there," Dian said.

"I don't like this." Deborah added. "And I'm guessing whoever lives here won't like it, either. We have deferred to your judgments until now, but I feel I must speak up. Late company is usually most unwelcome."

"We're out of options," John whispered in a stern tone, apparently in no mood to chance Sol's campground, no matter what lay inside this house.

"Are they even here?" Rachel asked in a groggy voice.

"I don't know," Sri said. "But I do know that if they are, they will be friendly to our cause, and we will be safe. Ecbatana is a long stop for these men, and I have traveled with them before. My only regret is that I did not greet them upon our initial stay in town. Custom and other business dictated my initial reluctance, but now, we have no choice."

Sri dismounted. He walked up to the dwelling and knocked on the door. No one stirred inside.

"Knock louder," Sejal whispered.

Just as Sri was going to give a good rap, a light spilled from under the wooden door, which creaked open to reveal a short man of medium build, bathed in the light of the oil lamp in his hand.

"Bo?" Sri asked.

The man's eyes widened as he recognized his friend, who removed his scarf. "Sri?" The men embraced. "Sri, what are you doing here?"

"We need your help, Bo."

"Come in, everyone. Hurry!" The group let out a collective sigh of relief and dismounted. James, John, and Sri took the camel tethers. Bo scanned the street as he ushered the remaining party inside. "Your camels," Bo said. "All others please wait inside." He walked out with his lamp and led the men to the side of the dwelling. There was a small corral that held the camels for the tea caravan.

They bedded the animals down, and when they returned to the house, the women, turbans removed, stood in the silent darkness. Bo hurried past them to a small stove in the corner containing the lingering embers he had used to light the lamp. They heard the thump of logs as he built a roaring fire to take the chill from the night air. The firelight cast shadows down a narrow hall, where the guests could make out three closed doors.

Bo took in his company properly for the first time. A bewildered look crossed his face as he studied the men and women in their odd garb.

"Sit, sit," Bo directed. "I can see I am in for quite a tale."

He invited his guests to rest on mats scattered about the room, then busied himself at the stove. John could smell the intoxicating Turfan tea, his mouth watering. He looked over at Sri, who winked. Bo happily served his guests and spoke excitedly.

"Sri, my friend, I've been expecting you. Although I admit, not quite in this way."

"I am ashamed to say this is my second visit in less than a week, my friend."

Bo had a confused look. "You travel fast, Guruji. And silently, for I did not hear your steps on my porch before this night."

Sri laughed and explained to Bo how he had met up with James, John, and Flavus, and how they had arrived in Ecbatana. His voice turned grim as he told of their stay with Sol and their run-in with Philip. The women filled in details about the pilgrimage site and their current plans, or lack thereof, to ascertain Philip's whereabouts.

"And so, I have returned," Sri said, now on his second cup of tea. "Or, that is to say, we are all here now."

"You are looking for this Philip?" Bo asked.

"Yes," John replied, feeling a new sense of purpose as the tea moved through him.

"I know Philip," Bo said. "I remember him from your sermon...Brother John."

"My ser— wait...Bo? Bo! Yes! I knew I had heard the name before. You greeted me so warmly at the church. We spoke so briefly. I was distracted that night for reasons of which you are now aware. I'm sorry. So much occupies my mind. I did not remember you, and I should have. I would blame the darkness, but I cannot. Please accept my apologies."

James was incredulous. "You two have met?"

"Well, casually," John said. "He was at the tent meeting that night. He came and went so fast, it's no wonder you and Sri did not see us talking."

"Were you there, Sri?" Bo asked.

"Indeed, I was. I am sorry I did not see you, my friend."

"So mindful, Sri, yet so unobservant." Bo winked. The party laughed. It was amusing to see Sri with a fellow scholar with whom he had so much history. John was happy for Sri, who now had a companion to whom Sri's life was not a total mystery. "I was touched by your words that night, John." Bo refilled everyone's cups to the brim. "I travel with this group of tea traders as historian and scholar, teaching Buddhism and Taoism, among other subjects. I know of your Christ, but have not heard about him from one so passionate as yourself."

"Thank you, Bo," John said, tipping his head. "I appreciate that."

"Speaking of your tea caravan," Sejal said, "are they here? Are they sleeping? We do not in any way wish to disturb or impose."

"Your company is no disturbance, I assure you," Bo said. "Only a fool considers pleasant company an imposition. No, they are not here.

They have dispersed eastward, trading in nearby camps in small parties. Ecbatana is a good base of operations, but they need to make connections with those who are already on their way to Merv and Samarkand. Not every caravan stops in Ecbatana, and my friends need product to precede them east. Good leads are good commerce, as they say. The groups are one to two days' ride from here, on the slowest camel. Luckily, their beasts are fleet of foot. The tea traders come and go from this house for a few months, before starting the trek back to our homeland."

"Why do you stay behind when they are gone?" Dian asked. She and James sat close. James took the kettle from Bo and refilled her vessel.

"I teach here," Bo explained. "Shapur's harsh arrows have, thus far, missed my mark. Sometimes I work in the teashop, although, regrettably, I did not have the fortune to see any of you in there. I spread the good word of Buddha and Laozi, and the tea from Turfan. They fit neatly together, as a puzzle of joyful pieces."

"How did you come to know Sri?" Deborah asked.

"We met in this city years ago. He attended a lecture I was giving on the life and teachings of Laozi. He asked a question on an obscure point of philosophy, and we retired to the teashop for hours, discussing it. I invited him to join the caravan to Turfan to attend a gathering."

"A gathering?" John asked.

"Tea in Turfan," Sri said with a smile.

"What is that?" Rachel asked.

"Tea in Turfan, Sister Rachel," Sri beamed, "is when every one thousand two hundred and seventy-nine days, a gathering of scholars meets in the Chinese city of Turfan to discuss philosophy."

"That is an interesting amount of time," James said. "How did you decide on that number?"

"I did not decide," Sri said. "Nor did Bo. It adds up to the number one. One plus two plus seven plus nine equals nineteen. And then nine plus one equals ten. Then, one plus zero equals one. Of course, the number ten is also the first number with two digits, representing both the unity – and multiplicity – of scholars. Furthermore, one is knowledge and zero is receptivity. In that way, ten is unity, wholeness, and balance all in one numeral. It is a regular cycle, unbroken for generations. It represents ancient roots, new beginnings, and a fresh perspective, Master James."

"Very interesting," James said, as he pondered the symbolic elegance.

"You see, this gentle caravan of tea traders is more than company," Bo added. "They are among the greatest patrons of the Turfan meeting – as were their ancestors before them. Its occurrence is the culmination of two trading rounds on the road. They blend their tea, adding and taking away spices and essences so that it is slightly different each time. They serve it to the scholars and solicit their learned opinions on the new brew. We discuss religion, philosophy, politics, and tea for one month, before once again dispersing into the deserts, mountains, and jungles of the world."

"My goodness!" Sejal's eyes grew wide. "That sounds amazing."

"It does," John agreed.

"It is, my friends," Bo continued. "This year marks the 264th conference. Legend says Laozi, Buddha, and Confucius started the first one."

"Incredible," Dian said.

"It may be the longest continuous gathering of its kind in history," Bo said. "It is even rumored," Bo cast a playful glance to John, "that your Christ – Jesus of Nazareth himself – was once in attendance."

All eyes turned to see John's reaction.

"Well," John said, "it would certainly have been an adventure for him, and I hope he held his own against all those scholars." He quietly enjoyed the image of Christ debating philosophy with the greatest minds of the East. He wondered how the Turfan brew had tasted in Jesus's day.

"The point of the gathering is not to convince anyone of a

worldview," Bo said with a serious air. "Indeed, we do not seek to 'hold our own,' as you say. The deepest wisdom is beyond such competitions. It is alive and growing. Like a child, it is birthed, changing and maturing under the watchful eyes of time. Sometimes wisdom seems immortal, like a bronze statue or steely warrior, and at other times, it dies, suffocating under the weight of its own grandeur. The purpose of Tea in Turfan is simply to witness the maturing process of wisdom and to revel in the presence of knowledge."

"And tea," John added, lightening the tone.

"And good company." Sri raised his glass to Bo. "I hope I live to see another one."

"Why do you say this?" Bo asked. "You know we convene this year. You are here now. You will come with me as we had planned last time." Sri bowed his head. "Sri? Sri, what's wrong?"

"Bo, I have a duty here," he said. "I have a calling in Ecbatana. I must stand with this group and help them with their precious work."

John put his hand on Sri's shoulder. "You don't have to stay with us, my friend. This is my fight. It is a fight for a small piece of the West. Go and pursue your peace in the East."

"No, John." Sri was adamant. "It is a fight for us all. You see, the joy of Tea in Turfan is that we all come together to relax and talk about those that have come before. We marvel at how their feet walk among us still, through evolving texts and wisdom. Then, we step back into the world and carry their knowledge with us – to commoner and emperor alike. But here in Ecbatana, right now, there is a disagreement that is beyond the pages of books. It is real and dangerous. It threatens the safety of those I have come to love. I must remain here and stand with those in whom I believe. You came to the road to talk, John, but now you must act. So must I. I stand with you."

"Sri…" John was at a loss in the face of such loyalty to principle and person.

"There is no discussion," Sri said, waving off any remaining arguments.

Deborah, Sejal, Dian, and Rachel wiped away tears from their eyes. James watched with a look of silent satisfaction. He had come to appreciate Sri's quiet courage and to find great pleasure in his company.

Bo's eyes narrowed. "I stand with you, too."

"Bo, this is not your fight," Sri protested. "Besides, you are a man of peace. You do not believe in violence."

"Neither do you, my friend. I do not think any of us in this assembly stand for violence, Sri. But when it lays its menacing hand upon us, we have an obligation to confront it. We cannot ignore it, for it is an ill-tempered guest."

"I am involved through a debt of friendship, Bo," Sri said.

"So am I," Bo retorted. "You fight to understand a powerful opposition, and that is a mighty feat. Do you know what I was going to speak on at this year's gathering? *Yin-yang.*"

"What is that?" Rachel asked.

"It is the very essence of friendship," Bo continued. "Perhaps you have seen the ancient symbol. It can be drawn many ways, but it looks like two swirling fish, or two teardrops," he explained.

"I've seen that," Dian said. James looked at her in surprise. She delighted in his shock. "A Chinese pilgrim at the mountain had a parchment depicting it. There is a light side and a dark side. Each one has a drop of the other in it."

"Exactly," Bo said. "One can draw the symbol, meditate upon it, and come to realize that the world is a mix of action and passivity, of doing and allowing, of motion and rest."

"But why the drops of one in the other?" James asked.

Bo's eyes expanded in radiance. "That is to remind us that no side can exist without a hint of the other. If we live a life free of fear, we may come to embrace an opposite as a brother. When we divest ourselves from the anxiety of losing the power of our point of view, we open up to others. We expand our vision. Half a circle cannot roll, but when complete with its opposite, it can travel infinitely."

Rachel looked at John and nodded. Suddenly, the emotion of their discussion on the camel hours before came rushing back in vivid, vibrant detail.

"Bo?" Rachel asked. "Are you saying that we need our opposites?"

"That is exactly what I am saying. We do not always need to agree with those who oppose us, but we need to understand that we carry within us the same capacities as they."

"How do you mean?" John asked.

"We are all human," Bo continued, "but we express our humanity in different ways. We need to acknowledge the opposite, rolling along with it and joined to it. Could Christ's work be revealed so powerfully without Satan concealing it in the world? If Jesus did not embrace the capacity for temptation, would he have been able to show how to resist it?"

"That's interesting," Sejal said. "In many ways, Jesus was the essence of balance. Christ was proof that someone can reach states of truth through love *and* discipline. A love for all mankind, despite their worldviews, and the discipline to examine truths in light of opposing arguments." She looked over at Sri. "Much like the Hindu guru."

"Moses held my people together for years in the desert," Deborah added with enthusiasm. He was afraid at first. He had been born a slave and risked returning to that condition upon his return to Egypt – a risk he took on God's Divine promise. He was reluctant to take up the mantle and lead his people, and even after he agreed, he was tested. But he overcame his fears and encouraged a great nation. He did not want to return to Egypt and the threat of slavery, yet he embraced his mission. He was only able to liberate the Hebrews from Pharaoh by identifying with their bondage, even though he was free."

"Philip…" John muttered.

"What?" Bo asked.

"Philip," John repeated. "Maybe he can see himself in me. Maybe he can learn to embrace me as a complement to himself and not as his enemy."

"Possibly," Bo said.

The room was quiet as everyone anticipated John's next words. "But what if he cannot?"

All eyes fell on Bo. "We are at a point in our discourse that is difficult to hear because we often stand in our own truth, convinced of it to the exclusion of all else. In actuality, this philosophy is even harder to live out than to accept. But here it is for your ears. Unfortunately, not all who oppose us can embrace us. That is the sad legacy of war, and why violence persists in the world."

"Sad but true," John said. "One of the oldest truths."

"But take heart," Bo said. "The possibility of an embrace is there, and the situation will flow only as it should. If you cannot embrace Philip, or he you, you may still embrace the situation and find another solution in your heart. I would be honored to take part in this project, difficult as it may seem."

"That's not very reassuring," John said. "But I will try, Bo. Thank you."

"I feel as if I am in Turfan, old friend." Bo patted Sri tenderly on the shoulder. "And so, we have come full circle. Remember the great discourse we had on *wu wei* in Turfan so many years ago?"

"Yes," Sri replied.

"Well, I am planning to speak on it again this year."

"Wait," John said with a laugh. "*Wu* what?"

Sri smiled with delight. "*Wu wei*." Sri turned to John. "*Wu wei* is the idea that we should do that which is appropriate…spontaneous in the moment."

"Indeed, my friend." Bo addressed the group, who still appeared confused by the term. "It means that we should not overreact to a situation, or avoid it, but rather, embrace the flow of life as it comes." Bo made waves with his hands, then clasped them together.

"It sounds like an extension of *yin-yang*," Sejal said.

"It is," Bo said. "Balance requires a skilled and even-handed knowing."

"How does it work?" Rachel asked.

"Take me as an example," Bo said, tapping his heart with his right hand. "I have much practice in knowing when to be still and to meditate." Bo smiled, as if uncomfortable describing himself. "But just this evening I was working on my discourse, praying for a good story to tell in Turfan of when to take action. I was pondering the idea that my actions in this life are mostly consumed with riding on camels and teaching. These can be appropriate, of course, as the camels take good tea to good people and the teachings may help someone. But I was reviewing my life to find a time when I took an action that was unexpected, yet necessary, in a particular situation. Then, in the early hours of this morning, your party here assembled knocked at my door." Bo looked at each member of the group. "I see here a band that stands for truth and is struggling with a powerful opposite. I see a group that is at a crossroads. You stand in the swirl of the shadow of *yin* and the light of *yang*, and you are deciding what your next move will be in the calmness before the storm."

"What are you saying, Bo?" Sri asked, sensing the gravity of the moment.

"I am saying, it is time to act."

Chapter Forty

The first light of day crept under the wooden door. John's eyelids resisted opening as though made of lead. He rubbed the night from his gaze, sat up, and looked around the small house. His friends lay sleeping. Exhaustion clearly permeated them. They were peaceful in slumber, and he was grateful for the reprieve from the terrors of the road. He was amazed that he had known all of them for such a short time, yet they had what seemed a lifetime of adventures.

He tiptoed gingerly among the sleeping bodies to give life to the few remaining embers in the stove. Their revival breathed warmth into the morning. He looked at Rachel's face, her head gently resting on her hands, pressed together as if in sideways prayer – a child supplicating God before bedtime.

"I hope all of your dreams come true," he whispered.

He noticed empty spaces on the floor and took a brief headcount. James and Dian lay close, with Deborah pressed next to Dian. Sejal and Rachel slept soundly. Where are Sri and Bo, he wondered?

He carefully opened the door so as not to attract attention from any passersby. He peered left to see that early morning had brought so much life to the streets. Trading started before sunrise so travelers could procure supplies and get an early start east or west. Merchants and buyers crowded the roads in the distance. Animals lumbered and lingered among them. To the right was empty land and stables. A light haze enveloped the valley beyond. The camels grazed in their enclosure under an ascending sun. John stepped back inside, closing the door with an unintended clunk. The sound roused the rest of the group.

"Good morning, all," Dian said with a long yawn. She knocked James on the head. "Hey! Wake up, lazy!"

"I hear Dian," Deborah groaned. "It must be morning."

Everyone acknowledged Dian in a groggy tone.

"Good morning, friends," John said from beside the door. "I'm sorry. I didn't mean to wake you. I was just looking for Sri and Bo. It's early. I don't know where they are."

"Wherever they are, I'm sure they will know how to open and close a door much more quietly upon their return," James snapped.

"That's alright." Rachel stood and stretched. "We needed to get up anyway."

"Why?" Deborah asked.

"Because…" A broad smile crossed Rachel's face. "Well, just because."

Rachel went over to the stove and started the morning tea. John happily watched her busy herself with a pot. Rachel of Turfan. Just then, the door slowly creaked open. Sri and Bo peered inside and, upon seeing the morning activity, walked in with bread and vegetables. John was relieved to see Sri dressed in women's clothing, his face hidden by a scarf. Bo looked somber.

"We met up with members of one of my trading parties at the teahouse," Bo said, avoiding small talk. "They have returned with news."

"News?" Dian's voice held an unveiled concern. "What news?"

Sri looked at Bo, then down to the floor.

"They traveled two days east and have come back two days west after a small trading venture," Bo continued. "They stopped at the pilgrimage site at the mountain. I always ask them to stop and make an offering. They gave bread and tea to two bedraggled women there." Sejal, Deborah, Dian, and Rachel exchanged glances. "Apparently, men arrived at the site on the heels of rumor and speculation about John and started asking questions of a group of four women. The men searched the camp and found your dog, John."

"No. Bo, no." John's blood ran cold. The color drained from his face – fear gripping his body.

"The women..." Sri's voice trailed into the empty space of sadness.

"The women refused to say where Flavus came from," Bo said. "The men bound them, beat them..."

"No!" Dian buried her face into James, who wore a look of stone. Sejal held Deborah and Rachel close as they cried.

"They murdered two of the women, slitting them open, and..." Bo paused, looking ill, "and battered two others in the tent to within an inch of their lives before Flavus was able to run them off. Those are the two survivors my party met. Fate brought us this news."

The women wailed, the devastating announcement bringing them to their knees. Deborah slumped to the floor and tore her robe. Rachel, Dian, and Sejal comforted her through their own grief and a storm of tears.

"I'm sorry," Bo said. "The other women at the site gave them a proper burial and are caring for Flavus. Apparently, he was heroic." John's face was frozen in shock, as the news penetrated him. Bo approached with utmost care. "John, he saved lives. He saved two lives. And he protects many more."

John looked into Bo's face, but could not see or hear through the fog of stunning devastation. It was as if the world had become a cave, black and cold, with no hint of warmth or light. Only a word separated John's mouth from a trail of horrible curses and vomit.

"This..." he muttered through heavy breath.

"What?" Bo could not decipher the utterance. "John, what did you say?"

"This was mine," John said in a whisper. "This was mine!" he bellowed, his voice paralyzing everyone into a moment of pause. He beat the door with his fists, his back to the group. Bo placed a hand on him.

"What do you mean, Brother?" Bo asked. "How is this terrible deed yours?"

"This battle with Philip." John turned to face the group, intense. "It was mine. And now all of you…and innocents…are all involved. I killed those women. For the love of Christ, I killed them!" John roared in frustration, his seeping emotions for Philip running over, carving boiling pathways of hatred in his mind. Rachel rushed to John, hugging him through her grief.

"Listen to me," she said, as he melted into her. "John, listen. This is not your burden, do you understand? This is not your fault. We came with you of our own free will. We chose to fight this battle with you." She looked at Bo, the group, then back to John. "We chose to act…we chose to act on this, do you hear me? We chose to come and be a part of this just cause. We knew there would be consequences. Danger. But we need to do this." She forced him away from her body, holding him firmly at arm's length. His head slumped in anguish. Rachel suppressed her own grief and shook him hard until he looked into her eyes. She willed her words to penetrate his sorrow and extinguish his guilt. "John of Antioch, listen to me. We are here for you. We are here with you. Do you understand? You are not alone!"

John's body, now an empty shell, slipped through her arms to the floor as if made of sand. Rachel knelt beside him and stroked his hair with smooth, gentle motions. She pressed her face against his bowed head. No one was sure what to do. Sri consoled Deborah and Sejal, while James cared for Dian. After a few minutes in silence, loud sobs transformed into quiet tears. Shock oriented itself into the slow process of reflection and acceptance. Bo went to pour a cup of tea for John, who was nearly catatonic in Rachel's arms.

"Everyone, listen to me," Bo said. "Please." Bo offered the tea to John, who reached out a trembling hand and, with Rachel's aid, took a small sip. "Everyone, please. You heard Rachel. We are here to support each other, and to support the casualties of this unintended war. I told you this news and the details not to hurt you, although I knew you would be aggrieved to hear it. I told you because these were your friends, and you deserve to know."

"Thank you," Sejal said. "As hard as this is for us to hear, I am sure it was hard to say. You honor their memories, and our bonds of friendship, by sharing this news."

Bo nodded to her and continued. "You have returned to Ecbatana, and things appear to be more dangerous than you thought. My full caravan returns in a few days. You will be safe at this house until then. If you wish, you may join us on our way to Turfan. We will protect you as you make your way there, or place you with caravans heading to your homelands." Bo searched each face. "Or, wherever you may wish to go."

Dian looked up, teary-eyed. "Bo, did you not talk last night about taking appropriate action? And now you ask us to leave? To abandon our cause?"

"I advocate neither approach," he said calmly. "I am only suggesting that you have options, as your lives are now in serious jeopardy. We know your foe's intentions. We have no reason to believe their actions upon us will be merciful. One must know when to act. I cannot pretend to know for you. You must follow your hearts."

"We appreciate your sincere counsel Bo," John said, still shaking in Rachel's arms. Relief at the sound of his voice showed on the faces around him. "We are privileged to have your support and your friendship."

Bo nodded with a smile. He brought food to the solemn circle. "Please eat. I know food is not the first thought, but no matter your course of action, you need to keep up your strength so your courage might follow."

The group partook in the light meal, though it went down hard. Sejal looked with pity upon her companions. In her lonely life they were her only lasting family, and they understood her as only sisters can. Her heart wept for them and their predicament, but something stirred deep within her, pouring forth into encouragement.

"Everyone, look up for a moment." The group met Sejal's gaze. "Hold your heads high in this difficult time. This news is devastating, but it has shown us something. It has shown us the power of hate. We owe it to those women to stay here and finish what we have started."

"So much pain," John said. "So much bloodshed. I do not want to see any of you hurt. This has gone beyond a fight for the body of the Church, everyone. We have strayed over a line into a battle for the soul of a man. Again, I must urge caution."

"We may be crushed," Sejal said, "but we must not crumble. We must stay, John."

John regarded the tear-stained cheeks of his companions. They had the look of battle scars, yet everyone now sat taller on their mats. The grief was real, but the path was clear. He knew they were already invested to a degree greater than he could imagine.

"If we are thus resolved, we need a new plan," Sri suggested. "We are not dealing with a mindless mob from Ecbatana, but a group on a mission. Clearly, they will not stop until John is captured."

"They may not stop even then," James said. "They seem to be capable of any ill deed."

"You must decide what you are going to do," Bo added grimly. "And you must do it now, through your sorrows. These men will not rest for dawn or dusk, and you have precious little time for grief."

The group nodded in assent.

"We cannot rely on the local Sassanid authorities for our safety," John said, moving the conversation to action. "Their disdain for Christianity suggests they will not take our plight seriously. Perhaps Roman officials in the city can help…if we can access them."

"What is your first step?" Sri asked.

"We need to set about figuring out how big Philip's network is, and if he is still alive." John took another sip from his cup and felt a blaze of life follow the tea into his body, as if an unseen coal was searing through him. He knew he had to cast aside his hesitations for the sake of his church, and his friends.

"What then?" Dian asked.

"We need to get word to Meletius about what is happening out here," he said. "That is probably most important. I do not believe he intended things to get so out of hand. He needs to know."

"But John, who is going to get that message back?" James asked. "It could take weeks, or months, and I am not going to leave you here to do this dirty work alone. I'm sorry, but I will not return to the West without you, even with an important message."

"Fine. Then we need to find out who is loyal to Meletius in this town, but has not fallen under Philip's madness," John said. "I will try to contact the church leader, Luke. He may still be friendly towards me, and he may have connections with local Roman officials. I cannot believe every Christian soul in this town is now against me. I know there must be some Roman presence, even in the company of Shapur."

"How can you know for sure?" Rachel asked.

"I cannot. I can only pray."

"I will go to the teahouse and sit watch," Bo said. "I remember Philip from your sermon, if indeed he was the man behind me in the greeting line. I heard one of his friends address him by name that night."

"That was him," John said.

"Then I will keep a lookout for him. He does not know me, and that is an asset to you. I will take Sri in disguise."

"James," John said, "you and I must risk a walk through the heart of the city near the secret meetinghouse to assess what is going on."

John rode this new energy, the terrible news from the mountain igniting courage within him. He was ready to cast his fate into a swift-moving and uncertain current. Everything else be damned, he wanted to act now.

"Wait," Deborah said, slowing the momentum into reality. "You can't just go walking through Ecbatana."

"I will be in disguise," John said, in no mood for trifles.

"Well, when you get to the meetinghouse, are you just going to walk up to the community leader dressed as a woman and start talking?" Deborah's sarcastic tone smacked John back into caution.

"I had not thought of that," John said.

"Send us," Sejal said. "We will once again don our own clothing and walk through town. On the road, it was necessary to appear as men leading a caravan, but here, no one knows us. We will pose as pilgrim church members and find out the situation."

"That's fine," James agreed. "But go in the afternoon when Luke will likely be preparing the church for evening devotions. John and I will simply monitor the streets. We will all meet back here at sunset."

"If you are being watched or followed," Sri said, "go directly to the teahouse, but do not acknowledge Bo or me. Duck inside and wait until we can create a diversion to get everyone to safety. The afternoon start will bring us closer to cover of darkness should anything go ill."

"What about me?" Rachel asked. "Every Christian in town knows that I am Philip's wife." Her frustration surfaced as her circumstances now threatened her participation.

John's heart sank. This was the moment he dreaded, when he would have to face the cold fact that Rachel wanted to be a part of such a dangerous mission, even as her previous one had almost claimed her life. He approached her, taking her hands in his – their support roles now reversed.

"Rachel, stay here at Bo's house," he said quietly.

"No!" she cried. "I want to help."

"Then stay. That would help me."

"This is not about you, John. It's about something much more!" Bodies shifted and eyes wandered, as the situation became awkward. John led Rachel into a back room and closed the door.

"Rachel, I—"

"John, I'm a married woman and I want to know where my husband is. Can't you understand that?"

"Rachel, please—"

"I don't know why you and I are so close, anyway. It's not appropriate. Besides, I'm just as capable as you, and I won't stay here while my friends are out there risking their lives. I can fall on a sword for the ones I love, as well."

John was silent against his will. He wanted to tell her everything in his mind, to express his soul. His heart ached in disappointment, his thoughts in disarray. Rachel, suddenly panged with regret at her words, stepped close and tried to touch his face, but he turned away. She placed a hand on his cheek and guided him back.

"John, I'm sorry. I should not have said that. I'm just so scared and confused. You promised you wouldn't leave me, so let me go. Let me go into the streets to assist you. I have just as much invested in this as you, and I know these streets. I know a henchman's face. I can help." She kissed him softly on the lips.

"I thought you were married," he said, trying to sound nonchalant.

"I am. But I don't know if my husband is alive or dead. The Lord will forgive me in my ignorance."

John leaned in and kissed her passionately. He pulled her close in a tight embrace and prayed this would not be the last moment they shared.

"Rachel, I'm afraid…" he began, but Rachel again pressed warm fingertips against his lips, stopping the inevitable protest in its tracks.

"You won't lose me, John, nor my friendship. Maybe this is a time when I need to act. Maybe I need to face my opposite. Come. Let's join the others."

As they emerged from the room, everyone was busy preparing. Sejal cleared her throat as Rachel picked up a pile of men's clothing. Dian cast a bewildered look at John who wore an expression of bemused resignation. He knew better than to question Rachel now. He picked up his teacup and made for the kettle, knowing he would need more than courage on this day.

Chapter Forty-One

Rachel was protected in a turban, face scarf, and a solemn promise not to talk. After the women left for the church, the men donned fresh dresses and undergarments. They once again squeezed themselves into the uncomfortable clothing and submitted to Bo for inspection. After some minor adjustments, they wished each other good luck, and Sri and Bo set out for the teahouse.

John and James patrolled the busy afternoon streets. They walked up and down the roads on the lookout for signs or clues. At one point, they noticed Roman guards at a stall sorting through silks and made a mental note of their presence. They risked passing the church to see if the women had met their objective. They saw them sitting inside the meetinghouse with the church leader, talking animatedly.

"That looks like it's going well," James said, with an optimism John did not believe.

"I hope so," John whispered. "Although, he could be talking to them about killing me."

"Keep your spirits up," James said in a mock woman's voice. He sounded ridiculous, but John did not dare laugh.

As they passed the church, John spied parchments with an official Church seal in a leather sack, hanging from a hook. He slid one from the holder and concealed it under his dress. He and James made another circuit through the streets near the church, with no sign of Philip, Simon, or Mark. John knew Philip had to have more confederates lurking, but did not know what they looked like, steeping the already tense mission in heightened anxiety.

"There is nothing out here," James said. "Let's meet Sri and Bo for tea."

"We can't risk that," John hissed.

"We're in women's clothing. No one is going to recognize us. Come on. Besides, it will give us a view of the church so we can check on the women."

"But Rachel—"

"John, come. She is still in disguise and, as you can see, she is sitting in silence."

John followed James to the teashop. The prospect of watching Rachel across the street was too much to resist. He was relieved to find the shop empty, save for the table where Bo sat with a disguised Sri. John nodded politely to the tea man who smiled with a weak nod.

"Well?" Bo asked as they sat down. "You were not followed, I trust."

"Not that we could tell," John said, holding the scarf to his face with his hand and looking around anxiously. He spied the church and saw the women were not in sight. "Gone already? Where are they?" he asked.

"They left the church as you turned your back to cross the street," Bo said. "Luke left not long thereafter. We decided to remain here so as not to arouse suspicion."

"And Rachel?" John asked.

"From what I could see at this distance, Rachel remained perfectly disguised the whole time, and did not appear to speak. I didn't even recognize her."

"No sign of Philip or his men," Sri said, answering John's next question without him asking.

"That bastard has to be in this town somewhere," John said, casting an uneasy eye toward the street. "Or, in his grave."

"His grave!" James exclaimed, a bit too loudly.

"The Pit!" Sri declared.

"Let's go!" Bo urged. "Hurry. It is almost sunset."

"I'm going to stay here for a while," John said. "I'm going to keep watch on the church to see if Philip emerges. I will head back to the house near sunset and meet you all there."

"Wait," Bo said. He handed John a parchment. "Take this."

"What is it?" John asked.

"A map to Turfan. I created it quickly today during Sri's lookout. If this all ends well, maybe you will come. I know we discussed it earlier, but consider this your formal invitation and a good omen for all of us. I know the timing is awkward, but I am casting a bright coin into a dark well. Maybe now is the time for a wish."

Sri, Bo, and James left the teahouse. John set Bo's parchment on the table and regarded it, as if expecting it to come alive and speak to him. Suddenly, he remembered the scroll he took from the church. He unrolled it and read the shocking announcement:

From Meletius, the Holy Bishop of Antioch, A Decree: Meletius of Antioch has issued a recall of Antioch missionaries on the road. It is their Christian duty to return to the Motherland upon receipt of this parchment. Any official Antioch missionary found on the road in due course, and after unreasonable time after receipt of this parchment, is subject to excommunication and will lose his status in the Church. It is your duty as a Christian to pass this decree to any missionary you encounter. Local church authorities and militia will take charge of receipt and registration, and will provide guidance for your return through Sassanid lands. Missionaries are to register at churches in each large city along the route back, and state their express intent to return. Missionaries will receive their timetables for return from local church authorities, and must present them in each town.

John dropped the announcement next to Bo's map and reflected on them. He thought about how his life had come full circle. He had been sent into the world, onto this road, with a mission – a mission now diminished. Replaced. How had it come to this? Had he come to the end, or was this a new place to start? His eyes moved to the small church across the street, as sweat dripped down his face.

The heat was murderous.

John now sat quietly in the empty teahouse, a warm cup cradled in his hands. Gazing beyond ripples of heat at the dusty streets beyond, a racing mind was his only companion – a mind unmoored from what was once a very secure faith.

"The very fires of hell," he muttered.

He was certain his shallow measure of tea would evaporate if he did not drink in haste. The steam that arose from the rough, clay vessel was more moisture than he had seen in days, and he was sure the surrounding air was grateful for it. But he knew better than to rush. He relished this uneasy peace, determined to savor this moment. "Brew patience the way the tea master brewed this tea." That was his mantra in this moment. His only hope.

The cotton tarp encircling the teahouse whipped wildly in the dry wind – a broken sandal under determined foot, marching nowhere. Unwelcome veils of dust blew into the tiny shop, settling around the little wooden table. John awoke to the realization that he had not seen fluffy clouds for days. The constant breezes here blew them away, long before they could provide relief. The promise of cooler salvation in the mountains was broken in this unusually hot season. He wondered if Shapur himself would stay away from his royal summer home. It was so hot in Ecbatana, John could hardly think. But a blank mind was a luxurious jewel buried deep. Right now, he had to think. He had to focus. This decision was not going to make itself. After all, delay would not placate the two parchments that lay before him on the table.

As he turned his attention toward the setting sun, he knew his homeland lay in its wake. For so long, he had thought about nothing other than home. There, on the shores of Antioch, John longed to preach and teach the word of the Lord. Maybe he would even venture back to the Holy Land itself and win converts. The possibilities were endless. But now, sitting in Ecbatana, John faced his destiny plain and simple. He closed his eyes for just a moment and reflected, as if knowing how he arrived at this point could help him move on from it.

When he opened his eyes, he had a burning feeling in his gut. He crumpled up the map to Turfan and walked out of the shop.

"Philip first," he said, as he made for Bo's house. "Then I will go home."

Chapter Forty-Two

Hello?" John walked into the house and found the front room empty and dark. "Hello? Is anyone here?"

"Bo?" A door from a back room swung open. A man's voice, quick and sharp, addressed John, giving him a start.

"No. I'm John. Who are you?"

"I'm Chen, the tea trader. You are Bo's friend, John?"

"Yes. Have my friends not come back yet?"

"Yes and No. Why?"

"Why–? Wait…yes and no? They were all supposed to be here at sunset."

"Men dressed as women came back and met the women dressed as women and the woman dressed as a man. The group left together."

"They left together? The women went to the Pit with night approaching? Why?"

"I do not know. I have not seen them since. You can wait here if you like."

Chen receded back into his room and shut the door, leaving John in silence. John went outside and looked up and down the street. No sign of anyone. He paced nervously on the front steps.

"I must go to the Pit!" he proclaimed, as if speaking directly to his own impatience.

He ran to the farthest edge of town and followed the rocky gorge that skirted the valley. His only mission was to get to the graveyard as quickly as possible. His feet quickened when he heard yelling and screaming in the distance.

"Christ, have mercy!" John yelled, as he came flying into the Pit.

He ran to where the men were pulling down a crucifix. John tripped over a pile of three other crosses as he made his way to their side. Sol's groans were barely audible. He had been hanging for a day in the blazing sun, his body dehydrated. Blood from his wounds was baked onto his skin.

"Sol? Sol!" John was near panic.

"He can't respond, for God's sake!" James yelled, as the men pulled him down. "Get the hell over here and help us, for the love of Christ!"

The women stood by and kept a lookout while the men tilted the cross partially out of the deep hole, so it was resting at an angle. Using their feet, and brute strength born of desperation, they cracked the wood backwards and released the tension, guiding it flat. The crucifix toppled to the ground with a thump. Sol landed face up, yet still nailed down.

"What happened?" John asked Rachel, as she stood lookout with the women.

"The church leader met with us today," she said. "We posed as converts. He told us that Philip had caught a Jewish criminal and crucified him. He said Philip was a hero around here now."

"A *hero*?" John shrieked as he worked furiously to free his friend.

"We wanted more details," Sejal said. "We asked what the crime was, and the leader said it was attempted murder. Philip has been telling anyone who will listen that a Jew led a band of blasphemers who tried to kill him and his friends. Apparently, Philip is missing an eye. He shows his wounds to everyone and tells his version of events. Everyone is looking for you."

Bo directed the men to various duties in a calm fashion, completely focused on Sol. He gingerly extracted the long spikes from Sol's hands and feet, liberating his limbs. They fell limp under their newfound freedom.

"Come here and hold his head, John," Bo instructed. His steady voice kept everyone on task, despite the gruesome scene. "James, you hold his feet down. This is not the first man I have pulled from a cross in Shapur's empire. Freeing his limbs does not free his body. Sol is having tremors, and we need to make sure he remains still, so he does not injure himself further."

"Where is Philip now?" John asked with a sense of distracted urgency, holding Sol's bloody head in his hands.

"No one is sure," Sejal remarked, still scanning the horizon. "When we left the church, the leader seemed nervous. He ran across into a little house and we walked quickly in the opposite direction toward home."

"It's the house where they kept you captive," Rachel said to John.

"Bo, Sri, and James stopped at the tea traders' home on their way here," Sejal continued, "and we told them the story. We all just ran here a little while ago."

"John, please." Sri redirected him, "I need you to focus. Bo?"

Bo poured water into Sol's mouth as Sri placed his hand over Sol's face. Sri recited a prayer, and Sol slowly opened his eyes and started to struggle.

"Hold him," Bo barked. "Hold him still! He will struggle under the force of freedom. We must bind him a moment more." Bo fought gently to keep Sol steady.

"Sol!" James screamed. "Sol!"

"Calm, Brother James," Sri said. "Quiet energy."

"Sol," James voiced softly. "Sol, can you hear me?"

Sol lay still, trying to take in the scene. He recognized his friends and tried to smile, but his parched lips would not move. A slight huff and blink of the eyes was all he could muster in acknowledgement.

"We need to get him back to the house," John urged. "Now!"

"Too late!" Dian yelled.

John looked into the distance and saw a cloud of dust under torchlight moving towards them. A group of townspeople was closing in fast on the Pit. Too fast. There was no way to escape with Sol.

"Women!" James yelled. "Women, run! Get out of here!"

"We're not leaving without Sol!" Deborah shouted back. "Or without all of you!"

"Fine. Then get behind us. Hurry!" James's voice was authoritative, and the women moved quickly at his command.

Philip appeared first. He led a group up the hill to the site. A mob, numbering about thirty strong now, stood between the group of friends and Ecbatana. John's heart was pounding in his chest, but he stood his ground, resisting his every instinct to attack Philip.

"Well, well." Philip grinned and surveyed the small gathering as the mob crested the mound behind him. "Look what the merciless wind blew in. John, good to see you again, old friend." John stood tall in front of Rachel. She hid behind him. Philip came to within six feet and stopped. "I see you brought my whore of a wife back to me."

John, unable to contain himself any longer, lunged at Philip with a determined fist. Philip ducked the blow. A group of men ran forward and grabbed John. Members of the mob took hold of the others in the party before they could enter the fray. James struggled to get free, but an anonymous, swift punch to the stomach stopped him.

"Nice clothes, John." Philip flicked at the dress and eyed the stockings and scarf. "You turned from Christ, and now you turn from manhood?" Philip clicked his tongue with unbridled sarcasm. "You've gone through all kinds of change out here, my friend. I see you gave Rachel your clothes." Philip approached her and ripped the turban from her head before tearing her robes at the neck. He rubbed her hard on her breasts while she struggled. "No. Not a man," he yelled at the mob, with a tone of triumph. "I had to check." He sneered at John. "Still a whore, I see," he hissed at Rachel. "Glad that has not changed."

"That's enough, Philip!" John screamed, struggling to break free. A man went to hit him, but Philip stayed the punch.

"I see you've added another pagan to your party," Philip said. "Oh, and in case you were wondering Bo, I recognized your face from the tent meeting. You may be insignificant, but you are not invisible. God blessed me with a powerful memory for enemy faces. You didn't need a group of disguised and stupid women to give your presence away." Philip looked over at Luke, then back to the party. "I figured something was amiss when I noticed you all watching the church from that cafe." The group exchanged looks of shock. "That's right. You are not the only masters of disguise in Ecbatana." Philip came close and pushed on Bo's stomach. "Besides, I know you don't have the Buddha belly to hold all that tea. What else would you be doing in there all day?"

Philip paced up and down the line of captives and came face to face with Sri.

"And Sri. Dear, godless Sri. You make an ugly woman." Philip slapped him across the face, but Sri's gaze calmly returned to meet Philip, unyielding and unfazed.

"What do you want from us, Philip?" John said, barely containing his rage.

"Ah, this conversation is so familiar, isn't it, John? You always make me sound so greedy." The mob laughed. "What do I want? I want my eye back." Philip stepped close and lifted the cotton bandage over his socket to show John the empty space. John winced as he stared into the void. "I want my whore of a wife back." Philip came uncomfortably near. "But, most of all, I want Christ back!" Philip kicked John in the stomach and the guards let him fall backward to the ground. "I want back what you are trying to destroy. Speaking of wanting things back, perhaps you heard Meletius has called us all home?" John's friends looked at each other in surprise. "Oh, you didn't hear? John didn't give you a copy of the parchment I watched him take? Apparently, due to the reverse conversions, Meletius has called us from the road thanks to bastards like John!"

Philip kicked John hard in the ribs, grinning at his cry of pain. The mob voiced a low roar of cold solidarity. John rolled in a heap next to Sol who lay motionless, except for a wheezing breath.

"No better than your pagan friends, John," Philip hissed. "Fitting that you will have the same end." Philip kicked the pile of crosses.

"No!" Rachel cried. "Philip, you can't!"

Philip walked to her, imposing his arrogance. "Can't I? I can do whatever I want. Meletius has placed me in a position of great importance. I am here to weed out dissent and to clear the way for our future missions. I intend to do that, at any price. We all have made that commitment." Philip, in a grand gesture, swept his hand across the angry crowd. "And to that we hold, even in a hostile empire under the worst circumstances."

"Philip, what you're doing is immoral," James said. "You cannot just kill at will."

Philip walked over to James and whispered in his ear so no one else could hear. "I haven't killed anyone. I have others do it for me. I just watch. Guide. Think of me as a camel driver of sorts, like yourself." Philip turned to survey the women. "I see each man has a girlfriend now." He grabbed their cheeks hard, one by one, turning their faces, as if considering a purchase. "Pagan prostitutes," he yelled to the mob.

"Monster!" Sejal cried.

Philip looked her up and down. "You must be Sri's whore counterpart. I hear from Luke you have a mouth that enjoys the strength of its own tongue. Maybe it will be silenced once you see your friends' fates."

Philip nodded, and his henchmen pushed the women aside before dragging the men away. Another group heaved three crosses over and dropped long metal stakes and mallets beside them.

"I have to say, John, I find this irony simply beautiful." Philip tapped the spikes with the tip of his foot, showing little regard for their piercing points. "I showed you such hospitality back home and now you have done the same. You've given me your friends, your mission, and the satisfaction of furthering Meletius's noble work. I don't know how I can ever repay you. We will put Sol in a grave tonight and I'll see that Bo lives to tell of your fate far and wide…though his words may not make sense, since he will soon be missing his tongue."

John looked up from the ground where blood spilled in a raging river from his lip. In the distance, a cloud of dust and torches silently broke the horizon behind the assembled mob. He did not know if it portended trouble or salvation, but as it neared, he knew he needed to stall for time to save his friends.

"You can repay me by doing your best, Philip," John said.

"Stop!" Philip raised his hand to his henchmen. They ceased dragging the men to their crosses, and let them drop in heaps at their feet. "I want to hear what this pathetic excuse for a Christian has to say."

John gathered himself and tried to focus.

"I said, do your best, Philip. Any man willing to go this far for a cause must truly be dedicated. It is an honor to be in your presence."

"Are you mocking me?" Philip made to kick John in the face, but John put up his arms in supplication against the blow.

"No! No, Philip. I realize now that you are a man who is passionate about Christ and his work. You are my opposite. You are right. I was trying to befriend people on the road instead of converting them. I let myself get lost in relationships and not in my mission. I owe the Church more than making friends."

"Oh, so you see that now, do you?" Philip spat.

"I…I do." John winced at the pain in his sides, but knew he had to maintain his strength.

"Why should I believe you? Why should I think you are not just saying this to save your own life?"

"Forgive me, Philip. I forgot my place in the Lord's kingdom."

"You've certainly caused a lot of trouble, John. When I first saw you here in Ecbatana with the Hindu, I thought you had gone mad. Now I see you with these new pagan friends and whores and I simply do not know what to think."

"I understand, Philip. I know you are just doing your job."

Philip looked down at John and for a fleeting moment, pity washed over his face. However, he shook it off to make room for the madness once again.

"This is crazy!" he yelled. "Enough of this pointless and false begging. Pound the stakes!"

Just as the henchmen started pulling their struggling prisoners onto the crosses, the mob began to stir as the mysterious dust cloud reached the Pit.

"Stop where you are!" a voice yelled.

In the dim torchlight, John could barely make out the shape of Chen, Flavus trotting at his side. Men from Chen's tea caravan accompanied him, as did Roman guards from a local garrison, and two women. Simon and Mark were also among them, their hands bound.

"Release these people," a guard yelled, gesturing toward John and his friends.

"On whose authority?" Philip asked. "We are on Sassanid ground."

"By authority of Rome," the guard replied. "Until the uneasy treaties break, we still have power here."

The women from John's group ran to embrace their newly arrived sisters. John stood, with some difficulty, under Sri and Bo's assistance. James ran to Sol, now lying face down, motionless. James turned him and held him up, dabbing blood from his mouth with a scarf. Flavus ran over to John and licked his hand before nuzzling Sol in a warm greeting.

"But how…?" John stammered in surprise at the new arrivals. "How did you know where we were?"

"You have interesting friends, Brother John," the guard replied. "And you have stupid ones," he said, looking at Philip.

Chapter Forty-Three

People of Ecbatana, listen to me." The head guard held up his hands and ordered silence. "This group of men is not to blame for recent events. You have heard talk of assault and murder. You have heard talk of conspiracy. I say to you, it is not the men for whom you came." The mob made a rabbling sound and looked angrily at Philip who eyed the new party, and his confederates, uneasily. "Emissary Philip and his men have murdered and tortured in the name of Christ!" The crowd searched from the guard to Philip, trying to discern the truth. "These men," the guards shoved Simon and Mark forward, "assaulted a group of women and murdered two of them, gutting them like fish. These two women," a guard led two wounded women forward, "were brave enough to join a caravan from their home and come here to Ecbatana to seek justice. Justice for crimes committed on the orders of this man." The guard nodded his head to two of his cohorts, who grabbed Philip's arms.

"Let me go!" Philip lashed about wildly, trying to fight off his captors. "Let me go! I've done nothing!" His eye was wild, as he thrashed about like a demon of ancient tales, the very embodiment of an unrelenting foe captured by some long-forgotten hero.

Eventually the guards subdued him, and their leader continued. "Hear me now," he said with authority. "I know Shapur stands against Roman and Christian alike. I know we have seen emperors and military campaigns come and go. I know we live in this city under constant threat that treaty and uneasy peace will again succumb to violence. But until that time, we must stand together, good citizens. We must not allow Roman justice to wane amongst the Sassanids, even as our presence here wanes."

The crowd cheered their assent. Meanwhile, James struggled to get Sol to his feet, his wounds weeping with infection. Sol stumbled and two members of the Chinese trading party rushed to give assistance.

"Get him back to town," Bo said to a man in the party. "Take him to our house and see to these wounds." The men supported Sol's limp, bloodied body and carried him off. Bo uttered a quiet prayer as they walked away, then turned to John. "Those men are part of the tea trade group. I am guessing they are responsible for saving us."

"I beg your pardon," the head guard said to Bo, "but you should thank this man."

It was difficult to see in the firelight. The small, unassuming man from the teashop stepped forward out of the shadows. John, overcome with surprise and gratitude, reached out his hands, as the man started a bow. Both men simultaneously exchanged customary pleasantries in a way that looked like a fumbled dance, especially as John's tender ribs shrieked in protest as he tried to bend his body low in respect.

"Sir, we owe you a debt of gratitude." John smiled, tears welling in his eyes. "But, how did you know about all of this?"

A shy grin appeared on his face. "You spent so much time in my tea shop, I came to find out as many of your secrets as *you* know. I am quiet and often unnoticed, save for my brews."

"What is your name?" John asked.

"Please…you can simply call me Lao."

"Well, thank you, Lao. You are truly our savior this night. May the Lord bless us that we may someday serve you in similar fashion, though not in similar circumstance."

Chen stepped forward. "More of my men made their way back from their brief journey on your heels. They, like the party before them, heard of the unspeakable deeds near the sacred mountain."

"When they came into my shop to bring me tea," Lao interjected, "they told me the news, and that they had two injured women and a dog at a safe house in Ecbatana. I realized your party was connected to this. This afternoon, I overheard your plan to come to the Pit and I raced to the guards for help."

"And we are here," the head guard said, stepping close to John and placing a hand on his shoulder. "Not every soldier has abandoned Meletius and the church in Ecbatana for military duties alone, and not all Roman Christians are loyal to Philip and his men. We have our own minds and keep our own sworn duty to the Church."

"Philip?" Luke confronted him. "What is all this about? We believed in you. You led us with a promise in this savage place. What did you and your men do?"

"Nothing!" Philip yelled. "I've done nothing but serve Christ!"

"That's not what your friends Simon and Mark tell us," the guard said.

Philip fell silent. Sejal came forward. "Philip, did your men attack and murder our friends?"

"Whores!" he screamed.

"Philip, tell us!" Rachel interjected. Her tone appeared to surprise even her. Never did she possess the courage to speak to Philip in anger, although she had felt the urge many times and for many years.

Philip squinted his eye at her, but did not yell back. "They...they were only supposed to find John." He looked at Simon and Mark who had their heads bowed.

"Three men..." The guard looked at Philip and his companions. "Three men and three fresh crosses," he said to the angry assemblage. The guards pushed the captives into the dirt as the mob closed in.

"We're sorry!" Mark wailed, his hands raised, as if begging God for mercy. "Please!"

The crowd turned violent and surrounded the three, lying helpless on the ground. Kicks and punches flew from all directions.

"Murderers!" voices from the mob yelled. "Monsters!" A man put a foot on Philip's throat and screamed, "You are no better than

Shapur! You are worse! You persecute your own!" The guards stepped back and let the group exact justice.

"Stop!" John yelled. The mob ignored him as the men howled in pain under the blind torment. John fought his way through the violence and thrust his body as a shield upon Philip. "Stop! Stop!" he yelled, indiscriminate blows landing on him.

"They're killers!" A clear voice rang out from inside the chaos.

"And if you continue, you will be, too!" John yelled. He fought to protect the accused from a cascade of fists and feet.

"John!" James stepped forward to try to extract his friend from the melee. "Let them get what's coming to them."

"It's no less than they deserve," Dian said.

"No!" John insisted, and stood to address the crowd who had backed away, at least for the moment, leaving the three prisoners writhing in agony. "Listen to me! Philip convinced you that I tried to murder him and that I had turned my back on Meletius and Christ. I know he blames men like me for the missionary recall to Antioch. You had little evidence, save for his word, and you were ready to draw my blood, thinking I had undone the noble work of the Lord. Convinced that I had betrayed you. I understand how you must feel now that you have proof of their vile crimes against the Father. I know your passion and your thirst for justice." John looked at Sri and Bo, then to the crowd. "But this is a time we must know when *not* to act." John was now pleading, as if fighting for his very own brother. "If we kill these men here in this dirt, in this way, in this anger, then truly we are no better than they. Only Christ and the Father can pass judgment unto death."

The mob looked from one to the other, then to the three men on the ground. There was an undertone throughout the crowd as they considered John's words.

"Please," John continued. "Blood is plentiful in these days in both mountain and desert. But mercy…mercy is the beloved spring and the eternal well that can save us all. Please. Stop." Everyone moved back, leaving the cowering bodies exposed in the flickering firelight. John turned to the guards. "Men, take them away. I'm sure a trial will make known the truth." John looked down at the accused. "I'm sure there will be a just punishment."

The guards dragged them off. Sejal, Dian, Deborah, Rachel, Sri, James, and Bo stood bathed in the light of the torches, facing the lingering crowd. There was a hush, pregnant with bewilderment and sadness, as everyone tried to come to grips with what had just taken place. The overwhelming silence spoke its peace and the mob gradually disbanded. The group of friends retired to Bo's house.

Chapter Forty-Four

Any news?" James inquired of John. It had been a week, and the group was eager for an update. James had stayed in the small house with the women while John and Sri went to the jail seeking information on Philip and his men. James and Flavus were now on the front step, waiting like expectant parents.

"Nothing new." John, Flavus now at his heels, walked past James and through the door. He took off his sandals and sat on a mat next to Rachel. "Their trial is still set for tomorrow."

"They will try them in Ecbatana, then?" James asked.

"Yes." John scratched Flavus behind the ears. The dog was happy to again be in the presence of his master, and John made sure that Flavus knew of his own delight to be in his faithful company once again. "With unrest growing daily in the region, there is no other way. Ecbatana may not be a Roman city, but there is an official in this town under treaty. It is the only way."

"So be it," James said.

"This has been a long week," Sri added. "Philip, Mark, and Simon are locked away with the small garrison until the trial."

"What are the charges?" Sejal asked.

"Assault and murder," John said. "The trial has been delayed because officials have gone to find more witnesses of the attack at the mountain. The two survivors who made their way to Ecbatana are also safe and are being kept in secret."

A few minutes later, Bo arrived from town with bags and put them on a small table.

"Tea!" Rachel rushed over to smell it.

"It's a token from Lao," Bo said. "He wanted to show his appreciation for your patronage these past weeks."

"He is showing *us* gratitude?" John said in surprise. "I feel as if I have not thanked *him* enough."

"The man is a saint," Sejal said. "We owe him our very lives."

"He has not had his shop open for a few days," John said. "Where has he gone?"

"He has decided to devote his life to study," Bo said. "He will travel with my party to Turfan. He says there is too much excitement here for him now and he wants to retire in peace. All are leaving tomorrow."

"Tomorrow?" John did not hide his shock.

"We must go," Sri said, stepping forward.

"We? Sri, you're leaving with them?"

"John, I joined with you because I needed aid. I needed assistance." Sri took John's hands with an intimacy reserved for kin. "You have given me so much more…so much more than you will ever know. I will always value your friendship."

"Sri, I…" John's voice weakened in the face of such a strong bond, and he was at a complete loss.

Rachel stepped in. "Sri, thank you. For everything." She embraced him, throwing her arms around his neck. John thought he detected a hint of bemused discomfort from Sri, who, of course, was too polite to refuse the gesture. And he was too much a friend not to reciprocate.

James now stood in front of Sri, who tentatively put out his hand to shake. James did not take it, but instead, put his hands together as if in prayer and bowed. Sri returned the gesture with a smile.

"Sri, it has been a pleasure," James said. "One of the most unexpected pleasures of my silly life. If I had not met you, I would never know I was a Hindu. You have saved me from my ignorance and my karma."

Sri smiled and looked around the room. Catching Sol's eye, his body still bandaged and lacerated, Sri came to his side and knelt next to him.

"Solomon," he said with an air of respect and deference, "I want to give you something."

Sri nodded to Bo, who went over to Sri's belongings. He picked up a small sack and handed it to Sri, who placed it gently in Sol's bandaged hand.

"What is this, Sri?" Sol asked.

"Take a look and see."

Deborah, who had not left Sol's side since the night he was pulled from the cross, untied it for him. A green stone fell out.

"Sri, this is beautiful," Deborah said, holding it up so everyone could see.

"What kind of gem is this?" Sol admired it in the light, dazzling and bright green.

"It is jade," Sri smiled.

"Jade?"

"Yes. Gurudev gave it to me before his passing. He called it the heart of Shiva. It is one of the few possessions I kept from my time with him."

"Sri, I can't possibly accept—"

"Ah, ah." Sri cut off Sol's protest. "You must. Gurudev gave me this stone after he imbued within me the power to heal with the hand. He said, 'Sri, all hands have holes in them. We can fill them with hate, and hit, or we can fill them with love of the very heart, and heal. When you find a hand with a void that is truly holy, fill it with this.'"

"Sri, I'm just a campsite manager." Sol looked at his bandaged wrists and then up at Sri with tears in his eyes. "Albeit an injured one. I have no special gifts. Besides, it's my wrists that have the holes."

"That is a fact of small significance, my friend," Sri said. "Gurudev spoke of a metaphorical hand. Of everyone present," Sri directed his gaze and hand around the room, "you bore the heaviest physical load on this leg of our journey together. That kind of experience marks a man. His scars leave him not unfortunate and suitable for pity, but transformed.

"Transformed?" Sol laughed. "I don't know if I'm on par with your great guru, Sri. That was a man who sounded transformed."

"You will find, when you are healed," Sri looked from Deborah to Sol, and then continued, "that you will also be at peace. That was the joy in another Jewish man's noble journey. Jesus's story appears tragic on the surface, but to the third eye," Sri tapped Sol on the forehead between his eyebrows, "it is revealed that He did not suffer as one alone. Instead, He set an example of how we all may find ultimate redemption in transitory suffering." Sri touched Sol's wounds with his hand and recited a prayer. "You hung on that cross and persevered, my friend. You stand taller for it."

"Sri, we cannot thank you enough," John said. "In your absence, there will be a hole in our hearts for your sacrifices and friendship that no gems can fill."

Everyone nodded in agreement. A small tide of tears crested from the deep ocean of Sri's normally placid eyes.

"I am not leaving right away," he said, keeping his characteristic composure. "We still have the evening. Why don't we enjoy these refreshments, and all have one more wonderful night together in this home? John, it is still light outside. Walk with me to find some sweets to accompany the tea."

Chapter Forty-Five

Sri and John stepped out into the streets. The day was fading and life in Ecbatana had returned to normal after recent events. However, there was still a buzz in the air about the impending missionary recall and Philip's trial. Luke, in a gesture of sincere contrition, had asked John once again to speak at the community church. Since the incident at the Pit, the church had become an unexpected haven for local religious devotees of many faiths, where all could gather for spiritual conversation and tea. John was more than happy to oblige before departing again for Antioch. He had developed a small following of spiritual seekers eager to discuss and debate his insights, and to hear of his recent trials.

The men walked in silence. John wrestled with his feelings. So much had happened. So many surprises. So much uncertainty.

"When were you going to tell me, Sri?"

"Tell you what?"

"That you were leaving with the caravan. I mean, I guess I always knew, but still."

"The time never felt right, John. But then again, perhaps my silence was just right for the times. As you say, you always knew I would continue my journey. You knew I was going with Bo to Turfan. In fact, you have known this in some form since our very first meeting."

"I know. You did say you were heading east, past Samarkand. I guess now that the moment is here, I don't want to believe it."

Sri paused to take in his companion. "Brother John, we have been through so much together. Since we have made each other's acquaintance, you have made significant changes. We both have. But our lives were always going to take us in two different directions. You are going back to your home, correct?"

"You saw the parchment from Antioch, Sri."

"Maybe someday we will meet again, Brother John. Maybe someday we will share tea in Turfan."

"I hope we do." John turned his gaze to the ground, his mind at once full of thoughts of home and thoughts of foreign lands. He felt both distant from the familiar, and close to the new. "Sri, do you believe in destiny? Or fate? Do our choices matter?" John kicked a stone down the way and the two men walked on.

"How do you mean, John?"

"All of this excitement. The bloodshed. My purpose on this road. Our paths crossing. Our adventures. The people in this town. The travelers on this route—"

Sri laughed. "So many activities! You want to know if it is all out here by divine decree, or if we make it happen through our choices."

"Yes."

"Why should you be troubled by this question, John?"

"I'm not sure. I think about all the things that have happened. I think of Philip sitting in that cell, his deeds stained upon his conscience like wine on crisp, white robes. But did he have a choice?"

"A choice?"

"Yes. I've been considering what Bo said about my going with the flow of life. What if the waters get rough through God's Divine command just to test how well I swim?"

Sri stopped again, turned to his companion, and smiled. "My friend, where are the teacups? Indeed, you are in the wonderful heart of Turfan at this very moment!"

John smiled. "I'll really miss these chats."

"I as well, my friend, I as well. But your question is here for us now, so let us take a look at it. You want to know if the events that pass before you are there for you as they are, or if you have control over them in some way."

"I think that might be a clearer way to state it."

"Perhaps the question is not answered in one direction, John. Perhaps the truth is somewhere in between."

"In between? How can a choice between fate and free will be in between, Sri? It either is, or it isn't."

"Is it?"

"Isn't it?"

Two grown men looked at each other and rolled their eyes — schoolboys disputing a rule of some ancient game with boundaries long forgotten.

"John, what if a situation arises that has a certain number of possibilities that will lead to the same destination?"

"How so?"

Sri held up his hand, fingers together, all pointing upward. "Do you see my hand?"

"Yes. It's right in my face."

"Describe it to me."

"You have a palm with lines on it. And five digits radiating from the palm."

"Which way are the fingers pointing?" Sri asked.

"Up. To the sky."

"Yes. No matter which finger you choose, if you follow its path long enough, you will end up in the clear air of heaven. You can see by the varying lengths of the fingers that if you take this route," Sri wiggled his middle finger, "your journey will end higher, but will be considerably longer and with more trials in the material world than if you take this route," he then wiggled his pinkie. "And if you take this path," Sri wiggled his thumb, "you will have the longest journey of all."

"But—"

"Ah, my friend, you are going to tell me the thumb is a short route, but do you see how it spreads to the side? It will take you up, eventually, but you will have a slow, rising course in air, over much distance, to reach the heights of the other choices before you. It is a trade-off. All of life is a trade-off – more earthly experience to get more height, or less earth-bound adventures and more floating to catch up. You will not grow as tall on the pointer finger as the middle one, but you will grow, nonetheless. Same destinations, yes, but different ways to get there, with different amounts of growth."

"So, what is the palm?" John asked.

"The palm of my hand is the work of God in this world. The palm is the pool of possibility that spawns these five great rivers!" Sri wiggled all his fingers, smiling as he regarded their action. "Do you see how the palm stays still as the paths move? I can bend them, cross them…it is my choice. But they all come from one place."

John felt the faint echo of comprehension, but still struggled to sort it out in his mind.

"Sri, if I see this correctly, you are saying that our choices are fated, as they radiate out from the palm – the source – but the choice is free will. The road up is, well, up to us."

"I suppose that is a way of looking at it. Yes. The source of all things creates for us a human dimension. A world of space and of time. There are many choices that were set before you since you entered the world naked, crying, and with no earthly markings on your consciousness. That is fate. In the end, we will all merge with the origin of that source, or be at its hand, as you might say. That is the space above the fingertips. The silence after *Om*. But how we get there? The route we ultimately choose? That appears, at least to our limited thinking, to be free will."

"The choices are fated, but the choice is free will…" John held his own hand in front of his face. He spread his fingers, curled them in, and stretched them out. John put down his hand and regarded his friend. "Sri, what about Philip?"

"What about him?"

"Can we really say his cruelty was part of a master plan? Can we really say that his actions, and those of Simon and Mark, are really from here?" John pointed to his palm. "Were such deeds really always within a realm of some universal possibility?"

Sri stepped closer to his friend and looked him straight in the eye, with no wavering in his gaze.

"John, if you believe in the divine origin of this world, and if you believe your Father in Heaven created this world of possibility, including space for deeds of evil, and if you believe that these five fingers radiate out of a world of divine potential, then you have to make room in your mind for the possibility that Philip's actions are just as important to the world as your desire to stop them."

"I'm not sure I like that possibility."

Sri did not flinch. "I do not think you have a choice in the matter, my friend. I think Philip's acts are just as much a part of your journey as your own thoughts. Who can say why bad deeds and poor choices walk among us?" Sri once again opened his hand and spread his fingers. "Maybe terrible tides rise from pools of peace to test the methods we will take to stem them." John once again looked at his own hand. He pictured Philip swimming along one of his fingers. "Which river will you take, John?"

John stood rooted to the spot, taking in a long meditation at his hand. "I don't know, Sri." John frowned, a smirk of resignation crossing his lips. "I simply do not know."

"Come, my friend." Sri grabbed John's fingers from the air and pulled him toward a bakery. "So many choices," he smiled. "I feel we cannot go wrong!"

Chapter Forty-Six

Everyone settled down to comfort. James held Dian close. Deborah sat beside Sol, and as had become customary for the pair, she simply held his bandaged hands in hers as they smiled and gazed in perfect silence at the group.

Sri, Sejal, and Bo talked with spirit and animation. Sejal had decided to join the caravan to Turfan after accepting Sri as her guru and pledging her spiritual life to him. Bo indicated she would be the first female ever in attendance at Tea in Turfan through formal invite. He gave her translations of Chinese philosophy to read on the long trip ahead. John presumed their discussion also included the logistics of traveling in the larger tea caravan, now reunited after being splintered into short-distance trading parties.

John turned his attention to Rachel, sitting next to him. She was scratching Flavus behind the ears and talking with the normally reserved and reclusive Lao, who had accepted an invitation from Bo to this small gathering before heading out to Turfan. Rachel revealed to him intimate details of her life and how she had come to Ecbatana, and it took much of John's self-control not to eavesdrop on their quiet conversation.

Her casual demeanor was a departure from the usually awkward moments she and John had shared since discovering Philip alive. Rachel had been close, yet distant. John knew she was still married to a living soul and, knowing her mind on the issue, he did not want to push her in an uncomfortable direction. Though they had not discussed her marriage, he could sense the uneasiness. Ever since the events at the Pit, he resolved not to disturb her undoubtedly delicate conscience.

The members of the tea caravan had packed their bags. John knew it would not take long to prepare the camels in the morning. He surveyed his own bundles lying in the corner, awaiting his journey ahead.

When the tea masters came in from the corral, Sri and Bo rose to prepare sweets and drinks. Lao served the entire house, now bursting at the seams to contain the gathering. He proceeded to pour, simply smiling and laughing over loud objections that he was merely to be a guest this night.

There was life in the air, full and rich. There was excitement for new journeys, feelings of youthful love, and a congenial atmosphere. Still, John felt detached. He honored the distance and stepped out to the porch, a cup of tea nestled in his hands, at once desperate for isolation and comfort. Rachel excused herself to follow. She stood beside him, allowing her proximity to speak for her in the moment. John's heart beat faster whenever she came near, and although lost in his thoughts, this time was no exception.

"John, what's wrong?" she asked, releasing him from the silence.

"Nothing. Nothing you need to worry about." He smiled at her, and she returned the warm gesture. Behind them, John could hear laughing, and he envied his friends, totally consumed in the freedoms of joy.

"Are you worried about the trial tomorrow?" Her voice barely disguised the sound of faint anxiety about the much-anticipated event.

"I don't know, Rachel. I don't know what I'm feeling."

"Talk to me about it."

"It's just…It's something Sri said to me today. That the events in our lives are there to see which road we take. Will we do what we know is ultimately right and grow tall, or will we do what is expedient, and then live in regret that we made the poorer decision?"

"John, I don't understand."

He searched her gaze and found in her an expression of genuine caring. He had come to depend on her gentle nature for his nurture – a nature that seemed to so eagerly accept his limitations and frustrations.

"Rachel, I don't know what I am going to say tomorrow."

"About what?"

"About Philip and the others. I must bear witness at the trial, but I do not know which plea I will make to the magistrate."

She rested her hand on his arm. It was their first intimate contact since that fateful night at the Pit. John closed his eyes to her hand. Her skin and her countenance were perfectly warmed, countering the cold desert night.

"You will know," she said.

"How?"

"Just ask, 'What would the Lord do?'"

"Christ? I don't know what He would do."

"Yes, you do. John, many people think they understand His teachings. They have commentary and opinion. They have built empires upon His name, and executed horrors in His memory, separating themselves from others, believing that to be *His* will. But look…" Rachel turned John around with tender patience and showed him the crowd enjoying the party. "Look at the gifts of His Father's world. In that room steeps the sweet, simmering pot of Jew, Buddhist, Taoist, Christian, Hindu, and those still on the search. There is love in there, and understanding. There is caring and healing. There is gentle master and devoted student. There is conversation, debate, and laughter. You say you are not sure which path to take? Take the one that feels right. Take the one that flows easiest. Do not create waves where they need not be. After what we have seen and heard, after the friendships we have forged, how could we ever say the dictates of the heart are wrong?"

"I'm scared, Rachel. What if I can't read my moral compass?"

She moved her hand to his chest, pressing gently on his heart, as if holding his infinite life force. "Follow this."

Chapter Forty-Seven

John and Rachel rejoined the party. The group made a joyous noise as they stepped through the door, and Flavus barked in unison with the revelers. John surveyed the scene. He was amazed at how many friends were in this one place. He knew this would be the last time they would all be together, and the ensuing swell of emotion was difficult and inspiring. For a moment, he imagined an ark, his friends aboard, adrift in a flood sent to cleanse the world.

"Everyone!" John tried to get the crowd's attention. "Everyone, I want to say something."

"Uh oh," James said. "I've heard that before. Keep it short, Brother. Early day tomorrow." Dian hit him on the arm. "Ouch!" He shot her a playful look.

"Let the man speak," Dian said with an air of false sternness. "Please proceed." She gestured ceremoniously at John.

"I should have had you with us from Tyre," John said. Dian grinned and James mocked annoyance. "Friends," John continued, "many months ago I began a journey. I ventured from Antioch to carry a message to the desert. I came to the East to light a fire in Shapur's lands. But now, as I look at all of you, I see faces I could not have imagined when I walked through Tyre for the first time." The group smiled. Rachel wiped away a tear and James rolled his eyes at John in jest. Dian made as if she was going to hit him again. Sri simply nodded to his friend in honor of their first meeting. "We have come through many trials." John met each eye. "There has been pain. Some tragedy. I know there were friends out there who suffered on our account. Friends I never knew, but who are dear to me nonetheless. However, I know we did some good out here. As I return home, I know one thing…" The group exchanged glances. Few in the room were sure of John's final decision, and some were surprised. "I know that I will have memories for a lifetime, and as I continue to carry the Word, I will always have your voices speaking with me."

John sat down, eyes misty. Rachel rubbed his back and then stood up.

"I'd like to say something as well," she said. The group looked at her with some astonishment. Rachel was not always comfortable sharing her feelings with individuals, much less in a group setting. "Months ago, when Philip dragged me to this place, I was scared. Then, I was scarred. Then…" she looked at John and to her female companions, "I was saved. But I also lost sisters. I lost friends. Tragically. However, I have confidence that tomorrow, a trial will bring justice." Rachel looked down at John and continued. "We have a responsibility to the victims' memories to continue to speak kindly, to show mercy, and to love deeply. I intend to carry on in this life in service of Christ, who has shown me so much blessing. I love you all."

The room was silent. John thought for certain they were thinking about both their fallen friends and his relationship with Rachel. He laughed quietly to himself as he looked down at his radiating fingers. God, he thought, why did you bring me the possibility of Rachel? You know it is a path I cannot take.

No one else stood to speak. The mood grew somber in the difficult knowledge that the next day would bring separation with the departure of the caravan, and that Philip, Simon, and Mark would stand trial. The group sipped tea and ate sweets in relative quiet.

"Nice speech, John." Sol broke his silence, and everyone was delighted to hear the sound of his voice.

"Thank you, Sol. Can you ever forgive me?"

"For what?" Sol pulled himself upright with Deborah's help, under her ever-watchful eye.

"For what? For what you went through. Your wrists…your feet."

"John, listen to me. I'm lucky to be alive, I know, but I am also fortunate in another way. My experiences with all of you brought me more than just wounds." Sol placed a bandaged hand on Deborah's knee. "You showed me kindness and friendship – true friendship, beyond our differences. And there is joy in that."

"I appreciate that, Sol," John said. John smiled at Sol, who returned his attention to Deborah and her care. John had often wondered how Christ felt on the cross, looking out at the world. Was there joy in that pain? What can I learn, he wondered, not from the Jew who lived and died over three hundred years ago, but the one before me in this room? "I guess we don't know when we will be called to serve," John mused. "Or how."

"No," Sri said. "We do not. Ours is to embrace the flow of life, not to struggle against it."

"That reminds me of a story I once heard from a Taoist scholar," Bo chimed in.

The group grew silent again. Stories had become customary. Special events providing hope and comfort. Everyone, in his own way, had experienced the tales' significance in shaping their journey, and felt how the narratives so powerfully influenced their life choices. All ears turned attention to Bo, eager for his words.

"A poor farmer sat upon a rock in a raging river, thunderstorms bellowing overhead. The banks at this particular spot were holy, and many came here to pray. As the man sat upon the boulder, the waters splashed around him, dousing him mercilessly. White water foamed, sending cold spray high into the air. He was completely surrounded. There was no way out as another crash of thunder boomed above. To step into the water and attempt a swim for safety would mean certain death.

"After a long while, a pilgrim appeared on the riverbank. 'Hello!' he called out to the farmer. The farmer waved back from the rock.

'What are you doing out there?' the pilgrim hollered, his voice barely audible over the storm and rushing waters.

"'I walked out here not long ago when the riverbed was dry,' the farmer replied.

"'Why?' the stranger yelled back.

"The farmer pointed to the tree under which the pilgrim stood. 'Do you see that tree there? It has flowers on it. They are strong medicine to cure my sick child. I cannot afford a healer, so I walked many miles to gather them myself, as they only grow near this riverbank. I came to meditate beneath the tree and to pray for a flower. You see, like me, this tree cares deeply for its children and does not relinquish them lightly.'

"The pilgrim picked up a browning flower. 'Why not simply take one from the ground?' he asked.

"'Once dead and fallen, the flowers are of no use,' the farmer replied. 'They must be gathered in their prime. The tree presents a puzzle. Where do I exert great energy to gain the greatest benefit?'

"'But you are in the river,' the pilgrim pointed out. 'The tree is here on the bank! What good are your efforts out there?'

"The farmer looked at the water around him. 'When the sky was bright and clear, I had a feeling in my meditation that I should come out to the riverbed. I saw myself in a vision stacking rocks upon the shore so I could reach the tree's canopy. I did not want to throw the rocks up into the branches, because I did not want to damage the flowers.'

"'So, why are you sitting out there?' the pilgrim asked.

"'I was walking back and forth with heavy rocks to stack on the bank, when I twisted my ankle. I crawled to this spot to tend to the wound. As I sat, another traveler, weak and weary, came to the banks to pray for water to swell the rivers and quench the lands. His family was dying of malnutrition and his crops were dry, threatening him and his loved ones with starvation. I could not make it to shore, and he was too weak to carry me back, so I told him to pray for rain, despite my predicament. I joined his prayer as if I was he, and my own life and family were at stake – as if his were my kin and my fields.'

"'I understand,' said the pilgrim. 'That is very noble of you. But now you are stranded. I see by the torrent the other man's prayer was answered. However, how can you be so calm when your own go unanswered?'

"'I think that should be obvious,' the farmer said. 'I have no other choice than to accept this situation.'

"At that moment, a lightning bolt raced from the sky and struck the tree, cracking it at the base. The tree toppled, canopy first, into the river, narrowly missing the boulder. The farmer upon the rock calmly collected the fresh flowers now easily within his grasp. Meanwhile, the pilgrim traversed the long trunk to reach him, carrying the stranded man to safety.

"'You have your flowers,' the pilgrim said as he fashioned a cane for the injured man from the tree's branches.

"'Indeed,' said the farmer. 'Thank you for your assistance. If you do not mind, may I ask why you have come to this place of pilgrimage?'

"'I was told it was a fine place to find great teachers,' the pilgrim answered. 'Men of great wisdom and enlightenment.'

"The farmer called back as he hobbled away, 'I hope you find one.'"

Chapter Forty-Eight

Are you sure you don't want to stay?" John tried all night to convince the caravan to delay until after the trial. Now that morning had arrived, Sri approached him with a look of resolved resignation. A decision clear in his eyes.

"I'm sorry, my friend. We must go if we are to reach Turfan. This unusually hot summer in the mountains will soon give way to bitter snows. It will take many months, and we can delay no longer. If I have learned anything out here on the road, it is that time often appears to walk faster than my camel. We must do what we can to keep up."

"Don't you want to see the trial?" John implored. "Don't you want to know the truth?"

"Brother, I already know it. Besides, in the end, there is only divine justice." The men embraced warmly. Sri got down on his knees and stroked Flavus, who licked his face. "Take care of my companions, Flavus. You are an unusual friend, and they are fortunate for your company."

Sri mounted his camel with ease. He motioned for Sejal, who was currently engulfed by a sea of arms and tears.

"We'll miss you, Sister Sejal." Dian hugged her friend. "You show those men in Turfan that we women are ready to make our name in their world."

"I will," Sejal said, wiping away a tear. "I feel confident Sri will see to that. I will never forget all of you."

Sri helped Sejal into the saddle. The tea caravan lurched forward, making its way for the city gate.

"Your camels are where you left them in the stables, James," Bo called back. "They await your next adventure. Thank you for letting me take part in this one."

The group thanked Bo and his caravan. Sri, Sejal, and Bo turned around often to wave at their friends. The group's mood dampened as the camels melted in with the crowds and disappeared. There was a palpable void where kind and loving faces had been. Sol leaned on Deborah, and a surprisingly emotional James consoled Dian.

"Okay friends," John said, trying to replace sadness with duty. "We have a trial today. Let's get ready."

Chapter Forty-Nine

The friends took their places in the crowded amphitheater. Under an agreement with the Sassanid authorities, and considering the grave circumstances, the Roman citizens were accorded permission to conduct the trial.

Because John was slated to speak, and the group members were potential witnesses, they were given special seating. The trial for the three men would take place in front of a local magistrate, a member of a nearby garrison who still held some influence over Roman citizens under treaty. So many had come from Ecbatana and the surrounding areas that crowds gathered outside the entrance were being turned away. John saw many familiar faces, including local church patrons. He greeted them with a nod. The women nodded solemnly to friends across the aisle, two of whom were victims still nursing injuries.

"Who are the women with the survivors?" John whispered to Rachel.

"They are from the mountain. They are my Sisters."

"They are here to support the survivors," Dian said to the group. "And they are probably here as witnesses, as well."

A drum beat directed attention to the stage. The Roman magistrate asked for the accused to come forth. A guard that John recognized from the night at the Pit escorted Philip, Mark, and Simon onto the stage. They were made to kneel and face the assembly. Their hands were bound behind them.

"Men." the magistrate's voice bellowed about the amphitheater.

"You are accused of conspiring in crimes against the Roman Empire, the Church, and your fellow man. Though we reside in foreign lands, you will be treated as Roman citizens and tried as such." The official unrolled a parchment and read the list of their alleged crimes. "It is hereby charged that you did willfully authorize, perform, or cause to take place, the assault, attempted murder, and murder of innocents." The magistrate put down the scroll and glared at the men, their heads bent low. "What say you to these charges?" he asked.

Silence. Nothing could be heard in the amphitheater except the eerie quiet of expectation. No one breathed. No one moved.

Philip slowly raised his head and looked out at the crowd. He spied John and Rachel, and his gaze narrowed, his brow furrowing under the weight of his wrath. John looked at Rachel who turned away in the face of Philip's menacing stare. A tear streaked down her face. John squeezed her hand with a comforting intensity that matched Philip's ire.

"What do I say?" Philip broke the silence, his voice slithering through the crowd like a cobra. "What do I say? I say these charges are just." The crowd gasped. The women from the mountain widened their eyes in amazement and confusion. "I say these charges are just, and I say my cause was just." Philip's voice oozed an arrogance that confounded John.

John willed his thoughts to reach the condemned man – Philip, save your soul if you cannot save your life.

John had hoped that Philip would show remorse, opening a new chapter on this day to guide the hand of clemency. Deep down he wanted to believe that the Philip who showed him hospitality on that night in the valley so long ago would reappear and take a new direction under the Father's watchful gaze. John closed his eyes and envisioned Philip and Rachel in the small hut, pouring wine, serving hot bread and oil, and tending to John's wounds from the road. There was talk of conversion. Talk of Christ. Talk of new community in the old world. John wanted Philip to live, even if it meant he could lose

Rachel forever.

John opened his eyes to greet the cold reality of the deep chasm between the liberation of brotherhood and the bondage of power. Philip's lust for his own ideals had clouded his vision. Now, he could only see the fog of institution, and not the peace in its message.

John could feel Christ's heart break in this moment.

Simon and Mark did not look up. Their heads drooped lower as they realized the man who had directed their actions and masterminded their crimes had now sealed their fate. The crowd's initial shock turned to rage in the face of Philip's indifference. Men and women stood, hurling insults at the stage. Rocks flew from the stands, and it appeared as if a massive riot would erupt. The magistrate and the head guard urged quiet, and the crowd settled.

"Let him speak," the judge said.

Philip looked out at the crowd with disdain as he continued. "I say whores were killed. I say scoundrels were assaulted. I say a Jew was punished. I say a lie was avenged. I say a truth was preserved."

The crowd once again crested into a roar. John remained seated and silent, still clinging to Rachel's hand. Her head was still hanging, and he felt her tears rain down on their interlocking fingers. He looked far into the distance to three crosses erected at the Pit – barely visible, yet imposing. Crucifixion had been abolished in the Roman Empire, but John knew the practice still continued in Sassanid Ecbatana, and other places to the east. The three crosses were a sure indication that this magistrate would use that tactic.

He knew Philip and his men had made those crosses to hold himself, Sri, and James. But John knew for whom they now stood, and he prayed again that Philip would come to his senses, as Philip could not rely on the customs of Antioch to bring painless death in the hostile frontier. Only contrition could do that. He looked back to the stage and saw that Philip's deranged look persisted, his body writhing.

"I, Philip of Antioch, say the Father and Son are one, and I say I speak for Them!" Suddenly, Philip's hands broke free of their ropes.

In an instant, he snatched a blade from a guard's sheath. Before anyone could react, he lunged at Simon and Mark, slitting their throats. Their heads lurched back, blood and life draining from their necks in crimson rivers. With the Roman guard now in pursuit, Philip jumped from the stage to the witness box and grabbed one of the women from the mountain. He held the blade to her throat. "Stay away!" he yelled, his anger transformed to savagery. "Stay away, or I'll cut this pagan whore's throat!"

"John, what is this new madness?" Rachel looked on in horror. Terror had replaced the sadness in her eyes. John jumped up and ran to Philip.

"Stay away from me, John!" Philip cried. The hostage thrashed about in his arms. A trickle of blood ran down her neck where the sharp blade rested on her skin.

"Philip, stop!" John ordered.

"Why, John? Why stop now?"

"Philip," John's voice softened. "Philip, it's not too late. It's not too late to repent and start a new life...even now. Even in this last effort."

"My life is over, John. What's left now?"

John stared Philip straight in the eye. "Eternity."

For a fleeting moment, John thought he saw the rage disappear from Philip's face. For a fleeting moment, he thought Philip had recognized the gravity of his deeds and how they ran so counter to his original purpose. Maybe…

"I won't watch you destroy Constantine's work, John." Rage once again consumed Philip. "I won't watch you sacrifice Meletius's pure teachings on Valens's and Julian's filthy altars!"

"Philip, please," John implored. "I beg you. See reason. I am not against Christ. I am for Him, and for His mission of kindness, love, and brotherhood. What you and I used to have for one another, I want for all men in all places."

"And what did we really have, John?"

John looked around at the crowd. Everyone was now quiet. Still.

They did not watch as spectators anymore. John sensed their reliance on this response, a clear mirror of Philip. Hope, not just for the Church, but for an empire, could spring from a careful sentence, and John knew he had to choose words wisely now. There was more in this moment than justice.

"Faith, Philip. First and foremost, we had faith. My friend, we are not out here for powerful men. We are not out here for ourselves."

"Then why are we out here?" Philip tightened his grip on the woman's neck.

John's head was buzzing. He did not know whether to speak his heart and risk inflaming Philip's rage, or to say what he thought Philip's anger wanted to hear to win the captive's safety. John looked back at his friends. They clutched each other tightly and hung on the precipice of his silence.

"Do you not know, Philip?" Philip moved the blade along his hostage's skin. She sniffed in, quick and sharp, and shut her eyes. "Philip! Do you not know?"

Philip's face went blank. As if his hand was struck numb, he loosened his grip on the woman's neck and dropped the blade. It hit the stone floor, sending an echo about the amphitheater. He dropped to his knees and began to cry. No one moved toward him, captive in the drama. Struck dumb. Frozen in time.

"Father," Philip wailed as he raised his hands to the sky. "Father, forgive Your son!"

In a flash of light and confusion, the woman picked up the fallen blade.

"No!" John yelled, running toward the praying Philip.

The guards came in from the other side, but it was too late. She drove the long blade into Philip's chest. It passed through until the blood-soaked tip almost touched the ground behind him as he fell backward. The guards grabbed the woman and pulled her away, leaving the blade in Philip's chest. John ran toward him and knelt down.

"Philip!" John cried. "Philip, oh my God!" Philip's face was pale. He bent his head to study the wound. He slowly moved his hand to the sword and touched it. It was a cruel spike, yet far more a blessing than crucifixion. This was no grand martyrdom. Only the end of a tortured man and his deeds. He held his bloody fingers to his lips and smiled. His body shivered and rocked as life drained away. "Philip. Philip, I'm sorry." John placed a hand upon him.

"John...John, I..."

"Philip? Philip, speak to me." John held Philip's head in his hand, as feeble words penetrated his bloodied lips.

"John, we bleed."

"I know, Philip. I know we do."

"John, we bleed. We bleed as He bled."

"Yes. Yes, old friend."

"He bled as we bleed, John. He is here."

"He is here, Philip. Go and be with Him."

"John, I..." Philip gasped. "John, I know why we are out here."

"Why are we out here, Philip?"

"To say what we know. To say...to say it...for each..."

"We are saying it. You are saying it."

"John, we are not in His hands." Philip's eyes fluttered. "We are not in His hands...I see it is not as we think. He is here. It is not what we..."

"Philip. How is it, Philip? If we are not in His hands, where are we?" John choked back tears. It was real now. The potential of this man – his life, his love, his crimes, and his hatreds – collapsed into the void of this moment. The past became present, as a future was erased before John's eyes. There was no judgment here. There was only death in this moment. "How is it, Philip?"

Philip looked into his blood-stained hands. "Christ...we are not in His hands. He is in ours. We...we care for Him. Care for...care for Him, John. Care for each oth..."

"Philip! Philip!"

Philip's lifeless head fell back. John closed Philip's remaining eye with his hand and uttered a prayer. Rachel ran to the stage and knelt by her dead husband. She took his cold, pale hands in hers and looked up to the sky.

"May God show you mercy," she said quietly.

John saw in her face only pity. No tears ran now.

Chapter Fifty

The group sat at Bo's house. No one spoke. The specter of the day's events hung in the air, Philip's ghost hovering about them.

"I was going to be a witness in his defense," John said, Flavus's large head fast asleep in his master's lap.

"Honestly?" James made no effort to hide his shock. "John, how?"

"I don't know!" John took a defensive tone, but pulled it back. "I don't know, James. It felt right. I saw those crosses in the distance. Crosses meant for us. I could not bear to see another hang."

"He's right," Sol interjected. "No one should hang. There is more power in the simple act of forgiveness than in all the effort one exerts to crucify another."

"But Sol," Deborah interjected, "after everything he did to you? After all the pain Philip caused?"

Sol regarded her with great tenderness. "I think sometimes we suffer so that we know what others must never experience." Sol looked to John. "Maybe that is why your Lord had to suffer. So that He could be a lasting example of why we need to be kind to one another."

Sol's comments drifted away into the room.

Rachel had been listening quietly and now had a look John could not interpret. She was at once blank, but at the same time distant, as if heeding the call of a far-off and calming voice. He wanted to find out how she was faring in the aftermath, but he also wanted to respect her silence. She had not shed a tear since the amphitheater, and he was not sure if that was a positive sign, or the beginnings of an emotional breakdown.

"Rachel, will you walk with me?" he asked with a tentative air.

"I'd like that," she said. A smile washed over her face, bursting through the uncertainty, relieving his soul.

They headed for the outskirts of town. John packed a mat, blankets, a canteen of tea, James's fire-starting tools, and some bread. The two sat on a ridge overlooking the valley, watching in silence as the sun sank to the horizon. John started a small fire to stave off the impending chill of the evening.

"I never thought it would end this way," she said.

Her head was thrown back toward the sky, flowing black curls gently dangling down her back, touching the ground beneath. Her feet were stretched before her, and she kicked them together like a child.

"What do you mean?" John had the fire blazing and came to sit next to her.

"Philip. My marriage. Life."

John brushed her fingers gently, as casual and accidental as the night breeze. When Rachel did not pull away, he rested his hand upon them. She looked at their hands, John's on top of hers, as if she were examining something new and strange.

"John, do you know why I didn't cry at the end?"

"Tell me."

"It was something Sri and Bo once said. They were having a conversation about expectations. Sri said that to have an expectation is to have an open door to disappointment."

"How so?"

"He said when we open the door to a guest we expect, we have the idea they will act in a certain way or share our company in a certain way. Maybe we want them to bring us a sweet or make us feel special. We are waiting to be fulfilled in their presence, to be completed through their acts and words. But when the unexpected guest comes…"

Rachel fell quiet, taking her eyes westward as the sun made its last efforts of the day, painting the sky orange. She breathed in the color, exhilarating and penetrating.

"Yes? Rachel, what about the unexpected guest?"

She looked him squarely in the face. Her features were radiant, with an ever-broadening smile anchoring what John felt was a deeper inner peace so near to the surface, but just behind the exquisite veil.

"When the unexpected guest arrives, anything is possible." Rachel fixed her attention back to John, leaning in close and squeezing his hand. "John, when Philip walked through my door so many years ago, I had so many expectations. Our marriage was about our desires. When we didn't fulfill them, I guess we felt like failures. At least, I did. I cannot speak in full for Philip, though I am sure his actions speak volumes. But for my part, when my expectations went unmet, I suffered for it. Then you arrived. Unexpected. You were possibility. So full of fire. So full of passion. I did not long to be with you at that time, as I did not want to leave Philip. I just wanted a taste of the freedom you had through belief and faith."

"Rachel, I—"

"Just a taste," she whispered, tilting her nose to his lips to stop his words. She lightly swept it around his mouth in a perfectly smooth oval before touching it to the tip of his nose, at perfect rest. "John of Antioch, I only expect one thing now."

"What is that?" he asked. His voice quivered. He whispered as though all the breath had gone out of the world and each word had to be carefully chosen. He could hear her taking in his breath.

She looked deep into his eyes. "I expect to flow with the river."

Rachel nudged John's nose to tilt his head upward. She took his face in her hands and kissed him with a passion John only knew from his commitment to the Church…a mere shadow to this. She pushed him back gently to the ground and undressed him slowly as if unwrapping a divine gift. She savored each layer as it peeled away.

She lay on him, her weight keeping him pinned to the ground, even though John would have laid there for an eternity without protest. She was sure of herself, sure of her actions, and knew that as she was with John, she was putting her life back on course. Their bodies pointed like one compass – heads east, feet west. Their union formed a bridge that spanned the great distances of their journeys apart, and together. She explored him like a map to Samarkand, tracing lines through his body as it rose and curved.

Rachel sat up tall, her silhouette cradled in the crescent moon behind her. She slipped from her dress as easily as a knot drawn out from a silken bow. Fantasy, fulfillment, myth, and legend were emblazoned upon her in the firelight. Her figure was a new testament open to his interpretation. She was more than he ever imagined, her sensual energy authoring a thousand psalms. She pulled her hair aside with both hands and let it fall in flowing waves along her back and across her face. John reached up and caressed her body as she arched her back.

Their bodies were warm together, like sun on sand. Naked. Exposed. As they merged, John knew he had his answers. There was no riddle or verse that could hold his attention now…no reason to solve further mysteries. Friction, as knife to flint, ignited a fire in the desert. One he hoped would burn on.

He did not need to know the truth. He was living it.

Chapter Fifty-One

They crept into Bo's house just before sunrise, taking care not to wake the others. The front room was empty, and the doors to the back rooms were closed. They had spent a warm embrace through the night on the cold ridge. John stoked the embers in the stove to start breakfast. Suddenly, as if on cue, a door opened in the back and Sol and Deborah emerged.

"Good morning, you two," Sol said groggily.

Deborah gingerly walked him over to a mat in the front room to change his dressings. Sol was now in the habit of not resisting her, simply giving her free reign over his wounds, and his healing.

"Good morning," Deborah said, as she looked Rachel up and down with a smile. Rachel blushed, taking a sudden interest in the stove. "These are looking better," Deborah said as she examined Sol's wounds. "You should be fine in no time. You'll be wearing Sri's exquisite gem as a necklace and not as a cork for these holes."

"Thanks to you." Sol kissed her and it was her turn to blush. She focused on the creamy white bandages and avoided eye contact with Rachel, who now grinned from ear to ear.

"What's all the noise?" James emerged from the second room and approached John with a smile. He patted his friend on the back knowingly.

"Good morning, everyone." Dian stepped from the room behind him, awkwardly adjusting her dress. Flavus was at her heels. "I see everyone is again assembled!"

"You two were out late last night," James said with a wink to John. "I suppose you're going to tell me you've been here since just after we all went to bed."

John furrowed his brow in embarrassed frustration. "Well, we—"

"I don't believe you," James laughed. "Flavus would have woken the entire house if he heard you come back." James patted John on the arm as he prepared his breakfast from a selection of bread and honey.

"We had a very nice night, thank you," Rachel said. She pushed James playfully and took his piece of bread. She popped a piece into her mouth, licking the honey from her fingertips.

The group ate and drank. The mood was light. It had been so long since everyone had seemed so truly free. They all took the morning's moments as a celebration.

* * * * *

"I need to go." It was mid-morning when John made the announcement he so longed to avoid. The group exchanged glances, John's words forcing reality into the small house on the edge of their dreams.

"Where?" Sol asked. "Into town?"

"No," John replied. "Onto the road."

John watched as his friends' eyes darted from one to another in a silent conference, seeking consensus.

"Do we have enough camels?" Deborah asked.

"Enough camels?" John looked over to her, eyebrows raised. "Enough for who?"

"For us, of course!" Dian lay in James's arms, as he stroked her hair.

"I hope you don't mind," James said. "I invited a few friends along for the journey."

"James, why?" John asked, his lips in a reluctant smile.

Rachel put her hand on his arm. "John, listen. We are a family now. Our lives are forever intertwined, and none of us is alone anymore."

"That's right, John," James interjected. "It's like you said the other day to Philip. We are not out here for men of power, and we are not out here for ourselves."

"We are out here for each other," Sol said quietly. "Or did you not listen when Philip answered your riddle? He had enough breath to carry about that amphitheater, even at the threshold of death. Did you not mean all that you said that day? Were you using empty rhetoric? What would Sri say to that?"

John looked at the group, dumbfounded. He was facing the trap of his own words, and the words of a departed man. He knew that to deny their company and companionship would be to deny everything he had learned since coming to the road to light the flame now burning before him, and within him.

"This may not be that simple, everyone." John stumbled around in the last remaining refuges of argument. "I may have some trouble out there. Besides, it's not an easy road, as you all know. Sol, what about your campsite?"

"I have friends here, John. I didn't run the whole place alone. It's my land, but a community business. Besides, I've been here for so many years, I want to see the world...a world free of Shapur's shadow. It's my turn to impose on James's horrid hospitality for a while."

"Did you hear that, John?" James said with a smile. "It's my chance for some payback...a chance for me to restore some balance. And it will give me someone else to torment. Who knows? On the way back, Sol and Deborah may yet convince us that we are not Hindu after all. Perhaps we are all Jewish."

"What about the mountain?" John cast a gaze upon each woman. "What about your sisters still there?"

"I have a feeling it will be well cared for," Deborah said. "New women are called there all the time, and the community has a life of its own. There is a natural flow from the springs of humanity, just as the springs from the mountain. That is its gift. That is its true refuge. It will live on long after we are gone. Besides, we arrived there seeking salvation." She looked at Sol and took his hand in hers. "I think we found that."

"Let's pack ourselves up!" Dian said, getting to her feet. "Don't give this simple missionary time to complicate things again."

"C'mon John," James said. "We'll tend to the camels. I think the tea caravan left us just enough."

Chapter Fifty-Two

The group arrived at the gates of Ecbatana where the rock lions kept their vigilant watch over the great city. It was still a young day. Life was in full swing. Merchants bustled about, and many caravans were making their way out of the city. Soon, frigid snows would return to this town, replacing summer's heat. Eventually, Shapur himself would take his leave for the winter.

The small group was once again part of something so much bigger, their time in this city passing into a larger history that only they might remember. John surveyed the men and women coming and going and saw in each of them the same hope he had so long ago when he arrived from Antioch. What were their stories? From where did they come? Who had they left behind…and who had they found?

John steeled himself in the saddle as he took in the paths before him. There was no anxiety in the fingers spread before him. The road that once stretched out ahead into nothing, now was a route to everything. He closed his eyes and pictured a pool of opportunity, radiating into rivers of possibility. He did not know where they all led, but he finally felt free to be excited about them. He looked back at Rachel, who gripped his waist. They both looked down at Flavus, tireless in strength and loyalty, and eager for adventure. Deborah sat with Sol, making sure he and his bandages were secured for the ride. James, relegated to the rear of his saddle, bantered playfully with Dian about her new position as camel driver.

John of Antioch smiled. As the leader of the caravan, he turned straight ahead, sitting as still as a statue, ever vigilant, ever solid.

"What's the matter, John?" James asked. "Paralyzed with fear? I taught you well enough. You know the road to Tyre. Let's move it."

"John?" Rachel whispered in his ear and kissed it. "John, my love, are you alright?"

"I am." John softened to her gently caressing hand. He was consumed in such inexplicable bliss, he felt as if his insides would burst if he understood it completely.

"What's wrong? You know the way, don't you?"

"No," John said, smiling. "Thankfully, I have a map." He pulled a crinkled parchment from his robes. "This should do it," he said.

Rachel looked closely at the parchment. "Wait. I thought...I thought you decided..." She grabbed the map and traced Bo's drawing to Turfan.

"Who wants tea?" John shouted back. He heaved the reigns and turned his camel to the East. Flavus barked his approval, running ahead down the trail. The others followed, talking excitedly.

"But...but how...?" Rachel stammered.

"Lao picked this up after I left it in the tea shop and gave it to me before he left Ecbatana. He thought I might need it in case I ever want more of his wonderful brew."

"I thought you wanted to go home," Rachel said through tears of happiness.

John kissed her tenderly on her soft, red lips. "You are with me, Rachel. I love you. I am home."

Author's Note

In every era, people seek to be free – to express themselves and live their lives according to their own truth. And, in every era, there are people who try to stop that pursuit. This is the cycle of the centuries, and the inspiration for this story of John and his companions.

As a student, scholar, and teacher of world religions and philosophy, I was often struck not only by the lengths some people would go to stop others from living authentically, but also by how many cultures and belief systems managed to live side-by-side through the ages. You see, the story of ancient wisdom is not only one of strife and persecution. There is also harmony and understanding in there, too.

Sometimes, you just have to search for it a little bit.

If you made it this far in the book, I first want to thank you for taking the time to read it. I also want you to take some time to reflect – not only on John's journey, but the journey of his friends, as well. What prices were they willing to pay to stop tyranny and live as they pleased? What price are you willing to pay to believe what *you* believe?

Long after you put this book away or download the next one on your to-read list, I hope you will take away one simple message: Find your Tea in Turfan. In other words, don't always take the predictable and easy path back to what's familiar and comfortable. Instead, challenge yourself once in a while. Take the invitation to a great adventure, whether it be a physical journey or one of the mind. Steer your camel right when others expect you to go left. Speak your mind even if it takes you away from the well-trod path of easy conversation.

Above all: Be kind. Not just to yourself, but to your fellow travelers. See, we're all on this silky road of life together, and to even make the journey takes courage. Remember that as you learn, teach, and travel.

Reading Group Guide

1. John took on the journey to the East because of his loyalty to Meletius and the Church. Do you have a loyalty in your life that you would do almost anything to serve or protect?

2. John is initially hesitant to befriend, or even travel with, Sri. Does that hesitation mirror anything from your own life? Do you have people you now consider close acquaintances, or even friends, you initially resisted?

3. There is often great excitement traveling to a new place...but also trepidation. How do you feel about leaving your comfort zone and trying new things? Are you an adventurous spirit or more of a homebody? Have you ever challenged yourself to get out there and explore?

4. Sri teaches John some deep and challenging concepts. John resists at first, but eventually learns to embrace some of these teachings and even incorporate them into his own worldview. Have there been times in your life when you've embraced a new philosophy or way or thinking, and it opened your mind or changed your life?

5. After all that happened between John and Philip, John was willing to lay it down to forgive, even until Philip's last breath. How has forgiveness played a role in your life? Do you carry grudges? Do you try to lay them down, so they don't fester into bigger issues?

Glossary of Terms

Arianism - Controversial teaching of the Alexandrian (Egypt) priest Arius (250-336 C.E.). This view claims that God the Father and Christ the Son are not coequal in substance – that God the Father alone is unique. Therefore, God created Christ the Son, suggesting there was a time when Christ did not exist, and that only God the Father is eternal.

Brahma - Creator god of Hinduism; one god in the Hindu triumvirate, including Shiva the destroyer and Vishnu the preserver. (*See* Shiva.)

Brahman - In the time of the Hindu Upanishads, it is the eternal, unchanging, absolute reality – infinite, divine source, considered the ultimate oneness. (*See* Upanishads.)

Buddha (563-483 B.C.E.) - "Enlightened One." Born Siddhartha Gautama, a prince of the Shakya tribe in northern India, he later became a spiritual seeker and the founder of Buddhism. In addition to the historical Buddha Siddhartha, it can also refer to one who has attained the state of enlightenment, ending the cycle of birth and rebirth.

Council of Nicaea - Council of Christian bishops in 325 C.E. Called by the Roman Emperor Constantine to promote religious consensus.

Ecbatana - Modern Hamadan (Iran); the summer residence of Persian kings.

Flavus - Latin word for golden or yellow color.

Ganges (Ganga): Holy Indian river that flows from the Himalayas 1560 miles to the Bay of Bengal.

Gregory of Nazianzus (330-389 C.E.) - Fourth century Church Father and noted orator.

Jovian (331-364 C.E.) - Also known as Flavius Jovianus; Roman

Emperor from 363-364 C.E., and a champion of Christianity. Humiliated by the Persian army when forced into a hasty treaty during Sassanid (Persian) campaigns. The terms required him to cede Roman-controlled lands, including territories east of the Tigris River.

Julian (332-363 C.E.) - Also known as Flavius Claudius Julianus, he was Roman Emperor from 361-363 C.E. Called Julian the Apostate for his attempts to resurrect paganism in the Empire. Died either at the tip of a Persian arrow in battle or at the hand of a Christian assassin.

Laozi (ca. 6th Century B.C.E.) - "Old Master." Also known as Lao Tzu, he is the traditional founder of Taoism and the purported author of the seminal Taoist text, the Tao Te Ching.

Mani (216-276 C.E.) - Iranian prophet who lived in Babylonia. He is the founder of Manichaeism, a religion teaching that opposing forces of light and dark are locked in struggle.

Meletius of Antioch (unk-381 C.E.) - Fourth century Bishop of Antioch and a supporter of the Nicene Creed over staunch Arianism. (*See* Arianism; *see* Nicene Creed.)

Molossian - An ancient breed of dog renowned for its hunting and protective prowess.

Nicene Creed - A profession of Christian faith for the Eastern Orthodox Church, the Roman Catholic Church, and various Protestant denominations. It took its first form at the Council of Nicaea in 325 C.E., but was approved in its final form at the Council of Constantinople in 381 C.E. Thus, it is sometimes referred to as the Nicene-Constantinopolitan Creed. It was written to explain the Trinity, to counter the Arian position, and to establish the divinity of Jesus Christ. (*See* Council of Nicaea; *see* Arianism.)

Om - The sacred syllable of Hinduism, used as well in Buddhism and Jainism. Its sound consists of three letters: A-U-M, and it is often recited at the start of prayers. It is believed to be the sound that was present at the inception of the universe, and the embodiment of all knowledge. The three sounds of "a," "u," and "m" are each considered to have a meaning: "a" is the consciousness of the waking world, "u" is the world of dream and the inner self, and "m" is the realm of sleep where all is one. The silence at the end is release and pure consciousness.

Placenta: Baking recipe from the Roman statesman Cato the Elder (234-149 B.C.E). It is bread filled with honey, cheese, and bay leaves, and was used as a Roman religious offering.

Samudragupta (unk-380 C.E.) - Emperor of India from 335-380 C.E; said to have presided over a time of unusual prosperity.

Sassanid Empire - A Persian Empire era dominated by the Sassanian dynasty for 400 years. Sassanid kings were patrons of the religion of Zoroastrianism. (*See* Zoroastrianism.)

Shapur II (309-379 C.E.) - Tenth king of the Sasanian Empire of Persia. Said to have been crowned in the womb. (*See* Sassanid Empire.)

Shiva – One of the three gods of the Hindu triad (along with Brahma and Vishnu). (*See* Brahma.)

Silk Road - Trade route of roughly 4,000 miles stretching from China to the Mediterranean Sea.

Torah - "Direction" or "instruction." Hebrew Scriptures consisting of the first Five Books of Moses: Genesis, Exodus, Leviticus, Numbers, and Deuteronomy.

Upanishads (ca. 600 B.C.E.) - "Sitting close" or "sitting down near," in the sense of sitting by one's teacher. The Upanishads are a collection of Hindu texts containing philosophical and religious insights.

Valens (328-378 C.E.) - Also known as Flavius Julius Valens, he was Roman Emperor for the eastern Empire from 364-378, and a proponent of Arianism. (*See* Arianism.)

Yoga - "Union" or "joining." A method for spiritual living to promote union with divinity. May include meditation (raja), devotion (bhakti), action (karma), or knowledge (jnana).

Zoroaster (unk, consensus 1000 B.C.E.) - Also known as "Zarathustra." Founding prophet of Zoroastrianism. (*See*

Zoroastrianism.)

Zoroastrianism - An ancient religion of Persia (Iran), founded by Zoroaster (a.k.a. Zarathustra). This religion claims that a high God (Ahura Mazda) created humans with liberty to choose between two moral sides represented by a spirit of light (Spenta Mainyu) and a spirit of darkness (Angra Mainyu). Contains belief in a resurrection, judgment day, and an afterlife. (*See* Zoroaster.)

Acknowledgments

Books are journeys — both reading them and writing them. The idea for this book arrived during a lunch I had with my dad many years ago, and it has taken many years since to find the page. I want to thank my folks for always being there for my ideas, start to finish (even the ones that end up in the trash bin). You're great sounding boards, editors, and idea-givers, and I appreciate it. I also extend my heart to my patient and amazing wife, whose skills steered the manuscript from unformatted, messy digital document to book. Thank you, Melissa! Without you, there would be no tea. And to my precious daughter, thank you for letting Mom and Dad have some time to get things sorted so we could get it published. We love you! Finally, I want to thank the journeyers on the road of life. It takes grit and courage to wake up and greet the day, and in that, we are all fellow travelers. Let's do right and good by each other.